LAUGHING
HEIRS

Legal thrillers by Michael Monhollon

A Robin Starling Legal Thriller
Volume 4

LAUGHING
HEIRS

Michael Monhollon

Reflection Publishing
Abilene, Texas

ISBN: 0971214255
ISBN-13: 978-0971214255

In memory of my mother, Patsy Lake

Chapter 1

In my front yard was a man peering through a window. Though it was not yet eight o'clock, it was February and dark but for the streetlight on the other side of the road a couple of houses down. Sleet had fallen for a couple of hours late that afternoon, and the streetlight glinted on the surface of the road without casting more than vague shadows on my house and lawn. I squatted by the curb, and Deeks ran over to me to see what I had found. I slipped my gloved fingers beneath his collar and gripped it hard.

"We've got company, boy," I said softly.

He gave my face a lick by way of reassurance. I reached into the pocket of my jacket, but my cell phone wasn't there. In my mind's eye I could see it on the coffee table inside my house where it wasn't going to do me a bit of good.

My visitor's vehicle, some kind of sports car, was parked on the curb, so my visitor wasn't being particularly surreptitious. Dissatisfied with what little he could see through my front window, he went back to the front stoop. It didn't help me see him any better: I hadn't left my porch light on, and he was wearing a hoodie.

Walking bent over so as to keep my hand inside Deeks's collar, I crossed the street to Dr. McDermott's house. Dr. McD was one of Deeks's favorite people, and the wiggle in Deeks's body tugged at my arm as his tail wagged. The grass was slick, but not as slick as the road, which made walking in my stooped posture a little easier. We went through the gate into Dr. McDermott's backyard. I let Deeks go and closed the gate as quietly as I could.

A tap on the back door didn't bring Dr. McDermott. I tried the knob, then knocked harder.

Still no response.

"Dr. McD," I called in a medium-loud voice.

"Robin?"

The door opened. Dr. McDermott was wearing jeans and a sweatshirt, and a crest of hair poked up from the back of his head. Deeks poked his nose between Dr. McDermott's knees, and Dr. McDermott scratched behind his ears with one hand. His other hand held a pistol. "What are you doing at the back door?" he asked.

"Trying to avoid the person at my front door."

"Who?"

"Don't know. I saw him peering in my window."

"You don't recognize him?"

"No. I can't see him too well, because I didn't leave my porch light on, but as near as I can tell, I don't know him.

"Did you call the police?"

I shook my head. "Left my cell phone in the house, too."

"That's not good."

"You go a few weeks without getting shot at, you get careless," I said.

"You certainly do."

We moved to the front of the house, turning out lights as we went. The man was sitting on my front steps, his forearms on his knees, his hands inside his sleeves and his face obscured by the hoodie that he wore under a dark jacket. He looked like he was waiting for something or someone—me, probably. The car by the curb looked like a Corvette.

"You don't want to take chances with this," Dr. McDermott said, moving toward his kitchen and his phone, which was a landline. "I'll call the police."

"Look."

A car was coming. It slowed and pulled to the curb behind the sports car.

"It looks like Brooke's car," I said.

The door of the CRX opened, and my friend Brooke Marshall got out.

"Crap. She's gonna walk right into him. You hold onto Deeks." I pushed Deeks toward him as I pulled open the door. Dr. McDermott bent to reach for his collar, but I hadn't given him enough time. Deeks surged toward the open door. Dr. McDermott staggered forward a step, losing his still tentative grip, and Deeks was out the door, streaking toward Brooke Marshall on the other side of the street. Brooke was another one of his favorite people. Of course, Deeks was a four-month-old chocolate lab. Everyone he knew was one of his favorite people. As he tore across the lawn, running all out, his head down, Brooke turned toward him. The man on my front steps was standing.

"Good grief." I leaped down the steps, almost going down when I hit the slick sidewalk, aware of Dr. McDermott coming through the door behind me as I angled across the grass toward my house. I hoped he hadn't put down his gun.

"Brooke, this way!" I called.

But she was bending to greet my dog. "Hey, Deacon. Good to see you, boy." The man was halfway down the sidewalk, moving faster. I hit the street, slipped, regained my balance, and shot between the Corvette and Brooke's car. The man was right there at the end of my sidewalk, and I lowered my shoulder as I plowed into him.

"Hoompf," he said as the air gusted out of him. We were in the air, then sliding on the icy grass, him on his back and me on top.

"Robin!" Brooke exclaimed.

The man under me was struggling to draw a breath, and I was gasping myself as I grabbed one of his wrists and pushed a forearm under his chin.

"Will you get off my brother?" Brooke said.

The hoodie still shadowed much of his face.

"How do you—" I began.

"I told him to meet me here. He needs to talk to you about a problem."

"Brian?" I said to the man beneath me. We'd only met once, and I had only a vague memory of what he looked like.

He gurgled, and I eased the pressure on his windpipe.

"Brian Marshall," he gasped. "Pleased to meet you."

4

Deeks shoved his head between us and licked his face. I got off Brian, and he sat up, holding Deeks off with one hand and sucking in the cold air.

"Robin Starling," I said. "And my dog Deacon. Sorry about the exuberance of our greeting. Did you hit your head?"

"A hug *and* a kiss," he said, still sounding breathless. "Quite a greeting." He had a light brown beard, short and silky, thick on his chin and along his jawline and pretty thin everywhere else.

I looked back at Dr. McDermott, standing at the end his sidewalk. His gun was pointed at the ground, but his left hand was still on the wrist of the hand that held it.

"Brooke's brother," I called to him. "False alarm."

He shook his head. "Good thing I've got a strong heart."

"I am awfully sorry," I told Brian. "I saw you looking in the window—"

"Brian!" Brooke said. "You weren't."

"—and I've been kind of jumpy lately."

"You don't have to convince me of that." He put a hand to the sidewalk, still holding Deeks off with his other hand, and got up. Seen up close, he wasn't very big, an inch or two shorter than I was, and I was embarrassed for having panicked at the sight of him on my front lawn. "I'm sorry. Brooke told me to meet her, so I was surprised no one answered the door. I rang the bell a couple of times, looked in the window to see if I could see a light, then sat down to wait."

I walked back across the street to Dr. McDermott. "You sure you're all right?"

"Sure I'm sure. Not having to shoot somebody isn't all that traumatic."

I put a hand to his arm. "You were there for me, as always. Thanks."

"I'll go back inside my house now, so I'll be ready and available for the next emergency."

"Since you're out, would you like to come over for some tea or hot chocolate?"

He shook his head, smiling. "It sounds like you might have business. I know enough about the law to know attorney-client privilege doesn't cover third wheels."

"You'd never be a third wheel."

I left him, though, and crossed back across the street to my house.

It turned out that no one wanted tea, hot chocolate, merlot, or even water, frustrating my hostessing instincts, such as they were. We sat around my living room, Brian on the couch, sitting forward with his forearms on his knees, Brooke beside him, and Deeks standing with his chin resting on the couch between them so that Brooke could scratch the top of his head and behind his ears. I sat in the leather club chair, my arms on the armrests, the posture feeling a bit queenly for the occasion, but it was the club chair or the floor.

"It's not my problem actually," Brian said. He tossed his head to get a shock of fine, straight hair out of his face. "It's my girlfriend Whitney's. Actually, it may not be a problem, but I'm thinking she should talk to a lawyer—and since my sister's best friends with one…"

"And she's not really his girlfriend," Brooke said. "Not in the sense that they're living together or anything."

He shot her a pained expression. "The relationship is developing," he said. "Can I go on?"

The circuitous approach to what Brian was there to talk about may seem unusual to you, but it's not. When people first come to a lawyer to talk about something, it can take them forever to come to the point.

"Whitney's uncle died last Saturday," Brian said. "They found him floating in his nephew's hot tub."

"Foul play?" I said, my interest kicking up a notch, but Brian shook his head.

"Evidently, he just passed out from the heat and slid down into the water. He was eighty years old, or close to it."

I wondered whether it was possible to tell with any certainty that someone had slid down into the water rather than being held down, but I let it go.

"Whitney has two cousins, Jared and Nathan, both older. They're brothers. Whitney doesn't have any siblings of her own."

"Their parents dead?"

"The brothers' mother is still alive, but their father, the uncle's brother, died a few years ago. Throat cancer. He had a pension—the mother's getting it, I think—but no savings. Whitney's parents are both dead."

"Nothing suspicious about their deaths, I suppose."

Brooke fixed me with a stare. "Will you give it up with the foul play?" she said. "People die of natural causes."

"Sorry. To a hammer everything looks like a nail."

"Three murder trials under her belt, and she's a hammer," Brooke said to Brian. "She's not a hammer really, though. She's a very versatile, all-in-one tool."

"Great. So now I'm a tool." Noting Brian's bewildered expression as he looked back and forth between us, I added, "Go on. We'll be quiet."

"She's very experienced in all kinds of business litigation," Brooke put in, speaking quickly, and I gave her a look.

"I'll be quiet, too."

"There may be some kind of monkey business with the estate," Brian said. "Jared's the executor. He's already hired a lawyer and filed the will for probate, but he won't give Whitney a copy of the will, won't give her a list of assets, won't tell her anything about what's going on. She's just a cousin, you know. Her uncle was a rich man, but I'm thinking she may come out of this with not very much."

"You're thinking, or she's thinking?" I said.

"I'm thinking. She should be thinking." He shrugged, tossed his head again. "She's just too nice, you know? Never thinks bad of anyone."

"If the will's probated, there'll be a list of assets. Who's the lawyer, do you know?"

"Rupert Propst. Do you know him?"

I shook my head. "I don't even know how to spell that. P-R-O-P-E-S?"

He corrected me, then gave me the uncle's name, which was Robert Walsh.

"I'll ask around about the lawyer," I said. "I've got a friend who does wills and probate."

"Anyway, I was wondering if you'd talk to Whitney tomorrow, and maybe come to the funeral, get a look at her cousins. It's at two."

"I could talk to her in the morning, see where we go from there."

Brian sat back, and his right knee began to piston up and down. "Well, no. She's the owner of Carytown Joe, the coffee shop. She'll be busy right up until time to go."

"Okay. Funeral first, Whitney after."

Brooke was watching his leg jiggle. She put a hand on his knee to still it, and he glanced at her. "Whitney's doing good business, but she's got a lot of expenses, too," he said. "She knew more about baking scones than she did about running a business when she bought the place a couple of years ago, probably still does."

"How did she finance the purchase?"

"Bank loan. Her Uncle Robert cosigned for it."

"Has he been equally generous with her cousins?"

"More generous. Cosigning a note isn't the same as giving Whitney money. The boys have gotten direct infusions of cash and as far as I know never paid anything back. He hasn't been out anything on Whitney's account. She's made her payments to the bank."

"Was the cash for the boys' own business ventures, or for living expenses?"

"I don't know. Both, I think."

Chapter 2

The last will and testament of Robert Wilson Walsh gave, devised, and bequeathed all property, real and personal and wheresoever situate, to his nephews and niece in equal shares, per stirpes.

At the risk of your eyes glazing over, I'll take a moment to parse that for you. Real property—land, fixtures to land, and interests in land—is *devised*; personal property—everything else—is *bequeathed*; and all property, real and personal and wheresoever situate, is *given*. *To give* is the catch-all, so it could take care of everything with no mention of devising and bequeathing. If lawyers started using one word when three would do, though, people might start thinking they could draft their own important documents.

Per stirpes is a Latin phrase—and without legal training who would think to use Latin?—that means if one of the beneficiaries dies before the will-maker, the beneficiary's children or grandchildren will receive his or her share, assuming the beneficiary has such. I didn't know whether any of Robert Walsh's beneficiaries had children, but I did note, among the definitions in the last section of the will, that *children* was not meant to include a man's illegitimate children unless those illegitimate children had been adopted by the father. The provision is a fairly common one and didn't necessarily mean that Robert suspected his nephews of sowing wild oats, but it was something to keep in mind.

On my way into work I had stopped by the courthouse to get a copy of the will. Jared was the executor, but Whitney was in for a third of the estate. Though there were a few pieces of real estate, most of the assets consisted of bank and brokerage accounts. There might be a few disputes over appraisals and division of property, but really I didn't see a lot of work here.

"Robin?" Paul Soldano, the short, somewhat overweight man whom I'd been dating, was in my doorway. (You may have noticed that I keep referring to people as short, but I'm a woman who's within an inch of six feet in height, so pretty much everyone is.) "You look deep in thought," Paul said. "I hate to interrupt."

I tossed the will onto the desktop. "Not really."

"You had that crease between your eyebrows."

"What crease between my eyebrows?" I fished in a side drawer and came out with a mirror. Sure enough, there was a faint vertical line between my eyebrows. When I brought my eyebrows together in pretended concentration, the faint vertical line turned into a trench. "Ah!" I exclaimed. "I'm turning into an old lady."

Paul dropped into one of my client chairs. "Hardly an old lady," he said.

"You're just being nice."

"Of course. It's the prospect of sexual favors that keeps me in line."

"You haven't been getting any sexual favors."

"I said prospect, didn't I? And you'll be happy to know the line between your eyebrows doesn't turn me off a bit."

"It would take a monkey wrench to turn you off a bit."

He held out his hands, smiling. "Where do you want to go to lunch?"

"The hamburger place on 12th?"

"I'll get Brooke."

Brooke was at her desk in the office next door. We had separate businesses—Brooke wasn't a lawyer, and I wasn't a computer geek—but we occupied two offices in a cluster of three in an executive suites that took up half the building's second floor. The executive suites was named, creatively enough, *The* Executive Suites, perhaps to distinguish it from all pretenders.

"I better not," Brooke said when we appeared in her doorway.

"You giving up red meat?" Paul asked. "The iron will help with your anemia."

"I don't have anemia."

"You might develop anemia if you don't eat red meat."

"Not today, okay? You two have fun."

Paul gave the elevator a sad look as we went by it, but we took the stairs down.

"It's just one floor," I said. "And it's been doing you good. You look like you've lost weight in the past month or so."

We emerged into the cold sunshine of a February day, and I sneezed.

"Sun feels good," Paul said.

"Gesundheit to you, too. So have you?"

"Have I what?"

"Lost weight." I took his hand and swung it between us as we walked.

"Maybe a pound or two."

"Well, you're looking good."

He didn't quite purr as we walked along, but he did smile with the smugness of a big tomcat.

I usually have a salad with a little deli chicken for dinner, which gives me license to order the occasional burger and fries. That's my position anyway. I did forgo the cheese, if you're counting calories for me. Paul ordered a burger without cheese, too, which was unprecedented, and without a bun, which was stupefying.

"No cheese, no bun, no Coke?" I said as we carried our food to a table.

"You're drinking water, too," he said.

"I always drink water. You drink Coke—and sometimes beer, if it's Friday."

"I've been taking the stairs, making a few positive dietary changes."

I took a bite of my burger. "How much weight have you lost really?" I said around the mouthful.

"Owmuwaitwilly?" he said. He cut his bunless burger with a knife and fork and took a bite.

I swallowed. "Come on. I didn't sound that bad."

He grinned.

"So?"

"I don't know. Ten, fifteen pounds."

I frowned. "In how long? A month?"

"Or so. I try not to obsess about it."

"That's too fast."

"Thank you, Dr. Oz."

"You do look better, though. Leaner, almost fit."

"Higher praise."

"Well…"

"I know. I've got a way to go. Tell me about this new case you've got. When I stuck my head in Brooke's office, she said it was something involving her brother."

"Actually, it involves her brother's girlfriend, or the woman he'd like to be his girlfriend. It doesn't look like it will be much, really. Her uncle died, she's a beneficiary, and there may be a little wrangling over the estate. A lawyer named Rupert Propst is handling the probate. I thought I might ask your friend Mike about him, see if he knows him at least by reputation. You still hang out with Mike, don't you?"

"Sure. Not as much as before I met you."

"That makes me feel kinda guilty."

"Mike's doing okay."

"Well, at some point I'd like to talk to him. I've never done probate."

"He'd be pleased to help you. He's a big admirer."

"Of me? Mike?"

"Of course. You've been in the paper, you know. And I've sung your praises a bit."

The photo that had accompanied the last newspaper article made me look like a longtime inmate in a woman's prison. It took me a while to recognize the outfit I was wearing, but when I did, I got rid of it. "I really don't like being in the paper."

"Oh, come on, the picture wasn't that bad—" He'd heard me complain about the photograph before. "—and how else are you going to build your business?"

"I know, I know. But picture aside, the article made me out to be some kind of super lawyer."

"And that's bad?"

"It can be. Eventually, I'll be going into court without my superpower."

He put down his fork and laced his fingers in front of him. "I don't think I've heard about your superpower."

"People look at my sweet face and my blonde hair, and they think I'm like that blonde who came across some tracks while hiking in the woods."

"What blonde is that?" He picked up his water cup.

"She was trying to figure out what kind of animal made the tracks when the train hit her."

He sucked water down the wrong pipe and choked on it.

"When people underestimate you, you don't have to be as good," I said.

"You don't have to worry. People will always underestimate you, because nobody can be as good as you are."

"Wow. You do see some prospect of sexual favors."

"Correlation does not imply causation," he said.

"What?"

"I think you're great *and* I see a prospect of sexual favors, not necessarily *because* I see a prospect of sexual favors. There doesn't have to be a causal relationship."

"Ah." In college I majored in English literature. Economics—Paul had double-majored in economics and political science—was evidently a whole other subject.

The day had turned colder. I had already told Paul about Robert Walsh drowning in his nephew's hot tub and what little I knew about Whitney Foster, so we walked pretty much in silence, each of us hunched against the cold. We stopped on the bricks outside the plate-glass windows of the Ironfronts, an office building that dated back almost to the Civil War. It was a cool old building to office in.

"I guess I'll leave you here," he said. "I've got a conference call in about twenty minutes." Paul was a bank examiner for the Federal Reserve Bank of Richmond, which was several blocks away in a twenty-four-story building next to the James River.

"I'm going to Robert's funeral. It's at Saint Stephens."

"Why would you go to his funeral?"

I shrugged. "I was invited."

"You're not thinking Mr. Walsh had help drowning, are you?"

"No reason to. It's really just that I don't have much else to work on right now." I had hung out my shingle only a couple of months ago after being fired from the law firm of Northrup, Hambrick and Larsen.

"Be nice if this turned into another big, fat murder case, especially since it sounds like there's a hefty estate involved that can pay the legal bill."

"There's no point in getting pigeonholed. Most of my experience has been on the civil side of the docket anyway."

"There just don't seem to be a lot in the way of legal fees on the civil side of this particular case."

I gave him a wry smile. "Too true," I said.

Chapter 3

I was late to the funeral. I parked near the far end of the narrow lot and walked down the sidewalk, which the sunlight patterned with the bare-limbed shadows of the leafless trees. I snagged an order of service as I entered the sanctuary, thinking I would slip into a back pew, but all the back pews were occupied. I kept walking forward as the video slideshow of photographs came to a close and the music ended abruptly. An old man stepped to the podium and coughed to clear his throat. Despite his lined face, he had broad shoulders, a big, square head, and a neck like a tree trunk growing up out of his shirt collar.

There were plenty of places to sit, but none of them on the aisle. "Excuse me," I said to an elderly couple and slid past them. I sat, and the old man at the podium coughed again.

He read, "For I consider that the sufferings of this present time are not worth comparing to the glory that is to be revealed in us." My cheeks still felt hot with embarrassment, and I took a few deep breaths as he continued, "For the creation waits with

18

eager longing for the revealing of the sons of God. The creation itself will be set free from its bondage to corruption and obtain the freedom of the glory of the children of God—and not only the creation, but we ourselves groan inwardly as we wait eagerly for adoption as sons, the redemption of our bodies." His voice cracked a few times, and when he finished he remained at the podium staring over our heads, his tears running down creases in his face so deep they might have been channels carved for the purpose. I had to look away.

Flower arrangements lined the front of the church, the casket there in the midst of them, its lid standing open. I was close enough that I could see a little of the waxy-faced man lying peacefully in repose. At the podium a younger man in a white robe replaced the old man. His role, evidently, was to tell a few stories about the deceased, and he told them well, though it sounded like he'd gotten the stories second-hand. I thought the old man might have done better if he could have kept from choking on his grief.

Brian Marshall was sitting just two rows in front of me beside a young woman with a mass of extremely curly, dirty-blonde hair drawn back into a pony tail. Whitney Foster, I guessed. She was wearing glasses with rose-colored frames and had a nice profile, though her mascara was smeared, and there was too much of it.

I wanted to turn in my seat to look around at some of the other funeral-goers, but I restrained myself. There was more scripture and a congregational hymn, but no more reminiscences of Robert Walsh, secondhand or otherwise. After about thirty minutes, the young woman I'd taken to be

Whitney Foster went forward and sang "We'll Meet Again." The order of service confirmed her identity. She had a low, rich voice and a polished enough delivery that I thought she must sing in a choir somewhere.

At the end of the service, we exited past the open casket. Robert Walsh had been a spare man with thinning white hair and a beak of a nose. I hadn't been at an open-casket funeral since my grandfather's death when I was seven, and I felt a shiver work its way up my spine and along my arms as I walked past the casket.

Brian and Whitney were in the foyer. The whites of her eyes were a disconcerting shade of pink that almost matched the frames of her eyeglasses, and her mascara had migrated still further down her cheekbones. Just beyond them were James Jordan and Ray Hernandez, two cops I knew.

"Hi, Robin," Brian said to me. "I'd like you to meet Whitney Foster."

I smiled at her and took her hand. "Robin Starling," I said. "You did a beautiful job with your song. It was very touching."

"Thank you."

"Maybe you could come by the coffee shop about five o'clock or so," Brian said to me. "Would that work for you?"

I nodded. "Sure."

There were, fortunately, other people who wanted to talk to Whitney, which gave me the opportunity to work my way around her and Brian. Jordan and Hernandez had left the church, but I caught up with them on the sidewalk outside.

"So did you know Robert Walsh?" I asked after we had shaken hands.

"Not during his lifetime," Hernandez said.

"What causes you to make his acquaintance afterward? Wasn't the death accidental?"

Jordan shrugged.

"Do you know it wasn't accidental?" I asked.

"No, we don't know it. Not at this time."

"Suggesting you're waiting for some tests to come back."

The two of them exchanged glances.

"You give dumb blondes a bad name," Hernandez said.

"Sorry. I'll try harder to live up to the stereotype. I'd assumed Robert Walsh was just an old man who stayed in a hot tub too long and passed out from the heat." Neither of them responded to the prompt. "Well?"

"What else do you assume?" Jordan asked.

"Bruising on the body suggesting his head had been held under water? Somebody's skin under his fingernails?" There were people exiting the church now, and we moved off the sidewalk to spare them my grisly speculations.

"How about postmortem abrasions that suggest the body was moved?" Jordan said.

"Really?"

He shook his head. "It's inconclusive. Drowning deaths often are."

"So what are you here for?"

He gave me a lopsided smile, still shaking his head.

"You're no help."

21

"What's your connection to Mr. Walsh?" Hernandez asked me. "Were you his lawyer, or are you representing one of the kids?"

"Or maybe you go to St. Stephen's," Jordan said. "And you go to all the funerals."

I smiled. "No."

"Which question are you answering?"

"Take your pick."

"I go to St. Bridget, right next door," Hernandez said.

"So this is your church?" I asked Jordan, then answered my own question. "No. If it was, you'd know whether or not I was a member."

"Jordan's a Baptist," Hernandez said. "How about you? What church do you go to?"

I shrugged. "I've never been too comfortable around churches."

"Too much of a social atmosphere?" Jordan asked.

"No, I'm a sociable person."

"Too many hypocrites?"

"No, I'm right at home with hypocrisy. It would be hypocritical not to be."

They waited for a fuller explanation, as if any of this was their business. I didn't have any reason to be close-mouthed with them on this particular subject; it was just my natural inclination.

"I guess I'm afraid of having an unexpected encounter with God Almighty," I said finally. "I have the feeling he'd disapprove of me."

"We like you," Hernandez said.

"Is that the way it works? God likes me, I'm in?"

"Well, no," Jordan said. "Everybody falls short. You have to repent."

"And change your carnal ways," Hernandez added.

What did he know about my carnal ways? I didn't ask. I said, "That's just what I need, to turn a corner one Sunday morning and run smack into the creator of the universe, only to find he's unhappy with the way I do things."

"See the woman who just came out?" Hernandez said. "Slender woman with straight blonde hair, wiping at her nose with the handkerchief?"

"Yeah."

"If we're ready to leave the subject of your spiritual shortcomings," he said.

"More than ready."

"She's Macy Buck, Walsh's therapist. A home health company called Mobilecare sent her to his house two, three times a week."

"What kind of help did Mr. Walsh need?"

Macy was wearing black slacks and a short coat over a white blouse. She was a pale blonde with delicate features and looked like she might be in her mid- to late twenties. Her eyes were clear and, except for the handkerchief she carried, there was no sign she'd been crying.

"He had a double knee replacement about three months ago," Hernandez said.

"Long recovery." Another group of people came through the door, and Macy stepped toward a sandy-haired man with a conservative haircut, putting a hand to the shoulder of the overcoat he wore over his suit. He gave her a grimace that suggested he didn't like being touched—not even by an attractive woman like Macy Buck.

"Jared Walsh," Jordan said in my ear. "Older nephew."

"And executor of the estate," I said, and Jordan raised his eyebrows.

Macy turned from Jared to embrace another man who had stopped just outside the church. This one hugged her back.

Hernandez said, "And here's Nathan, the younger nephew." He had long hair worn in a ponytail to expose the shaved sides of an undercut. He wore faded jeans and a black jacket that looked as if it might be silk.

"Macy really becomes attached to the families of her patients," I observed.

"Doesn't she?" Hernandez said.

"Nathan looks younger than Jared," I said. "I understand they're brothers?"

"Yes, sons of Robert's brother Harold," Hernandez said. "Nathan's thirty-two, Jared's forty."

"And Whitney?" I said.

"She your client?" Jordan asked.

I looked at him, and he shrugged.

"Twenty-four, daughter of Robert's sister—Francis, I think."

"Thank you." I squeezed his arm and drifted away toward Whitney's cousins and Macy the therapist.

"I'll miss him," Macy was saying to Whitney, who had just come out of the church, removing a pair of sunglasses from a hard case as she blinked in the sunlight. "He was a nice man."

"I always found him to be a difficult old man," Jared said to his brother, making no real effort to keep his voice down. "Jennifer couldn't stand him."

"Jennifer didn't seem to like you much, either," Nathan said uncharitably. His remarks were addressed to his brother, but his gaze had shifted to me, so I stepped forward and extended a hand.

"I'm sorry for your loss," I said.

"Jennifer's Jared's ex," Nathan said by way of explanation as he took my hand. "I don't believe I know you."

"Robin Starling. It's a pretty convoluted connection. My best friend's brother is dating your cousin Whitney there."

Somehow I seemed to have caught everyone's attention.

"I didn't know Robert," I said, "but I wanted to pay my respects."

There's nothing like a wall of silence to make a person feel unwelcome. Of course, as a trial lawyer, I was used to feeling unwelcome.

"He was what, eighty or thereabouts?" I said.

"He was seventy-eight," Jared said, a bit stiffly.

I said, "I guess he'd been having trouble with dizzy spells? Occasional faintness? It's just so sad he was alone when it happened."

Jordan and Hernandez had moved to within earshot.

"Tragic," Jared said. He looked as if he were trying to crack a walnut with his butt-cheeks.

"I didn't even know he used the hot tub," Nathan volunteered. "I'd have been more worried about him falling into the pool when he came over to help himself to Jared's tools."

I smiled at Jared, though he was the person who seemed least receptive to a smile. "Your yard seems to be full of attractive nuisances."

He stared at me.

"Pool, hot tub, tool shed…"

"Uncle Robert just held onto Jared's lawnmower," Nathan said. "Not that Jared uses it much himself."

"Will you for god's sake shut up?" Jared said, turning on him.

"Hot tubs can be so dangerous," I said to the crowd at large, "especially with kids and older folks. I know, seventy-eight's not so old, but when you've had your knees replaced, maybe still on pain meds that are making you loopy…" I shook my head.

"I may have heard him splashing," Macy said, sniffing, wiping at her nose with the crisp-looking handkerchief.

That got people's attention.

"I was across the street for our appointment, but nobody answered when I rang the bell. I was standing by my car with my cell phone, trying to call him—I had just talked to him not twenty minutes before to make sure he was going to be home—when I heard splashing, or thought I did. Jared's back yard is just across the street, you know. I thought, wow, it's February. Who would be using the pool? I didn't think about the hot tub."

"You went on to your next appointment?" I said.

"What could I do? Robert didn't answer his phone."

"I guess he was conscious enough to be trying to pull himself out. Was the splashing pretty violent?"

She shrugged. "I didn't really focus on it. I mean, I hardly noticed it at the time. It was only later…" Her bout of loquaciousness seemed to be at an end. A muscle in Jared's jaw was jumping; Nathan only looked bored.

Jordan and Hernandez intercepted me on the way to my car, one falling into step on either side of me. I looked at one, then the other, but I didn't break stride. "Gentlemen," I said in acknowledgment.

"You don't mind sticking your nose in, do you?" Hernandez said.

Jordan said, "What's your interest in the case really?"

"I'm still working on it. Whitney may hire me to represent her interest in the estate."

"And on the strength of that you're at the funeral pumping people for information?" Hernandez sounded incredulous.

"The police presence piqued my interest. Besides, business is slow."

Jordan said, "You've been on your own, what, three, four months now?"

"Two months. What did you think about Macy's story? Had you heard it before?"

"Unh unh," Hernandez said. "We had no way to prime the pump. Nothing like a nosy female making like a verbal fire hydrant to get people to talk."

"That sounds like a sex-based put-down," I said.

"It's a sex-based compliment. You've got a knack for getting people talking."

"My knack doesn't seem to be working on you two," I said.

"We really don't have anything to share."

"Which isn't the same as saying you don't have anything."

Jordan's mouth twitched. "I'm afraid it's close enough. You'll let us know if you stumble across something interesting, won't you?"

"Of course. I like doing volunteer work for the police and getting nothing in return."

It was not quite three, and I had nowhere in particular to be until five o'clock. I decided to run some errands. I couldn't buy ice cream or anything else from the freezer aisle, but it was cold enough that any other groceries would keep in the car as well as in a refrigerator. I turned on my car, turned up the fan on the heater a notch even though the air was still blowing cold, and cranked 96.1 The Planet, where Bob Seger was singing "Hollywood Nights." I rubbed my arms, rubbed my thighs, and sang, "Higher and higher and higher they climbed." Singing is not my forte, and no one would have recognized the song had Bob himself not been singing backup. In my defense, "Hollywood Nights" has some pretty challenging vocals, at least in my humble opinion.

Jordan and Hernandez drove out of the parking lot, Hernandez tapping his horn as they went by me. Brian and Whitney got into his rather battered-looking black Corvette and drove off, closely followed by Macy Buck in a boxy Honda Element. None of them noticed me.

Jared Walsh walked by with a white-haired man on either side of him, one short and curly haired, the other tall and nearly bald. They seemed to be telling him something, and Jared flinched visibly when the short man made a sudden movement. I turned off my radio. Bob Seger had given way to John Cougar Mellencamp singing his little ditty about Jack and

Diane, which didn't measure up to getting some lowdown on Jared. I lowered my car window about an inch to facilitate the eavesdropping.

"With you, it's always wait," the tall man said. "We're not going to wait much longer."

"Before I had no real prospect of paying," Jared said. "Now I've got prospects."

"Prospects don't pay the bills," the short man said.

"And we're not sure you even have prospects. What you've given us is a list of accounts and account numbers, but those accounts are virtually empty."

"You can't know that." Jared's voice.

"Virtually empty as near as we can tell," the short man said as the three of them passed out of my field of vision. "At the moment we're having to rely on some unofficial sources."

"Listen." Jared, sounding edgy. "There are assets. We just haven't found them all yet. You've got to trust me."

"Oh we trust you all right. That won't keep us from doing a little checking as we're able."

A group of women went by. They were chatting about flowers, which perhaps wasn't unusual for a funeral, but was certainly less interesting than a conversation about missing assets. I opened my door and stood to look out over the car roofs, but Jared and his companions were nowhere in sight.

Chapter 4

Carytown is a trendy shopping area in midtown
Richmond a bit south of the Museum District. A lot
of the buildings date from the 1930s, possibly
including the one that housed Carytown Joe. It had a
narrow storefront with plate-glass windows and a
recessed door.

In late afternoon on a weekday the parking
wasn't bad, and I managed to find a place on the curb
only a few cars down from the entrance. The store
was dark when I reached it, though, and the door,
when I tried it, was locked. I cupped my hands and
peered through the door glass. It was getting colder
again, and my breath fogged the glass. I rubbed it
with the sleeve of my jacket and held my breath while
I looked again. The floor was a checkerboard of black
and white tiles, and the stamped-tin ceiling was high
overhead. Benches lined both walls with round tables
in front of them and chairs across from them. Down
the middle of the room was another row of tables
with the chairs upside down on top of them. The
display counter was at the far end. Just inside the door

were a small wrought-iron table and two matching chairs, probably something they set out on the sidewalk to one side of the door when they opened each morning.

I looked at my watch. I had already been at the Kroger at the other end of Carytown and bought groceries enough to fill the back seat, but it was still just 4:37, more than twenty minutes early for my appointment. I was going to look like I was desperate for work, which I pretty much was. Certainly I didn't have anything else to do this afternoon that had the prospect of bringing in money, even as little prospect as this job had. Hugging myself for warmth, I stepped back. The lights were on in the wine shop on the corner just two doors down. I walked down to it, hoping for someplace warm to pass the time.

The clerk at the register greeted me with a friendly smile, asked if I had ever been in before, and invited me to browse. I did. I knew the names of a few grape varietals. I generally liked pinot noir and merlot, found cabernet a bit more challenging. The distinction I could make most readily, though, was price. Here I found bottles priced as high as thirty dollars—a pretentious little vintage, I thought, sliding one back into the rack—and as low as seventeen, still a bit pretentious for my budget, which was oriented more to the six-dollar bottles available at Food Lion. There was a wine bar at the back of the shop with a row of fancy stools in front of it and a smiling woman behind it.

"Can I offer you a taste of something?"

I thought she just had, but I returned her smile and shook my head. There were cards, T-shirts, coasters, and other knickknacks labeled with aphorisms like "Life is too short to drink bad wine." I passed them by and left the shop, exchanging more smiles and nods with the underworked sales staff.

It was still not yet five o'clock, so I went around the corner to the alley. As I turned into it, I heard a woman's voice say, "But they cost money, Brian. I just don't see the point."

I stopped walking. A man was saying something in response, but I couldn't make it out.

"What do you think she's going to do for me?" the woman said, emphasis on the *what*.

I thought I might be listening to Brian and Whitney, so I listened harder, hoping to hear what helpful thing I might do for Whitney, but Brian's response was too soft and in too low a register for me to make out the words. I retreated and walked back to the corner. It was 4:59. I waited five minutes, then walked down the sidewalk to Carytown Joe and pulled at the handle.

The door opened—though, except for a light at the counter at the far end, the shop was still dark. The chairs had been removed from the table closest to the display counter and were standing right-side-up around it. As I walked through the restaurant, Whitney, carrying a tray of mugs, pushed through a swinging door behind the counter and placed the tray on a long, white-wood table than ran along the back wall.

"How about a decaf latte?" she said, turning toward me. "Brian and I are having one."

"Sure. I guess you drink a lot of coffee, working at a place like this?"

She packed coffee into a little filter basket and twisted it on. "Not as much as you'd think." She touched a button. "Usually just a cup in the morning. Have a seat."

"I'm sorry about your uncle. It was a good service."

"Thank you. I'll miss him."

As the espresso machine began to sputter, Brian pushed through the door with another tray of mugs, which he set on top of the one she had brought in. We said hello.

"How long have you had this place?" I asked.

"Two years last October," Whitney said. "Almost two-and-a-half now."

"You own it?"

Whitney glanced at Brian. "Us, the bank, and a few silent partners—friends of ours that put in a few thousand dollars apiece."

"The two of you are partners?"

Brian said, "Actually, I'm one of the ones who put in a few thousand dollars, which was all I could raise at the time. Whitney's the one on the bank loan." He turned one of the chairs around to sit in it backwards, one forearm resting on the chair back.

"Me and Uncle Robert," Whitney said. "Just me now, I guess, unless the estate is still on the hook as cosigner. I'm going to make mine vanilla. How about you?"

"Vanilla's fine. My guess is the estate's still liable, but it depends on what the note says. I ought to have a look at it for you."

"Does it matter?" Brian asked.

"Probably not, but the worst possibility is that Uncle Robert's death constitutes a default on the note, making the whole thing immediately due and payable. You shouldn't worry, but on the other hand…"

"You should look at it," Whitney said.

"To be safe."

She began frothing the milk. It wasn't long before the three of us were sitting around the table, each with a mug in front of us. Coffee, like wine, was a recently acquired taste for me, but I found the latte sweet and good.

"I could get used to this," I said.

"We open every morning at seven," Whitney said.

"That seems late for a coffee house."

"When we started out, we opened at six, but we never had many customers in that first hour."

Brian said, "Now, we've usually got a few waiting at the door when we open up."

It wasn't enough to tell me the place was profitable, but it was early in the relationship to press for details about Whitney's finances. "Brian suggested you had some concerns about how your uncle's estate was being handled?" I said.

"Not necessarily. I understand the will leaves everything to us three cousins in equal shares—Jared, Nathan, and me."

"Yes, it's on file at the courthouse. I've seen it."

"Did you find out anything about the lawyer handling probate?" Brian said. It wasn't cold in the coffee shop, and he didn't seem agitated, but his right knee was pumping.

I shook my head. "Haven't had the chance."

Whitney said, "That's the one thing about all this that makes me uneasy. That lawyer keeps calling me, and he gives me the creeps."

"A creepy lawyer," I said. "That's one for the books."

They looked at me questioningly.

"Sorry. Little joke."

"That lawyer's not the only thing that makes you uneasy," Brian said. "They're planning to drill the safe tomorrow, and it's just by accident that we know anything about it."

"We heard Nathan and Macy before the funeral," Whitney said. "You met Macy, didn't you? We were standing just around the corner from them, and they didn't know we were there."

"What safe are you talking about?" I asked.

"Uncle Robert has a safe in his walk-in closet."

Brian said to Whitney, "If they get in that safe and you're not there, everything in it's going to disappear."

"We don't know that."

"We have every reason to suspect it."

"When is this supposed to take place?" I asked.

"We don't know," Brian said. "Sometime tomorrow."

"That lawyer seems to think I know the combination. That's one of the things he's been calling me about. I guess they've given up on finding it written down anywhere."

"Is the lawyer going to be there?"

"We don't know that either."

Paul called to ask if I'd like him to join me for dinner.

"At my place?" I said. "Sure, though I'm not quite there yet. Ten minutes."

"What have you got for us?"

"That may be a problem. I have the makings of a salad, but that's about it."

I thought he might offer to bring takeout, but he said, "A salad's good."

"I can mix in a little turkey I got from Kroger's deli counter, so there is some protein."

"Protein's good."

"Listen. Have you talked to Mike yet? I'd really like to get the lowdown on this Rupert Propst, if he knows him."

"How do you spell that?"

I spelled Propst for him.

"I'll give him a call. Do you think you and Deacon will be going for a walk after dinner?"

"At some point."

"I thought I might go with you."

Usually, he tried to time his arrival so as to miss any aerobic activity on my part, and, failing that, he watched TV—or me, depending on what I was wearing—until it was over. "Are you having some kind of midlife crisis?" I asked.

"I'm only thirty-two."

"So you say, but it occurs to me I've never seen a birth certificate."

"That's because I'm a man of mystery."

"Ah. So that's the attraction."

"That and my easy charm."

"I was forgetting your easy charm."

"Better keep it in mind. It's in the car and headed your way."

When I got home, I changed clothes and walked across the street to retrieve my dog from Dr. McDermott. I patted Deeks and rubbed his sides while his hindquarters wagged and he turned his head this way and that in a mostly unsuccessful effort to lick my hands. All the licking and the wagging wasn't enough to express his joy in the occasion, and he ran figure-eights around me as I walked back across the street, hugging myself against the cold.

We were wrestling in the living room—probably not the smartest thing to do with a dog that might grow to weigh a hundred pounds—when the doorbell rang. Deeks broke away to charge the door, dancing and turning until I got there. As soon as the door opened, Deeks pushed his head between Paul's knees, his tail wagging.

"Hey, Deacon. Hey, buddy," Paul said as he administered the expected ear-scratching.

I was eying Paul closely. "You have lost weight," I said.

He looked up at me, still bent to work on Deeks. "I'm glad it shows. I look at myself in the mirror, and I can't really tell."

"When did you say all this started?"

He gave Deeks a final pat and straightened. "You make it sound like I've been having an affair." He gave me a peck on the cheek, the sort of kiss that might have been administered to the forehead if I hadn't been five inches taller than his five-six.

"Sorry," I said. "Don't mean to cross-examine you. I haven't started on the salads yet, but it won't take a minute."

Paul watched as I made them. I sprinkled a little raspberry vinaigrette on mine and held the bottle over his, but he shook his head.

"I have some merlot open in the fridge. I usually have half a mug with my salad. Or you've still got a beer left from that six-pack of Dos Equis you brought a couple, three weeks ago."

"The Dos Equis sounds good."

"Well, that's a relief," I said as we carried our bowls to the table.

"What do you mean?"

"I thought I was going to have to tie you down and engage in some enhanced interrogation, find out who you are and what you've done with my boyfriend."

"As it happens, I did emerge from an alien pod just this morning."

"I don't think enhanced interrogation would be as much fun for you as you seem to think." I got the wine and Paul's beer out of the refrigerator and carried them to the table. When I sat, Deeks, who had been following me from refrigerator to table, sat too and fixed his eyes on the edge of my salad bowl.

"He looks like he's expecting something," Paul said.

"He shouldn't be. I've never fed him from the table."

"There's always a first time."

"Not in this case. I go through the door first, I eat first—Deeks has to know I'm the alpha dog."

"Okay."

"Okay what?" I said, noting the hint of a smile.

"Nothing. I just never heard a woman call herself any kind of dog."

I rolled my eyes. "I've made a concession in letting Deeks sit on the furniture. If he gets too controlling, I'll have to put a stop to that, too."

"You've got a whole system for keeping your men in line."

38

"He's a dog, Paul. It's a system for keeping dogs in line. I learned it from my veterinarian father."

"Point taken."

"Besides, I let you sit on the furniture."

After supper I put on a jacket and stocking cap while Deeks danced at the door.

"We are walking, aren't we?" Paul asked.

"Didn't you say you wanted to walk?"

"I was just making sure we weren't going to run. Don't you run with him sometimes?"

"It varies. Usually I do a little of both. I walk, I jog. Sometimes I do a few sprints."

"How about tonight?"

"Tonight I thought we'd just walk."

"Good. I'm up for walking."

I opened the door and Deeks took off into the night. By the time Paul and I reached the street, he was nowhere in sight.

"I take it you don't worry much about Richmond's leash law," Paul said.

"You can walk your dog without a leash if he's under, quote, 'immediate voice control.' "

Paul twisted to peer at the road on the other side of me. Of course, Deeks wasn't there. "I think I'm missing something."

"It may be a looser sort of control than immediate," I conceded.

I heard a clatter of toenails on the road behind me an instant before Deeks plowed into the back of my knees, almost taking me down. He caromed off me and disappeared again into the darkness. "You can see that he checks in with me periodically. And he's good about getting off the road when headlights are coming. That's the main thing."

"What do you do about his poop?"

I pulled a hand out of my coat pocket and showed him a plastic bag.

"Well, okay. I'm impressed."

"Unfortunately, Deeks usually poops up against someone's house, right under a window. That limits me. I can hardly go crouching in front of someone's bedroom window even if I am picking up poop. I'd be likely to get shot."

"So how long have you been carrying the plastic bag?"

"This particular one? Couple weeks."

"Ah ha."

"Ah ha?"

"That's the Robin Starling I know."

We did a two-mile loop and were almost home when Paul said, "I haven't seen Deacon in a while. Are you sure he's out there?"

"Pretty sure." I raised my voice. "Deeks! Deeks, old buddy!"

"Old buddy?" Paul asked.

"He seems to respond to it better than 'Come.' "

"He doesn't seem to be responding now."

I stopped Paul with a hand on his arm. The night was silent but for the distant buzz of a street lamp.

"What?" Paul whispered, but I held up a hand. You could hear it, almost a thrum in the air, a clicking of toenails, and Deeks was there, dropping into a sit with his nose almost against Paul's knee.

"You flinched," I said.

"Hard not to."

I took a treat out of the pocket of my coat that didn't hold the plastic bag and gave it to Deeks, feeling his teeth and tongue on my cold fingers. "Good boy, Deeks," I said. "Good boy."

He gave my hand another lick.

"Break," I said, and he was gone again.

"Break?"

"It means…" But Paul's cell phone rang and he fished it out of his pants pocket, spilling a few coins that clinked on the street in the darkness.

"Hello?" he said, as I bent to retrieve the coins I could see. "Yes. Sure. I'm with her now."

I stood and handed him the coins.

"Mike McMillan," Paul said. "He wants to talk to you."

I took the phone. "Hi, Mike."

"Hi, Robin. I understand you're going to be locking horns with Rupert Propst."

"You know him?"

"You know all those shark jokes they tell about lawyers?"

"Yes."

"He's the one who inspired them."

"He's good?"

"No, not at all, but he is unscrupulous."

"You sound like you know him well."

"Mostly by reputation—and of course he looks like a shark."

"Then at least I'll know him when I see him."

"I'll be interested to hear your take on him."

We had been walking as I talked and by the time I hung up were on the street directly in front of my house. Deeks was with us, now walking sedately at heel, his eyes on me as if he were the best trained dog in the world. Immediate voice control, I thought with satisfaction.

Chapter 5

The number listed for Rupert Propst looked like a cell number. I called it right at eight the next morning. It rang so long I kept expecting it to go to voice mail, but a man answered.

"Rupert Propst," he said, aspirating his consonants in an oddly breathy voice.

"Hi, Mr. Propst. My name is Robin Starling. I'm an attorney representing Whitney Foster."

"Yes?" He hissed the "s," and I began to get the mental image of a twisted, shadowed Mr. Hyde.

"I understand you're probating her Uncle Robert's will for her and her two cousins," I said.

There was a slight pause. "Jared Walsh is the executor."

"Understood. He's the executor, and he, his brother Nathan, and his cousin Whitney are the beneficiaries of the estate. Are you representing the estate, or Jared personally?"

"The estate, of course."

"There's a safe in the testator's house you haven't been able to open."

"Ms. Foster has the combination? I knew she must."

"She doesn't have the combination. I understand you're going to be drilling the safe open, though, and we'd like to be there when you do it."

He was silent.

"Sometime today, isn't it?" I said.

More silence. This time I waited him out.

"Two o'clock," he said.

"Great. If we're all there when the safe opens, I think we can avoid a lot of accusations being hurled back and forth—and lawsuits, and complaints being filed with the state bar. All for the best, I'm sure you'll agree."

"What did you say your name was again?"

"Starling. Think of the black-speckled bird."

"And your first name is Robin?"

"Yes. I'm afraid that would be the red-breasted bird." I hung up, reflecting not for the first time on my twice-avian name.

I took Broad Street Road into the office the next morning so I could drop in on Rodney Burns, who ran a detective agency located on the backside of a strip shopping mall. Actually, it would be more accurate to say he was a private detective and leave out the part about the agency, because the agency was just him. He did have room for help, though, an outer office with a computer desk from Costco and a secretarial chair that, as far as I knew, had always sat empty.

A bell chimed as I went through the door, and Rodney glanced at me through one of the plate glass windows in the wall that separated his back office from the front. He gave me a nod, which was a pretty subdued greeting coming from him.

I approached the inner doorway slowly, wondering if he had a client or was on the phone. "You alone?" I asked as I looked in, though I could see that he was. I stepped over a box of office supplies to stand by the client chair, which was piled with files. "Why so glum? You out of coffee?" I peered into his mug, half-full.

"No, I've got coffee. The building's been sold."

"The shopping center?"

"Such as it is. The new owner's going to tear it down and put something else here. He's not going to renew my lease."

"How long have you got?" Callously, I was wondering if a new restaurant might come in to replace the laundromat, the tanning salon, and the former karate studio that were on the front side of the building.

"End of the month. The sale must have been in the works awhile. Old owner kept dragging his feet about giving me a new lease. I've been month-to-month for almost a year now."

His head was down, giving me a good look at the comb-overs plastered against the dome of his head. I moved the files from the client chair and sat down. "At least business is good," I said, indicating the pile I'd just put on the floor. "I guess this is all stuff you're working on?"

He shrugged. "Some of it. My business has been kind of month-to-month, too." He sounded more lugubrious than I had ever heard him.

"Anything else going on? Ex-wife giving you hell?"

He turned his basset-hound eyes on me reproachfully. "I've never been married. You know that."

Actually, I did. "So. That's one positive, isn't it? No ex-wife to torment you."

He shrugged.

"I've got something you might look into, if you have time."

His eyebrows went up, and his mouth pursed beneath the short mustache that was just beginning to gray.

"Of course, payment is uncertain at this point," I said. "It'd be something you might work on in your odd moments, if you have any. You wouldn't want to set aside any paying jobs for it."

His eyebrows went back down.

"You've never seen my new digs, have you? I don't think you've been to see me since I hung out my shingle."

"You've always come here."

"Why don't you stop by? I'm in the Executive Suites on the second floor of the Ironfronts: 1011 West Main."

"Okay."

"Today, maybe," I said. "Or tomorrow. Brooke Marshall has the office next to mine, and there's a third office in the same grouping. It'd probably cost less than you're paying here, even if you have to pay extra to store all your files and, ah, stuff." I made a broad, sweeping gesture to include the stacks of files, journals, books, boxes, and whatnot.

"I don't know. I've been on my own a long time."

"You'd still be on your own, but you'd have a secretary out front, and you'd be a dozen feet from the door of your favorite client. There's even some sort of marketing consultant down the hall who's having marital problems."

"Why is it a plus that he's having marital problems?"

"She. When she finds out you're a detective, maybe she'll hire you to spy on her husband."

It earned me a weak smile, but really, the effort to cheer up Rodney was wearing me out. I gave him the names of Robert Walsh and his three beneficiaries, then added Macy Buck, Robert's therapist, as an afterthought. "Anything you can find out about them," I said. "I'm looking for background."

Robert Walsh had lived in a brick ranch house partially obscured by a huge magnolia. That afternoon I parked on the curb in front of it behind a Mercedes convertible and a late-model Nissan. Directly across the street from the sidewalk was someone's back yard—Jared's, if I'd understood what Macy had said at the funeral. The back yard was surrounded by a privacy fence, and the house itself faced a cul-de-sac that opened off Robert's street. Jared's house, if that's whose it was, was built in a more contemporary style than most of the houses in the neighborhood, with sloping roofs that didn't attach to each other.

The black Corvette that Brian drove stopped behind me, and I got out of my car and walked back.

"You ready?"

Brian nodded. Whitney shook her head, her eyes hidden by her sunglasses.

"Oh, come on. We've discussed this," he said to her. "We have to be there when they open the safe."

"It's going to be so unpleasant."

"You're going to have to put up with it, Mouse. It's the only way to be sure of getting a share of whatever's in there."

She sighed, looking out the window toward the house. *Mouse?* I thought.

"Whitney?" he said.

"I know. I'm ready." She popped open the door and got out, tucking her purse under the seat, but keeping a glasses case clutched in one hand. An image of a white, old-fashioned pair of glasses was printed on one side of the case.

I walked with Brian and Whitney up the sidewalk to Robert's house. Behind the storm door the front door was standing open, so I pulled open the storm door. "Hello?"

"In here."

I held the door for Whitney and Brian. She went first, changing out her sunglasses for a pair of glasses with clear lenses. I followed her and Brian into the foyer. Beyond it, the living room had a sofa, love seat, and coffee table all piled with clutter—books, magazines, catalogs, DVDs, and mail. An archway led to the kitchen, where the table and the sill of the window at one end of it were covered with scattered mail, some of it opened and some not, yellow pads covered with scribbled notes, and rows of bottles— some prescription drugs, but mostly nutritional supplements, from the looks of them. Jared Walsh was there, wearing a mock turtleneck and a houndstooth sports jacket. The other man was wearing a gray suit and a striped tie, and his scalp gleamed through the thin, dark hair plastered to his skull.

"You're Robin Starling," the man wheezed. "Rupert Propst." He extended a hand, grimacing at me with widely spaced teeth that struck me as, dare I say it, sharklike.

Jared kept his own hands in his pockets. "You didn't need to come."

Whitney shrugged, averting her gaze.

"Curiosity," I said. "Rumors of disappearing financial assets, a big safe no one can get into. Inquiring minds want to know."

Jared's mouth twisted.

"The locksmith should be here shortly," Rupert said.

I nodded, my gaze roaming over the bottles on the kitchen table. "What's Broccoli-Max?" I asked.

"What?" Jared's scowl deepened, but I picked one of the bottles off the kitchen table and held it up. "Broccoli-Max," I said.

Jared rolled his eyes. "God knows. Uncle Robert had an obsession with alternative medicine, and that therapist of his kept recommending supplements to add to whatever he was already taking. Made his obsession worse."

I put the bottle down, picked up another one labeled *ORAC-Plus*. The subtitle was Oxygen Radical Absorption Capacity, below it a bunch of numbers. I put it down.

"He bragged about being a health nut," said a new voice from the living room. Nathan, too, was there for the big opening. "Though we usually just called him a nut for short."

"We did not. He's only joking," Whitney murmured, looking a little pink.

"Oh, never to his face," Nathan said agreeably, his hands in the pocket of a gray overcoat he wore over jeans and a pocket T-shirt. "A rich man who can occasionally be talked into turning loose of a little money is entitled to respect, hey, Jared?"

Jared's mouth tightened, but before he could respond, Rupert said, "Why don't we go have a look at the safe? It's right back here through the bedroom. We might as well have a look at it, don't you think?"

"Oh, by all means," Nathan said. "Let's all have a look at the safe. That's sure to be productive."

Rupert was through the doorway, looking back over his shoulder and waving his arm in a come-along gesture. As interested in watching his efforts to maintain peace between the two brothers as I was in examining the recalcitrant safe, I followed Rupert through the door into a room that was dominated by a king-sized four-poster bed. The box spring and mattresses came up nearly to my waist, and, as I may have mentioned, I'm a tall girl.

"Right through here." Rupert reached through a doorway to flip a light switch and disappeared through it.

The next room was a small bathroom with two sinks on opposite walls, the counters covered with bottles of over-the-counter medicines and (mostly) supplements. The faucets and the sinks themselves were covered with a thick film of grime. Beyond making the bed, it seemed that not a lot of housekeeping got done in Robert's house. Of course, if I'd just had both knees replaced, I might be letting a few things go myself.

"What good is this going to do?" Jared asked, coming hard on my heels as if not wanting to allow a couple of lawyers to be alone with his uncle's safe.

Rupert already had the light on in the walk-in closet beyond the bathroom. Against the back wall was a chair, where, perhaps, Robert sat to pull on his socks and tie his shoes. Against a side wall, under a row of hanging slacks, was the safe, a massive cube about three feet on a side, a round disk with a number pad in the middle of the door.

"It's a five-digit combination," Rupert said, turning with a hand on the safe like a man about to demonstrate a new washing machine. "I called the manufacturer. Robert would have set it."

"Is there a default combination?" I asked. "Maybe he never got around to setting it."

Rupert was nodding. "There is. One-two-three-four-five, but that didn't work. Evidently, Robert chose his own."

Whitney was crowded in the doorway with Jared, beyond them a bit of Nathan's arm and a shadow that must have belonged to Brian.

"I guess you've tried everyone's birthday?" I asked. "Yours, Robert's siblings', his parents'?"

"Of course," Jared said.

Of course. "Anniversaries, any other number sequences that might have been significant to Robert?" No one said anything. "Does he have a desk? I assume somebody's been through it looking for a five digit number scribbled on an index card or a sticky note."

"Oh, I'm sure Jared's been through the desk," Nathan said.

"He used the front bedroom on the other side of the house as his office," Rupert said. "Of course we've been through it."

"What's the zip code here?" I asked him. "Have you tried that?"

"Oh, for pete's sake," Jared said.

I decided not to suggest the first five digits of Robert's social security number.

"We haven't tried the zip code, actually," Rupert said, spraying the side of my neck with a light coating of spittle as he said his "z."

"It's 23235," Whitney said from the doorway.

Jared, who lived right across the street and could have supplied the number, rolled his eyes. Rupert nodded, smiling at me with his shark teeth and his pale, colorless eyes.

I bent my knees—it was too crowded in the closet to bend at the waist without pressing my bottom into somebody's middle—and punched the zip code into the number pad, then enter.

"Keypad seems loose," I said, rising. "I thought I felt it shift."

"Leave it alone until the expert gets here," Jared said.

A bead of sweat broke free of my hairline and ran down my forehead. It was stuffy in the house, more so in the closet. We were packed in there like sardines, and we were going to be getting salty. I squatted again and twisted at the keypad.

"Don't break it, you idiot," Jared said sharply.

The keypad came away, trailing wires.

"Damn it!" Jared grabbed at my shoulder, but then let go. We were looking at a keyhole, a big one that looked like the sort of keyhole people used to peer through.

"Holy heck," Nathan said softly, taking a step into the closet.

"Well," Rupert said. "The man at Gardall kept saying that some of these models had a key."

"Why the hell didn't you say there was a key?" Jared said.

"There was no keyhole."

"The safe people didn't tell you it was under the keypad?"

"I thought he meant *beneath* the keypad, lower down on the door."

"So you've got a key?" I asked, looking up at them. "You know where it is?"

"No," Jared said.

"Then a keyhole doesn't help us, does it? We're still waiting on the safe man." I stood just as Whitney appeared in the closet doorway holding up a steel key with a long shank and an open bow.

"Where did you get that?" Jared asked belligerently.

"Top drawer of the bureau," came Nathan's voice, and Whitney glanced back at him.

"Underneath Uncle Robert's socks," Whitney said. "I noticed it not long after his surgery when I was helping him do his laundry. Uncle Robert couldn't remember what it was for, and I almost threw it away."

She snaked her way into the closet and handed me the key. I fitted it into the keyhole, and it turned with a satisfying clunk.

"Ready?" I said, my hand on the lever.

They all seemed to be glaring at me, so I stopped milking the moment for drama, pushed down the lever and pulled open the door.

The safe was empty. I emptied my lungs.

After a few moments of silence, Jared turned on Whitney.

"Where is it?" he asked her.

"Where is what?"

"You knew where the key was. You've been in this safe."

"I have not."

"What was in the safe?" I asked. "Do we know for sure?"

"No, not for sure," Jared said. "Our best guess is gold."

"What makes you think that? Did Robert collect gold?" I pushed up between them. Everyone was in the closet now, and I felt claustrophobic with the sense of breathing other people's air.

"No, but Uncle Robert's been converting all his assets into something," Jared said.

I looked at Rupert. "What does that mean, converting all his assets?"

Rupert cleared his throat, making a sound like the grinding of gears. "A couple of months before he died, six weeks or so, Mr. Walsh started emptying his financial accounts, even his retirement accounts. We haven't been able to track all of it…"

"We haven't been able to track squat," Jared said.

"Have you checked the banks?" I suggested. "Robert may have safety deposit boxes all over town."

"Not in his name," Rupert said.

"Why are you thinking gold?"

Jared and Rupert exchanged a look. "There are some brochures and invoices on his desk," Rupert said.

"How much money are we talking about?"

Neither of them answered. "Eight million dollars," Nathan said from the bathroom. "Maybe more."

"We don't want to go throwing numbers about casually," Rupert said, looking earnestly at the bathroom doorway. To me he added, "To tell you the truth, we're not sure how much money is missing, not exactly."

"The whole thing proves the old goat was senile," Jared said. "I've been saying that for months."

"He did trigger a lot of unnecessary tax liability," Rupert added. "The estate will owe money on everything he took out of his retirement accounts. Outside those accounts, his heirs have lost a big step-up in basis in everything he sold."

"How does the tax liability compare to the assets you have left?" I asked.

No one answered this time, though Rupert looked pained and Jared looked both angry and desperate.

"Ouch," I said.

Rupert's lips stretched over his big, square teeth.

"It seems to me there are a lot of people who could have been in that safe," Nathan said, wedging himself into the doorway.

"Just what do you mean by that?" Jared said.

"I'm just noting that you've arranged for a lot of witnesses to be here for the opening of the safe. Everyone can testify that when you opened the safe, it was empty."

Jared made a sudden movement, and beside him Rupert Propst lurched back against the hanging clothes, dislodging the clothing bar at one end and spilling a long row of Robert's dress shirts and slacks onto the floor in one corner of the closet. Jared stopped short of hitting Nathan, who hadn't moved, hadn't even taken his hands from the pockets of the overcoat.

"Shall I close the safe, or leave it open?" I asked as Rupert righted himself.

Jared and Nathan were looking at each other. The fist of Jared's that I could see was clenched, but Nathan was so nonchalant that I wondered for an instant if he had a pistol in the pocket of that open overcoat. "It hardly matters now, does it?" Nathan said to Jared. "Whatever was there is long gone."

"How much does gold weigh?" I asked. "Does anybody know?"

If anyone did, no one was saying. My eyes came to rest on Rupert, but he only smiled at me, or grimaced, or had a facial spasm. It was hard to tell. I thought I'd stir the pot.

"If the safe was full gold, whoever moved it had some heavy hauling to do," I said.

"He certainly did," Nathan said.

Jared's hands were coming up, but Rupert grabbed an arm with both hands. "We're going to need to work together," he said. "We can't start fighting among ourselves. It isn't productive."

"Can we move out into the living room?" I said. "I'm choking on human exhaust in here."

Somebody gave a nervous laugh. I pushed toward the door, and it started the crowd moving. When we got back into the living room, I wiped at the sweat on my forehead with the back of my wrist. Robert had an old cube of a TV in his entertainment center. Other than taking enough supplements to supply the nutritional needs of a herd of cattle, he seemed to have lived pretty cheaply.

Rupert took center stage. "We all have a common interest here," he said. "Can we put aside our differences and just agree to trust each other?" He bared his shark teeth at us, which I had to say didn't inspire a lot of trust in me. "If we can postulate that none of us is responsible for Robert's missing assets, no one in this room, it will suggest, I think, an obvious hypothesis. Am I right?" He was nodding, encouraging us to embrace the obvious. "From all reports, the therapist Macy Buck was in here all the time. She traded recipes with him, suggested supplements. Suppose he showed her the key before his death, and afterwards she took advantage of the situation to empty his safe."

"I wouldn't have seen her," Jared said. "She could have backed her car into the driveway—it's pretty secluded with all the privacy fences back there—and walked whatever was in there out through the garage."

"You really have no basis for that accusation," Nathan said. "Either of you."

"Or how about this one," Jared continued. "Robert told her what was in the safe, maybe even showed it to her. She saw where he put the key, then drowned him in the bathtub. We don't know. Maybe baths was one of the things she helped him with."

"You're just being gross," Whitney said, at the same time that I said, "I thought he drowned in your hot tub."

Jared looked at me. "In all the time he's been living right across the street, he'd never been in my hot tub. He had all kinds of knee pain leading up to that surgery, and he never asked to use it. I think Macy drowned him right here, loaded him into her car, drove him over to my place, and dumped him in the spa."

"She's not that big a woman," I said.

"She wasn't necessarily acting alone," Jared said.

"I resent that," Nathan said.

"I don't see the point in moving the body," I said. "It increases the risk, and Macy gets nothing out of it. She could walk the contents of the safe out past Robert's body just as easily as if he weren't here."

"Thank you," Nathan said to me.

"How about this one?" Jared said. "Macy talked him into going across the street with her, told him they were going to do some water therapy or something. She got him in the hot tub, held him under, headed back across the street to empty the safe."

"You keep going on about your damn hot tub," Nathan said.

"I just don't know what he was doing over there."

"Gentlemen," Rupert said. "I was merely suggesting a hypothesis. All of it is pure speculation at this point. Before we do anything, we should talk to Ms. Buck. If that isn't productive, we can put a private detective on her, see where she goes and what she does. We have suspicions…"

"You have suspicions," Nathan said.

"…but before we can act on them, we need to ascertain whether those suspicions are justified."

"I think you're grasping at straws," Brian said. "If Uncle Robert was hiding his money, there's no reason Macy would have known anything about it."

"What do you mean, Uncle Robert?" Jared said. "I don't even know what you're doing here."

The doorbell rang, and several of us started, but it was only the locksmith, there to drill into the safe.

"Sorry I'm late," he said. "I got tied up on my last job."

The conspiracy theorists broke up soon after that, and I was glad to get out into the sunlight and the cold, bracing air, out of the miasma of greed and suspicion. "Well, that was unpleasant," I said conversationally to Whitney as we stopped between our cars. Jared was getting into the Mercedes convertible two cars ahead of us, and Nathan was getting into a Ford SUV parked behind Brian's Corvette. Rupert's vehicle was the Nissan. They all started their cars and headed off immediately as if they had places to be. I rather thought Jared might drive his across the street and park twenty-five feet from where he started, but he was still accelerating when a bend in the road took him out of sight.

Brian and Whitney were still holding hands on the sidewalk. "I've got quite a family, huh?" she said to him.

"Don't you worry about them."

She pressed her face to his chest.

"I could talk to Macy," I said, and they turned to look at me.

"Or should we leave it to the others to fight among themselves?" I added.

"What do you think, Mouse? It wouldn't hurt for her to talk, would it?"

She gave him a squeeze, smiling up at him.

It seemed as if they'd be content to spend the rest of the afternoon standing on the sidewalk, hugging and smiling, but I hung around until finally they got into Brian's Corvette and left to go somewhere they could cuddle in private. I waved from my own car as they pulled away from the curb and drove past me, but when they had disappeared around the bend in the road, I got back out and crossed the street to the alley that ran behind Jared's house.

I couldn't see anything over the privacy fence, but once in his driveway I stepped up onto the lower rail of the gate and could see everything. There was a pool and a hot tub, some really nice decking, and Asian jasmine everywhere. Four sets of French doors ran along the back of the house.

I reached over the gate and undid the latch.

The first thing I did was go to one of the French doors and peer into the house. The living room had a high, vaulted ceiling and what I thought of as showroom furniture—big, nice pieces expensively covered and attractively arranged. I didn't see anyone, which was what I had hoped for. From what Nathan had said at the funeral, Jared was divorced, and no one had mentioned any kids.

I turned back around. The pool was a small one, shaped like a kidney bean, the hot tub set into the decking between it and the house.

I went to the hot tub, unfastened the strap that held down the front of the hot tub's maroon cover, and pushed it up. The water burbled gently, and the smell of bromine wafted out. It was a good sized hot tub, but I thought a man could push his feet against the opposite bench to keep his head out of the water. Of course, Robert didn't have good knees, and it might not have taken a lot of force to hold him under.

On the other hand, maybe he did just get light-headed in the heat, slide off the seat and quietly drown, the surface of the water bubbling just inches over his nose and mouth. There didn't have to be somebody's hand on the top of his head holding him under.

But there could have been.

Chapter 6

The next day was a Friday. Not long after I got to work that morning, my phone buzzed, and I picked it up. "Hi, Carly."

"There's a Mr. Rodney Burns here to see you."

"I'll come get him."

When I came out, Rodney was standing with his back to me. A slim briefcase dangled from his hands, which were clasped behind him as he studied a large work of abstract art on the wall opposite the reception desk. Actually, I can't tell you for certain that what he was studying was art: It might have been paint splashed on a canvas by someone with no artistic pretensions at all, but it was in a frame.

"Hey, Rodney," I said. "Come to check us out?"

His head bobbed on his thin neck. "That, and I have something for you."

"Let me introduce you. Carly, this is Rodney Burns. He's in the market for office space, and I told him about the empty office in my little cluster."

"Great! Pleased to meet you." Her enthusiasm was not everything you'd expect if she were being presented with a check from the Publishers Clearing House, but it was of the same order of magnitude. She stood and shook Rodney's hand over the counter, then came out through the door to one side of it. "I'm Carly Price, office manager, receptionist, and sometime data entry clerk. Let me show you around." She was tall—well, five-eight or so—and had warm, brown eyes and a hint of olive in her complexion. She might have been beautiful, but for a big nose and a mass of curly brown hair that made her face look even narrower than it was—and she had a predilection for tube skirts tight enough to show little saddlebags on what was otherwise a thin frame.

Okay, I'm doing Carly a gross injustice. In mentioning the minor imperfections that make Carly an individual, I've taken a pretty woman and made her sound like a Picasso painting. Certainly Rodney seemed mesmerized.

Carly had Rodney's hand again, and she continued to hold it as she talked. "Robin's one of our newer tenants. She's been with us, what is it, Robin? Not quite three months. We've got another lawyer here and a marketing consultant and a number of outside sales people. We offer them reception and the use of a boardroom and some secretarial services—we price those a la carte at twenty dollars an hour. What is it you do, Mr. Burns?" She fixed him with those big, brown eyes and waited for his response, her lips parted and glistening with lip gloss.

"I, uh, have a detective agency." He cleared his throat. "A small, one-man detective agency."

"A detective agency!" she breathed, leaning into him. "How exciting!"

"Stop in when she's showed you around," I said. "You can tell me what you've got for me."

I went back to my office and left him to Carly's tender mercies. It was about twenty minutes before Carly brought him to my door. "We're going to look at the empty office here in your cluster. It's just like this one of Robin's, Mr. Burns. Rodney." She smiled and ducked her chin. "It has the same wall of exposed brick behind the desk—isn't that beautiful? I think the last tenant left his desk and client chairs, and you can use those if you like them or you can bring in your own."

She swept him away again. She didn't sweep him far—the empty office was just on the other side of Brooke's—and I could hear the current of Carly's voice rising and falling, punctuated here and there by the silvery tinkle of her laughter.

They came back. "I'll leave you here with Robin, but here's my card. If you have any questions, or want to talk more about your particular needs—" Her voice became suggestively husky. "—a private detective must have any number of special requirements—please just call me."

When she left us, Rodney slumped into one of my client chairs. He seemed a little dazed.

"I'm sorry," I said. "Carly can be a bit overpowering."

"No, it's not that." One corner of his mouth quirked up. "It's just been a long time since a woman's paid quite so much attention to me."

"Well, it's not an act. You rent here, and you'll continue to be the most important person in Carly's life."

"Huh. That could be a bit..."

"Draining," I finished for him. "But it'll work out. It took me awhile to set some boundaries with her, too. Did you like the office?"

"Yes, I guess. It occurs to me that she never mentioned price."

"It's not bad. I pay five-fifty a month. It's a downtown location, and you can walk to anything."

He nodded.

"You said you had something for me?"

"Oh. Yes. It's right here." He pulled his briefcase onto his lap and took out a manila folder. From that he extracted a single sheet of paper. He handed it across.

The heading at the top of the document was Marriage License, and it began, *Virginia, City of Richmond, to wit: To any person licensed to celebrate marriages...* "Nathan Robert Walsh and Macy Gail Buck," I read. The license was issued by the circuit court clerk in Richmond.

"It's a certified copy," Rodney said, "which is probably overkill, but I was coming downtown anyway. That way it's admissible into evidence if you ever need it."

"They were married." I looked up. "Nathan and his uncle's therapist."

"I don't think so. No marriage certificate was ever filed."

"But they were going to be married."

"It looks like it."

"So there was no reason for Macy to run off with Robert's gold, even if she had the opportunity. She was going to share in a third of it anyway."

"What? What gold?"

Rodney didn't know anything about Robert's disappearing assets. I filled him in.

"When did he start emptying his accounts, did you say?"

"A couple months ago, evidently."

"And he was converting everything to gold?"

I tilted my head, shrugged. "That's what they seem to think."

"Maybe the romance was going sour on her."

I said, "Be a good way to get back at a no-good boyfriend, I guess. Haul his inheritance out through the garage door and disappear with it. Before it would do her any good, though, she'd have to sell it."

"Yes."

"She could keep it in her closet or underneath a floor board and sell a little at a time."

Rodney straightened in his chair. "On the other hand, maybe the romance was going along fine, but Robert looked likely to live another ten or twelve years. Maybe that's too long to wait before cashing in."

"So she talked Robert into going across the street for a little water therapy, and she drowned him in the hot tub. Now you sound like me."

"Sound like you how?"

"Suspecting evil of everyone. Carly showed you the kitchen, I suppose?"

"Yes, I saw the kitchen."

"The three-burner Bunn coffeemaker? Did she offer you coffee?"

"Well, no."

"Let me get you a cup of coffee." Rodney Burns was a big coffee aficionado. I left him in my office. All three burners were on, and all the carafes had coffee in them, though each was below half. The orange-handled carafe held the decaf. The two black-handled carafes held regular, but of different strengths. The label pasted on one handle said "4 SCOOPS" and the one on the other said "6 SCOOPS." According to Carly, the labels had resolved a raging debate the previous fall about the proper strength for coffee. The 4-Scoop tenants complained that the 6-scoop coffee was harsh and grainy. The 6-scoop tenants derided the 4-scoop coffee as brown water. Each had felt no compunction about pouring coffee of the improper strength down the sink and making fresh.

I sniffed at each of the carafes. Rodney, I thought, would fit in with the 6-scoop coffee drinkers, but the 6-scoop coffee smelled a little burned. I was making a fresh pot when Rodney joined me.

"Great Value coffee," he said, seeing the can.

"I know. Not up to your usual standards."

He picked up the can. "It just says coffee."

"What should it say?"

"It should say 100% Arabica, or at a minimum 100% Columbian, which would rule out that awful Vietnamese Robusta." He chewed at his lip while I poured in the water, his thin mustache looking like a light brown caterpillar trying to crawl into his mouth. Fresh coffee started draining into the carafe.

"I may be able do all of you some good," he said. "I'll talk to Carly."

"They go through a lot of coffee around here. I doubt you'll talk her into anything fancy."

"A good cup of coffee doesn't have to be fancy," he said with dignity. "Or more than marginally more expensive."

"It's good to see a man with a mission." The carafe was already half full. I switched it out with the 4-scoop carafe while I poured, then switched them back. I handed Rodney the Styrofoam cup.

"Some of them have their own mugs," I said, nodding at the peg-board.

Rodney sipped his coffee, and the caterpillar on his upper lip spasmed briefly. "I can definitely do you some good," he said.

We sipped our coffee, and Rodney examined the coffee mugs on the pegboard with their various jokes and logos. I thought his Edgar Allan Poe mug would fit right in.

He left, but I called him back a couple hours later, just before lunch. "So what are you thinking?" I asked him. "Will you be moving downtown at the end of the month?"

"I don't know. I haven't really looked at anything else."

"Time is passing."

"It always does." He sighed.

"Listen. Do you have a cell number for Macy Buck?"

"No. I can get it." I heard the clicking of a keyboard.

"So where can you get great tasting coffee for the price of Great Value?"

"I didn't say *great* tasting. I think you could improve the taste by fifty percent, though, with maybe only a ten percent bump in price."

I wondered how you quantified taste sufficiently to calculate a percentage.

"Do you think Carly would accept a ten percent increase in the price of her coffee?"

"Maybe. You ought to present the idea to her before you sign your lease. That's the moment when your ideas will seem most attractive. How do you know how much Great Value costs, anyway? Did you stop by Walmart?" I didn't think there was one between my office and Rodney's.

"I have a computer," he said with some dignity. "And, as it happens, Macy Buck's cell number is on the screen." He read it to me."

"Thanks, Rodney. I owe you."

"It will be on your bill."

With that unsettling thought, I hung up. I was continuing to devote resources to the case with little prospect of getting paid. Fortunately, most of the resources were my own time, and it wasn't like I had clients lining up to pay for that. I called Macy.

Macy met me for lunch at the West Broad Street Road Cafe, a combination cafe and gift shop on, as you might suspect, West Broad Street Road. It always struck me as strange that West Broad is identified as both a street and a road. You'd think there'd be a story to explain it, but if there is, I've never heard it.

The cafe is part restaurant and part gift shop. In addition to homemade soups, sandwiches, and pasta salads, it sells bracelets, gift cards, placards that say things like "Baby, It's Cold Outside" and "Eat Drink & Be Merry" in ornate lettering. I don't think it's a requirement that you have two X chromosomes to get in, but on the other hand, the one time I'd been there the only male I saw was in the company of a woman.

Macy was already seated, sipping iced tea from a Mason jar with a handle, when I slid into the seat opposite her. "I'm sorry I'm late."

"You're not late. My last appointment wasn't far from here, so when I finished I came on." She was a petite little thing, wearing crisp, navy scrubs that might have been starched and ironed. No ring on her left hand. "I'm glad you called. I was hoping to talk to you."

My eyebrows went up. "I didn't know you knew me."

"I understand you were at Robert's house yesterday when they opened the safe."

I nodded. "I guess you heard about it from Nathan."

"Why from Nathan?"

"Aren't you…I'm sorry, he mentioned a fiancé, and for some reason…are the two of you not engaged?"

She ran a hand back through her fine, blonde hair. "Nathan has a big mouth," she said.

"I guess you were keeping a low profile. Don't worry. I won't say anything."

"You were there on Whitney's behalf."

"It was a momentous occasion for everybody. Whitney was there with her boyfriend. Jared was there with his lawyer. I'm surprised you weren't there with Nathan."

"Somebody has to work."

"Everyone may have to. You should have seen the reaction when they opened the safe and found it empty. It was like a bomb went off."

"Whitney was close to her uncle," Macy said. "Closer than either of his nephews."

"Whitney has a good heart."

"So close she knew there was a key to the safe and where it was."

"Actually, I understood she'd seen the key, but didn't know what it was for until we found the keyhole yesterday."

"Until you found the keyhole."

"Ah." She suspected Whitney and me of complicity in making off with Robert's assets. "I guess it does look suspicious."

The waitress came by for our drink orders. When she left, I picked up the brown paper bag that had the day's menu printed on it. Macy pulled hers toward her, but her eyes were on me.

"What's good?" I said. "I've only been here once."

"They say all the sandwiches are good. I like the pasta sampler."

She waited until the waitress had come back with our drinks and we'd placed our orders before trying a more direct approach.

"So," she said.

"So," I agreed.

"Do you know what was in that safe and where it is now?"

"Macy." I gave her what I hoped was a disarming smile. "Whitney is not the executor of the estate, nor is she the sole beneficiary. If she and I had made off with her uncle's proof sets or his stamp collection or his bearer bonds, it would be theft, pure and simple."

"You didn't mention gold," she said.

"What?"

"When Robert died, there were pamphlets from Lear Capital and Rosland Capital and a couple of other precious metals companies on his desk."

"I think they mentioned that."

"But you didn't."

I shrugged. "Sorry. Gold, silver, platinum. Gem stones, maybe."

She was looking at me hard. Our food came, Macy's pasta sampler and my soup and half-a-sandwich. I sat back to give the waitress room to put it down. When she was gone, I picked up my sandwich and said, "I understood you were the one especially close to Robert, always conferring about supplements and holistic remedies for various old-person complaints."

She took a bite of her pasta and put her fork down. "We were close, but something happened just after the first of the year. He got really angry at Jared and started being just erratic."

"Angry at you, too?"

"Sometimes. Angry, suspicious…I began to think he was headed for full blown paranoia."

"Could it have been dementia of some sort?"

"It came in spells. Sometimes he'd be just a normal old man. At others, he wouldn't know Adam from Eve." She took another bite of her pasta.

"You ever do water therapy with him in Jared's pool or hot tub?"

She put her fork down carefully. "That's a lie."

"I was asking a question, not making an assertion."

"Jared told you that, didn't he?"

"Jared? Actually, what he's said is that Robert never used his pool or hot tub."

"Yes, he's pointing the finger at me just in case he needs a little CYA."

"Why would he need to cover his—" I checked my language. An old lady at the next table had her eyes on me. "—you know."

"Because he invited Robert over to use his hot tub." She put another forkful of pasta in her mouth.

"He did?"

"There's no other reason Robert would have been over there. Jared got him into the hot tub and made sure he didn't get out."

"You said something about that at the funeral. Robert wasn't home when you came by to do his therapy, and you heard splashing over in Jared's backyard. Was it splashing, you think, or just the jets in the hot tub?"

"It wasn't jets. And I heard voices, too. Jared was back there."

"I don't think you mentioned voices at the funeral."

"How could I? Jared was standing right there. I'd have been accusing him to his face."

"Have you told the police this story? There're a couple of detectives who might be interested."

"Who?"

I gave her Jordan's name. "His partner is Ray Hernandez. You could talk to either of them."

"Thanks." But her tone was grudging. Somehow, despite picking at her food, she had nearly finished her pasta. "I don't think I understand why you asked me to lunch."

"You should have asked me."

"Why should I have asked you?"

"It gives you the chance to pump me about Robert's assets and to spread the tale of the suspicious circumstances surrounding his death."

"But I didn't ask you."

"No."

"So what are you after?"

"Maybe the same thing you are. As you say, there seems to be a rather large estate that's gone missing."

"Have you talked to your client, her and her sweet boyfriend?"

"Sure."

"Don't let that phony niceness fool you. They're perfectly capable of…" She broke off. "Suppose Robert drowned in his own bathtub, and they found him there? What's to keep them from carrying him across the street and dumping him in Jared's hot tub? They maybe implicate Jared, and if he actually got convicted of killing his uncle…You see where this is going, don't you?"

I'd heard the same speculation from Jared with her in the starring role.

"He couldn't inherit. You're a lawyer, don't you see?"

"I thought it was Jared's voice you heard in the backyard."

"A male voice. It could have been Brian's."

"Or Robert's himself?"

"I don't think so."

"Whitney's no bigger than you are, and Brian's no bigger than average. It's hard to see the two of them carrying a body across the street in broad daylight."

She gave me a withering look. "They back a car up to Robert's garage, load him up, drive across to

74

Jared's driveway and carry him in through the back gate."

"I guess both driveways are pretty sheltered," I said. "You're better off sticking with Jared, though. Moving the body wouldn't cost Whitney her inheritance."

"You think I'm making it all up."

"Hardly matters now, does it? The estate's gone. Even if Jared were convicted and Nathan and Whitney split the estate, fifty percent more of nothing is still not very much." I smiled as I picked up the check.

"Do you really not know anything about the missing money?"

I stood. "If I did, I wouldn't be here talking to you."

"Your client does," Macy said. "Count on it."

I don't know why I picked up the check. This case was already costing me more than it was earning me in fees, at least on a cash flow basis. Of course, as Macy had pointed out, I had been the one to ask her to lunch.

I followed her out and watched her get into an orange Honda Element, a small, boxy vehicle that seemed appropriate for an in-home therapist. She started it and drove past me without waving. I didn't think we'd be doing any sleepovers.

I took a breath, then swung into my own car. It was early afternoon, so I headed back downtown, but after a half-mile or so, I circled the block and headed toward home. I had a dog there waiting for me. Technically, I guess he was waiting for me at Dr. McDermott's home rather than my own, but the point was, if I went home, I could go running with Deeks. That beat the heck out of playing spider solitaire on the computer while waiting for another client to walk through the door.

Chapter 7

So I got home about two-thirty that Friday afternoon and went on a two-mile run with my dog. Actually, I went on a two-mile run. Deeks probably ran twice that, dashing off on his little puppy legs to check out all the sights and smells apparent only to those whose eyes and nose traveled a few inches above the ground. If I worried about whether anyone seeing Deeks in daylight would object that my control of him was not immediate enough to satisfy the dictates of the leash law, I needn't have. Everyone was at work or school, and the streets were empty. An advantage to running in daylight was that it was not as cold as it was going to be after the sun went down—cold, but not that cold.

We got back, and I showered and walked with Deeks across the street to visit Dr. McDermott. He seemed pleased and a little surprised to see me.

"Are you going to leave Deacon with me this evening?"

I shook my head. "Taking him over to Paul's."

"You don't do that very often."

"No. I usually make Paul come here." I followed him into the kitchen.

"I was going to make myself a hot buttered rum a little later, but I'll have it now, if you'd like one."

I moved my head equivocally.

"No?"

"Oh, I'd like one. I only burned off 200 calories or so just now, though, and Paul is fixing me dinner."

"Say no more."

I took a seat at the table and frowned at the back half of a shoe sitting next to one of the table legs. "Did Deeks chew up one of your Topsiders?"

"Two of them. The first one's disappeared completely, and that's what's left of the second."

"I'm sorry."

He shook his head as he pulled out a chair and sat down. "No need to be. Labs need to chew, and that was just an old pair I used as slippers as I shuffled about the house. They fascinated Deacon from the first time he came over here."

"Some interesting smells, I guess."

He smiled. "Evidently. Once, when I was taking him out to potty, I was barefoot, and I could hardly get the door closed for Deacon running back inside for another sniff at those Topsiders, which were sitting just inside. I had to pick them up and carry them out with us before he'd go."

When I left, Deeks went with me. Dr. McDermott kept him weekdays; evenings and weekends were mine, except when I had to go somewhere that Deeks couldn't follow. Tonight, I was just going over to Paul's, though, and it would do Paul good to deal with some dog hair along his baseboards. After all, he was the one responsible for my having a furry little roommate in the first place.

Paul's apartment was on the Southside, a good twenty minutes from my house even when traffic was good, which, at five-thirty on a Friday evening, it wasn't.

He opened the door of his ground-floor apartment. Deeks started when he saw him, clearly surprised, but he recovered and raced past him into the living room, circled the weight bench in front of the sofa where the coffee table should be, streaked back past us through the door, and, turning in another tight circle, came back at us again.

"Whoa," Paul said as Deeks pulled up short in front of him. "I'm glad to see you, too, little buddy." He leaned over to pat him.

"You don't show it," I said. "You didn't run around in circles. I don't see your tail wagging."

I guess you get what you ask for. Paul turned around and wiggled his butt at me.

"What's for dinner?" I asked, ignoring the gyrating glutes in front of me. "I'm starved."

Paul turned around. "How about you, Deacon, buddy? Are you starved, too?"

Deeks panted at him, looking happy. It was impossible for him to look sad, really, with his mouth open and his tongue hanging out.

"I've got some chicken for him," Paul said as we followed him into the apartment. There was a barbell on the rack of the weight bench, two twenty-five-pound weights on each end of the bar—one hundred pounds, plus whatever the bar weighed.

"He's had some kibble," I said, "but I'm sure he'll be good with chicken, too."

"For us, I've got salad."

"Salad!" I eyed him critically. "What's gotten into you? You're losing weight, your coffee table's disappeared, and now you're eating salad."

"When I say salad, I don't mean just any salad. In addition to sliced chicken breast, it has cranberries and gorgonzola and sliced almonds, all sprinkled with a little balsamic vinegar and some dark, fragrant pumpkin oil."

"Sounds pretty good."

"Oh, stop. You're going to turn my head." He held up a hand. "No, no. That's all right. I'm sure there'll be more accolades when you've tasted it. It's all ready, and it's on the table. Do you want to eat there, or eat while we watch TV?"

"If we watch, we might miss some of the nuances of this divine salad."

"And we wouldn't want that. Good point." He led the way past the weight bench and around the corner to the small round table at one end of his galley-style kitchen. There was a white table cloth on the table, and a red candle in a pewter candlestick.

"Hey, fancy," I said.

Paul pulled out a chair for me, and I sat. Then he lit the candle using a long-nosed lighter.

"And for our canine friend," he said. With a flourish he set a stainless steel bowl of chicken chunks on the floor in front of Deeks, who gave him a quick nod of appreciation and immediately started wolfing it.

"You've thought of everything," I said.

"Have you ever seen American Horror Story?"

"Is that our evening's entertainment?"

"It could be. Netflix has the first two seasons."

"I've heard it's kind of twisted."

"Oh, yes," Paul said.

"You've seen it?"

"No. I've heard the same thing."

"All right then."

For dinner I usually have salad greens mixed with no more than a little torn-up deli meat, and this was really good. "I could do this every night," I said.

"We can. I don't think you've been to my place more than, what, a couple, three times? But my door is always open."

Deeks was sitting at attention now, his eyes on Paul. His head came forward as Paul reached for him, and Paul scratched him behind the ears. "You, too, Deacon, buddy. You're always welcome."

"I was really just referring to the salad," I said. "But your apartment's nice, too."

"Thank you."

We ate, we made small talk. Afterwards, we turned out the lights and settled on the couch across the weight bench from the TV, Paul on one side of me and Deeks on the other, his chin resting on my thigh—Deeks' chin, not Paul's, though I don't think Paul would have needed much encouragement. Paul did his magic with the button-studded wand, and the opening images of "American Horror Story" flickered across the screen. When his arm brushed mine, I noted its unexpected tone and squeezed his biceps to confirm.

"It's the weight bench," he said. "And a little change in diet."

"It looks good on you." I settled in next to him, putting my socked feet on the weight bench beside his, thinking life didn't get much better than this. That was when my phone went off, playing some majestic strains from "The Return of the King" soundtrack, my default ringtone. I silenced the phone and looked at its screen. Paul paused the TV.

"Brian Marshall," I said. "Brooke's brother."

"You better get it, hadn't you?"

I sighed. "I suppose. Surely it will just take a minute." I swept my finger across the screen.

"This is Robin Starling."

I heard only a heavy breath or two, not something I would have associated with Brooke's brother.

"Hello?" I said.

"Macy…" He was gone.

"Hello, are you there? Can you hear me?" I was standing, moving toward the sliding glass doors where the reception might be a little better, but I looked at the screen again and saw the call had ended rather than failed. I switched to the screen of my recent calls and touched Brian's name.

"Who is it?" Paul asked, but I held up a hand. The call went to Brian's voice mail.

"Hi, Brian. This is Robin. I lost you." I thought for a moment, but couldn't think what else to say. I ended the call.

"What did he say?" Paul asked. He was still on the couch, but Deeks was on his feet watching me, ready to follow wherever I might go.

"I don't know," I said. "It was weird." I told him about the heavy breathing and about the one word Brian had spoken.

"Macy. That is weird."

"Let me try Whitney," I said.

Whitney Foster picked up on the first ring. "Hello?"

"Hi, Whitney, this is Robin Starling. Is Brian with you?"

She hesitated. "Didn't he call you?"

"We got disconnected. Do you know where he is?"

"I...know where he was."

I waited.

"He went to Macy Buck's house."

"Yes?"

"She seemed to be dead."

"What do you mean, she seemed to be dead?" I realized I sounded shrill. I glanced at Paul, who was standing now, his hands gripping the barbell that lay across the rack of his weight bench. "How do you seem to be dead?" I said, making an effort to bring my voice down half-an-octave.

"There was blood all over her. Brian didn't tell you?"

I closed my eyes.

"I told him to call you and tell you everything."

"Didn't he call the police?"

"I don't know."

"Tell me everything he told you."

"There wasn't much. He went to see her, and her front door was open. He went in and...just found her."

"Was the door unlocked or actually standing open?"

"Standing open, I think."

"Wide open, or open just a crack?"

She was silent, which I took to mean she didn't know.

"Where does Macy live, do you know?"

"Somewhere on Patterson in the near West End, I think."

"Where was Brian when he called you? Back at his apartment, or still at Macy's house?"

"At Macy's, I think. I had the idea he was sitting in his car in front of the house."

"Why sitting in front of the house? Could he have been waiting for an ambulance?"

"I'm not sure."

"Why did he go to Macy's in the first place, did he mention that?"

"He's calling in. I've got to go." She ended the call.

I shook the phone in exasperation, and Paul said, "Macy Buck is dead, and Brian found her?"

"Evidently."

"Murdered, or just dead?"

"I don't know." I looked down at my phone, thinking about trying to get Whitney back, or Brian. Instead I went to Favorites and touched Brooke Marshall's photograph.

"Hey, Robin. Are you and Paul having fun?"

"Where does Brian live, do you know?"

"My brother Brian? Malvern Manor. Why? Are you not with Paul?"

The Malvern Manor apartments wouldn't be far from Macy Buck. "I need to see Brian."

"Why? What's going on?"

I put my phone on the weight bench and filled her in as I pulled my shoes on and tied them. "I've got a bad feeling, like he might be about to do something stupid. You don't know where he keeps his spare key, do you, in case we get there and can't get in?"

"I have a spare."

"Bring it. It'll probably take us close to fifteen minutes, but we're leaving now."

When I'd punched off, Paul said, "I'm going with you? Deacon, too?"

I'd spoken without considering Deeks, who wouldn't do well if left alone in an unfamiliar apartment—and who seemed to know it. His eyes were glued to my face, his expression anxious.

"Deacon, too," I said. "Let's go."

Marvin Manor consisted of a series of massive three-story buildings of red brick with rows of dormers protruding from the planes of the high, sloping roofs. I turned onto Malvern Avenue and pulled into a space along the curb. As Paul opened his door, Deeks leaped from the back seat into the seat Paul had vacated and from there out the door.

"Stay close," I called to him as I got out on the driver's side. Brooke's Honda was angling into the curb a few cars in front of me. Paul and I walked down to meet her, Deeks running ahead of us, then circling back.

When we met on the side walk, Deeks licked the leg of Brooke's pants in greeting. "Brian's in this first building," she said, pointing. "Third floor." As we started toward it, she added, "I'm pretty sure they don't allow pets."

"He's a brown dog in the dark," Paul said.

"Oh in that case I'm sure it's fine."

We followed her into the stairwell and up the stairs. No one answered the bell, and Brooke dug in her purse for the key. When she found it, she unlocked the deadbolt, then the knob. As the door opened, Deeks streamed past us into the apartment, bumping door and jamb as he snaked through.

"Deeks," I hissed. Paul shouldered past me and went in next. "Hey!"

"Brian?" Paul called. "It's Paul Soldano. I'm with your sister."

I moved into the apartment behind him. "We need to talk to you," I said.

There were sounds coming from the bathroom. As I started toward it, Deeks came out dragging a pair of jeans by the pant leg. I bent to take them from him, and he yapped once and wagged his tail, looking up at me.

"The leg's wet," I said. "Looks like Brian was trying to get a stain out." I sniffed at the darker splotch in the midst of the wetness. "It smells kind of like raw meat."

"Let me smell," Brooke said.

I let her and Paul sniff.

"I think it may be blood," Paul said.

"You know what blood smells like?"

"I think kind of like this."

"This is awful," Brooke said. "Where could he be?"

My phone played a bar from "The Bridge of Khazadum." "It's him," I said, swiping the screen. "We can ask him. Brian?"

"Don't try to find me."

"Don't be an idiot," I said. "You can't run away from this."

"You don't understand."

"I'm standing in the middle of your apartment. I understand more than you think."

He was silent.

"Brian?"

"What have you found?"

"A pair of jeans with a wet pants-leg."

"I didn't do it."

"Kill Macy? I know you didn't."

"No. I mean I didn't get blood on those jeans. They were thrown across my bed when I got home, a smear of something dark on the front of one thigh. I tried to get it out."

"They're not your jeans?"

"They are my jeans. That's what I don't get."

Brooke put a hand on my arm. "Let me talk to him."

I held up a finger. "You're saying you're being framed, and the frame's too good to beat, is that the size of it?" When he didn't answer, I said, "Who knew you were going to see Macy tonight?"

"Nobody. That's just the point."

"Whitney?"

"No." An immediate response, almost vehement.

"So somebody must have seen you there. Did you see anyone?"

"I didn't. It was getting dark, and…there was no one to see."

"A neighbor, looking out a window," I suggested.

He seemed to be thinking it over. "There may have been someone in the yard across the street, some kind of movement. I don't know."

"Movement as you drove away?"

"I don't know."

"When you left Macy's house, did you go straight to your apartment?"

"Yes, I did."

"Did you see anyone pull away from the curb while you were sitting there, someone who might have beat you to your apartment to plant evidence?" I sat on the edge of a camelback sofa with a worn floral print. There was a glasses case on the end table, a black case with cat-eye frames embossed in white on one side. I picked them up. "Does Whitney have a key to your apartment?"

He didn't answer.

"Who else?"

"Brooke."

"She's the one who let me in. Who else?"

"Nobody. There's a key under the potted plant by the back door."

"That's the door off the kitchen?" Tucking the glasses case into the pocket of my jacket, I moved toward it, a solid wood door painted white. I turned the thumb latch and pulled it open. Deeks went through the door ahead of me, turning back on the landing to wait.

Behind me Paul said, "She says the alpha dog always goes through the door first. I think she's confused about who that is."

I ignored him. The back stairwell wasn't as nice as the one in front: Linoleum on the landing instead of tile, and it was peeling along one edge. I saw the potted plant, a clay-colored plastic pot with a dead twig sticking out of the dirt. I put Brian on speaker and set my phone on the floor as I squatted beside the pot and picked it up.

"The key's not there now," I said. "I mean, the pot is, but there's nothing under it." The circular plate that had stuck to the bottom of the pot fell off and thumped on the floor. There was no key on the plate either—nor, I saw when I lifted the pot higher, was a key stuck to the bottom of the pot itself. Deeks sniffed at the pot, then gave my face a lick. I straightened.

"It was there," Brian said. "I think it was. It's been awhile since I've used it."

"Why so many keys?"

"I tend to misplace things. I've got one in my glove box, too."

"You had extras made? Where?"

"I don't know. It's been a couple of years."

Even if I'd found a key, of course, it might have been hard to prove anyone had used it, but at least I could have shown that other people had access to the apartment. "You're getting yourself into a mess," I told Brian as I examined the kitchen door for signs of forced entry.

"I'm in a mess."

"And you're getting deeper. Flight can be used to show consciousness of guilt. What you should have done was call the police from Macy's house and wait for them there. At this point, the best you can do is put in a call to the police and go back to the house to meet them." There were some scratches on the doorknob, but that was about it. No one had applied a crowbar to the door or kicked it in. "Call from a convenience store somewhere. You'd misplaced your cell..." That wasn't going to work. They'd get his phone records.

"It would be better if the police didn't know I was ever there."

"If you've been framed, then somebody knew you were there. Were you wearing gloves, or did you leave fingerprints?"

No answer.

"We need to meet," I said.

"I'll call you in a day or two."

"You can't disappear. It won't work. The second you withdraw money, or…"

He was gone.

"Crap," I said.

"What did he say?" Brooke asked.

I summarized as I went to my recent calls and pushed Brian's number. "He hung up on me," I said as Brian's number rang.

"What are you going to tell him?"

"The same stuff, but more convincingly. He can't run. The police will catch him." Somewhere in the distance, a siren wailed prophetically. My call to Brian went to voice mail, and I punched off rather than leave a message.

"What makes you think they'll be looking for him?" Brooke asked. "They may never connect him with Macy Buck's death at all."

"If this is her blood on his pants…"

"He said he wasn't wearing those pants."

"They've been worn." I took two steps to retrieve the jeans and held them up so they could see the creases at the hips and the poochy knees.

"Whoever framed him got them out of the laundry basket," Brooke said. "Or even hanging up. A lot of guys don't wash their jeans every time they wear them."

We looked at Paul.

"What, am I the spokesman for all guydom? Yes. It's true. We don't always wash our jeans. Listen, that siren's getting louder. Can we assume, while we're standing here, that Macy Buck's corpse is lying unreported in her house not very far away?"

"Maybe."

"If the body needs to be discovered, we could go discover it ourselves," Brooke said. "I can do it. There's nothing to connect me to Macy's death."

"It puts you in the position of lying to the police, unless you're going to tell them about Brian and his calls to us and all the rest of it. Lying to the police in a murder investigation is not good." Paul was right: The siren was getting louder. "Come on, we've got to get out of here. That siren sounds like it's right on top of us."

We went down the back stairs, locking the doorknob and deadbolt behind us. Brooke had her brother's jeans rolled up and tucked under her arm.

"You know those are evidence," Paul told her as we descended the stairs.

"That's why I'm taking them," she said.

The siren stopped abruptly just as we got to the bottom of the staircase. Paul held up a hand as he eased the outer door open and peered out. It was no good: we had a puppy with us. Deeks pushed his nose into the crack between door and jamb and pushed through.

"Okay," I said. "We've got to get to my car, so we have to be inconspicuous. Here." I took the jeans from Brooke and draped them over Paul's head. I started tying the legs under his chin, positioning the jeans so that they looked like a great, misshapen bonnet.

"I thought you said inconspicuous," he said, resisting.

"I meant innocuous. Be still and try to get into character. You're drunk as a skunk. We all are. I'm going to take one of your arms, and Brooke's going to take the other. We've been partying, and we're still going strong."

We pushed out through the door to where Deeks, thankfully, was waiting for us, but when he saw Paul with the jeans on his head, he started to bark. Inconspicuous we were not, but I laughed and patted Paul's chest, leaning on him heavily and throwing him off balance as I staggered forward. My behavior did nothing to reassure Deeks, who began backing away from us, darting from side to side and continuing to bark.

"Look at the cute little puppy," Brooke crooned, reaching for him. "Hey, cutie. Hey there, pretty boy."

Deeks didn't like that at all. He skittered away from her outstretched hands, barking at her over his shoulder as we managed to lurch a few more feet down the sidewalk.

"This is going to take forever," Paul said.

"Oh, you," I said. I pushed aside the jeans that covered most of his head and stuck my tongue in his ear. His neck straightened like he'd received a shock.

"Forever's good," he said.

Chapter 8

We went around the corner of the building and saw the flashing lights of a police car double-parked on Malvern, blocking my car in. Deeks, finally, had stopped barking, but he was keeping a wary eye on us and keeping his distance as we moved along the sidewalk.

"We'll take my car," Brooke sang out. "I'm the des-igna-ted driver." Her laughter sounded like a donkey's bray, not her usual laugh at all. It seemed to me she wasn't very good at pretended merriment, but who was I to criticize?

"Maybe I'd better drive," I said. "Give me the keys."

"No. I'm driving. I've had less to drink." Waving her keys, she let out a burp of legendary proportions, a talent that until now I hadn't known she possessed.

"Whoa," said Paul, who had taken the burp full in the face. He wiped his wrist across his forehead, knocking the jeans cockeyed. "That was enough to make you tear up. You're both wrong." He snatched the keys from Brooke's waving hand. "I'll drive. One of you can sit on my lap. The other one can sit behind me and rub my shoulders."

I smacked the back of his head, knocking the jeans over his face. "In your dreams, butterbean." I pinched his butt, and he staggered forward moving the jeans around in an effort to see.

"Can we take the puppy with us?" Brooke said, leaning toward Deeks again. "Can we take the pretty brown puppy wuppy?"

The puppy wuppy seemed to realize she was talking about him. He scooted further ahead of us, keeping his tail tucked and out of reach.

No one was at the police car when we passed it, and we didn't see a cop on the grass or sidewalk. Probably all our histrionics were so much wasted effort. Deeks jumped into Brooke's car as soon as Paul opened the door, and I ducked into the back seat after him.

"It's okay now, boy," I said to him. "We're back to normal."

He gave me a distrustful stare, then extended his neck to give my face a tentative lick. I hugged him to me and put my cheek against the top of his head.

It was Brooke's car, but Paul got behind the wheel, pulling the jeans off his head and tossing them on the center console. "You say Macy's house is on Patterson?" he said, pulling away from the curb. "It's right up here, you know."

"I'm betting the police are there," I said.

"I'll be circumspect." He slowed as we crossed Patterson Avenue, and we saw red-and-blue police lights flashing a block or two to the left. He accelerated again.

"Somebody else has found the body," Brooke said. "And reported it."

"And the somebody saw Brian there," I said. "And was able to give the police his license number, or maybe even tell them who he was."

"For anyone who knew him, that old Corvette's pretty distinctive."

Paul said, "Are you thinking that whoever saw him at Macy's house not only recognized him, but knew his address and was able to give it to the police?"

"Don't know." The only person I knew who fit that requirement was Brian's sweetheart, Whitney Foster.

"You're assuming the siren we heard was the police going to Brian's apartment," Paul said.

"We have to assume that, don't you think?" Brooke said. "Otherwise it's just too much of a coincidence."

"Coincidences happen."

"Maybe, but I don't like this one."

We decided we were going to have to wait until morning to retrieve my car from the curb along Malvern Avenue, so Paul headed west on Monument, the idea being to cross the river to his place and let Brooke take her car on from there.

"But your car's not at Paul's apartment," Brooke said.

"Paul can take me home."

"I could take you home," Brooke said. "I live closer."

I felt heat rise to my face. "Good point."

At the wheel, Paul turned his head to give Brooke a sharp glance.

"What?" Brooke said. "Oh. Sorry. I didn't mean to…"

"That's all right," I said. "It's late. It does make more sense for me to ride home with you."

"Sorry, Paul."

"That's all right. My designs are so deep and unfathomable…" He shrugged, giving up on the thought.

She touched his arm.

"These jeans worry me," I said, lifting them from the console between Brooke and Paul. "The police find them in our possession, and we're accessories."

There was a momentary silence as Paul and Brooke adjusted to the change of topic.

"They just look like jeans, don't they?" Paul asked. "Before the police thought to test them for blood and thought to match the blood to their murder scene, they'd have to first know Brian was at Macy's house…"

"Check," I said.

"And that we were at Brian's place."

"They may get there. It would be pretty obvious the jeans don't fit anyone in this car."

"Just holding them up, they might not realize that. You and Brian are about the same height."

"The odds of getting caught with them are low, I'll admit," I said. "But the consequences of getting caught are through the roof. Pull over."

He saw a space along the curb and pulled into it. I was craning my neck to look behind us. A couple of cars passed us, their shadowy forms appearing behind their headlights as they went past us. "I don't see anyone following us."

"No one could be following us."

"Let's hope not. Deeks and I will get out here and walk that way." Deeks, who was curled on the seat beside me, lifted his head from his paws as I pointed through the windshield at a street sign that identified the cross-street as Bevridge Road. "By the time you circle around to get me, I'll have disposed of the jeans."

"It's the middle of the night," Brooke's objected.

"All the better." I pushed her seatback forward, and she opened the door with one hand as she allowed herself to be pressed against the dash. In the seat beside me, Deeks was on his feet. He tried to wriggle out the door along with me, but I told him to stay.

He paid no attention. I pushed him back and held his chin to force him to look at me. "Stay," I said.

He looked forlorn in the dome light.

"Deeks, stay."

He sat back on his haunches, but jammed his body between me and the seatback in front of me as soon as my foot touched the pavement. He reached the pavement at the same time as my other foot.

"We're still working on stay," I said, leaning down to speak into the car.

"You're still working on who's the alpha dog," Paul said.

I closed the door and looked at Deeks, who stood looking up at me, his tail wagging.

"I wasn't going to leave you," I said.

His tail wagged harder, and I shook my head.

"Let's go."

After half-a-block on Bevridge I turned into an alley where my feet crunched on loose gravel. The darkness would have been near total but for the light from the occasional floodlight on the back of a house. At the third trash bin I came to, I pushed up a lid and wedged the jeans as deep into the pile of rounded trash bags as I could. I lowered the lid and kept walking, shoving my hands into the pockets of my jacket. There was something in the left pocket. I pulled it out, but it took me a couple of seconds to recognize it in the dark. It was the glasses case I had picked up in Brian's apartment, Whitney's glasses case. I switched it to my jacket's inside pocket, feeling the shifting of the glasses inside, and realized I'd lost track of Deeks.

"Deeks?" I spotted movement in the dark, a shadow among shadows. "Stay close, buddy."

My cell phone rang, and I fished it out of my pocket, expecting to see Brian's name on the screen, or Whitney's, but it was neither. I slid my finger across the screen.

"Hello, Jordan," I said, but there was no immediate answer. "Jordan?"

"I thought the number looked familiar. What have you been up to?"

"What number?"

"The number on Brian Marshall's phone. It looks like you talked to him not very long ago."

I felt suddenly even colder than the weather warranted. "How do you come to have Brian Marshall's cell phone?"

"It's customary to take possession of a man's personal effects when we arrest him."

"Arrest him! For what?"

"You do surprise very well. Want to tell me what the exchange of calls and missed calls was about?"

"He's my best friend's brother."

"Not to mention a client," Jordan said.

"It would be more accurate to say that his employer is my client. Whitney Foster. You remember."

"Uh huh. Does that mean you have no interest in Mr. Marshall's legal problems?"

I exhaled through puffed cheeks. "No, it doesn't mean that. Where is he?"

"Right now he's in a vehicle with Ray and me heading toward the house of one Macy Buck. I believe you met her at the funeral."

"Is she..."

"Is she what, Robin?"

"I'll meet you there," I said.

I'd come to the end of the alley. I tucked the phone into the pocket of my jacket and stood waiting, the wind blowing my hair and the cold seeping into me, body and spirit. A car appeared to my left, its headlights raking the houses at the corner as it turned toward me.

When it stopped, the door opened, Brooke leaning forward to give me access to the back seat. Deeks brushed my leg as he shot through the opening.

"They've arrested Brian," I said as I climbed in behind him.

Macy's house, a small cape cod that probably dated from the early days of World War II, was a block and a half from Malvern Avenue. Most of the parking seemed to be on the street, though there were a few driveways, some of them no more than cracked runners of cement with close-cropped grass growing dark between them. I parked my VW Beetle—I'd retrieved it from the street in front of Malvern Gardens—behind a police car illuminating the night with its silently flashing lightbar. I got out of my car alone, having with some difficulty left Deeks with Paul and Brooke.

Parked on the other side of the street was a white van with *Richmond Police Department* stenciled on the door—the forensic unit, I guessed. I took a breath and started toward the house, where rectangles of light spilled through the picture window and the open door.

The roots of a large oak had buckled the sidewalk, and the shade of the oak had reduced the yard mostly to dirt. A uniformed policeman stood on the front stoop, wearing a jacket and with his arms crossed over his chest against the cold.

I stopped, looking up at him.

"Who are you?" he asked.

"Robin Starling. Detective James Jordan suggested I meet him."

"He's not here."

"How awkward for me," I said.

He smiled. He was not very old, probably still in his twenties. "What's your connection to all this?" He jerked his head at the house behind him.

"A friend's brother has been arrested. Evidently they think he's tied to it somehow." I shrugged. "Jordan thought he might need a lawyer and was kind enough to think of me."

The cop lost his smile. "You're a lawyer? What did you say your name was again?"

I told him.

"Robin Starling," he repeated, uncrossing his arms and moving them back and forth for warmth. "Yeah, I've heard of you. Oh, golly."

"I don't guess there's any chance of us waiting inside," I said.

"You got that right. Nobody goes inside. Why do you think I'm standing here on this porch freezing my garbanzos off?"

"I'd wondered about that. Why did you say *oh, golly?*"

"What?"

"You said you'd heard of me, oh golly."

"Ah. Well." His mouth twisted. "You know Ray Hernandez, don't you? Jordan's partner. He says you're not an attorney, you're a hand grenade in a fox hole."

"Ray's a fan," I said.

"And Aubrey Biggs, from what I hear—"

I raised a hand to wave off whatever the district attorney had said about me. "Not a fan," I said. "What's your name?"

"Austin Maxwell."

"Good to meet you." I stepped forward and reached up to shake his hand. As he let go of mine, his gaze slid past me, and I turned. A Ford Explorer was pulling to the curb in front of the police car with the flashing lights.

"That's probably Jordan," Maxwell said. "The detectives all got new Explorers last month."

"I'll go see." I started down the sidewalk, my hands in the pockets of my jacket. Jordan got out on

101

the driver's side and stood looking at me over the top of his vehicle.

"You got here quick," he said.

"I was cruising the city on the lookout for malicious malfeasance."

He didn't smile.

"I left my cape in my car," I said. "But I can go put it on if it will make you feel safer."

He closed his car door and came around. "I'd give a lot to know what you've been doing the last couple of hours."

"So what's going on? They wouldn't let me in the house."

"Macy Buck is dead. But I guess you knew that."

"Let's say I feared it when I got your call. What makes you think Brian Marshall was involved?"

"We found a blood-soaked T-shirt in his apartment wadded up at the bottom of his laundry basket."

Deeks the Crime Dog had missed the T-shirt; taking the blood-stained jeans had accomplished nothing. "What were you doing rooting around in his laundry basket?"

The door on the passenger side opened. "We had a warrant," Ray Hernandez said, stepping out onto the sidewalk.

"What was your probable cause?"

"Your client's in the back seat, if you want to confer with him. We've got to go inside." Hernandez opened the back door for me and stood waiting. It felt like a trap, and I hesitated, my eyes going to his face.

"What?" he said.

Maybe it was just the yawning door and the dark interior working on me. I ducked my head and slid in, and Hernandez closed the door behind me.

Brian sat huddled against the door on the far side, his cuffed hands between his knees.

"I don't guess this has been the best night of your life," I said. "How are you holding up?"

His head turned toward me, but his face was in shadow.

"Where did they find you?" I asked, and this time I waited for a response.

"Bus station in Petersburg."

"Your Corvette was parked outside, I guess?"

He didn't answer.

"What have you told them?"

"Nothing."

"You haven't made any statement, answered any questions, anything?"

"I admitted I was Brian Marshall."

"I assume they've asked you other questions."

He shrugged. If his name was all he had told them, I was impressed. It's hard to remain silent when people in authority are demanding answers.

"Everything's happened pretty fast," I said. "When did it start?"

"When I found the body."

"When was that?"

He shrugged. "Just after dark. Six o'clock, six-fifteen?"

"How did you come to be here? Did Macy call you?"

"No."

"You just showed up at her house."

He nodded, but didn't elaborate.

"So Rupert Propst convinced you Macy had run off with Uncle Robert's money?"

"No."

"Did he convince Whitney?"

"No. She's busy with her coffee shop. If any money comes to her, she'll be happy to get it, but she doesn't lose any time thinking about it. She didn't want me to hire you in the first place, you know. I was just looking out for her, or trying to."

I nodded. "So you didn't kill Macy."

"No. She was dead when I got here." He scrubbed at the beard on his chin.

"Was the door standing open?"

"Wide open. Just inviting me in."

"The storm door, too?"

"No, the storm door was closed, but you could see in."

"What could you see?"

"Nothing really. The living room."

"No one in it? Nothing disturbed?"

"Just a normal living room. I rang the bell, knocked, pulled open the storm door to shout, 'Is anybody home?' But nobody answered."

"So you went in?"

After a moment he said, "I found her in the kitchen. All the lights were on. It was…She was lying on the floor, kind of on her side. The blood…" He stopped.

"Did you see any kind of weapon?"

"No."

"Could it have been underneath her?"

"I don't know. Maybe."

"Describe the room to me."

"It was a kitchen. Tidy enough. A drawer may have been open, a little rug rucked up in front of the sink. The main thing was the blood."

"Any chance it was an accident? That she'd gotten a knife or something out of the drawer, tripped on the rug, fallen on the blade?"

He seemed to be studying me in the darkness. "I suppose so."

"But you didn't react like it was an accident. You didn't call 9-1-1. You got out."

"It...there was an air of violence about the whole thing."

"And Whitney had been there."

"Who told you that?"

"You called her. Was it from here?"

After several seconds he said, "Right about this spot. I wanted her to know what had happened."

"Wanted to reassure yourself she hadn't had anything to do with it?"

"Look. She didn't. You need to leave that alone."

"Okay. When you were in the house, did you touch the body?"

"No."

"Did you get any blood on yourself at all?"

He shook his head. "I don't think so. Everything about it seems surreal now, but I don't see how I could have."

"How do you explain the blood in your apartment?"

"I can't."

"You just went in and saw the jeans. You changed shirts, and you left."

He shook his head. "I didn't change shirts. I was wearing what I'm wearing now."

"So the bloody T-shirt the police found in your apartment…"

"All I know is what they told me."

"Did you tell them it wasn't yours?"

"I told them my name. I figured they were going to get that from my driver's license anyway."

"When you called Whitney, was it on her cell phone?"

"Yeah. She doesn't have a landline."

"But she was at home?"

He nodded. "She lives in a duplex on Grove Avenue in the museum district." Not more than ten minutes from Brian's apartment, maybe no more than five. Of course, she could have been anywhere when Brian called her on her cell.

"When you got to your apartment, was the door locked?"

"Yes."

"And the blue jeans were…"

"Lying on my bed like someone had tossed them there."

"Not where you had left them."

"No, that's why I noticed them. I picked them up and saw the blood, and that's when I knew we were in trouble."

"We?"

"Me."

"How was Whitney in trouble?"

"She wasn't."

"But she had a key to your apartment, and her sunglasses were at Macy's house."

"She had nothing to do with any of this."

"So she left her sunglasses at your apartment? When?"

"Could have been anytime."

"But not this afternoon."

There was a tap on the glass behind me, and I jerked like I'd been shot. The door opened.

"Didn't mean to startle you, Counselor." It was Hernandez, and I was inclined to doubt him. "We're ready to go to the station. Your client going to make a statement?"

"No."

"Come on, Robin. We've got a murder to solve here."

"And if he told you he didn't do it, you could refocus your investigations on other, more promising suspects?"

"You know better than that."

"You're right. I do."

I turned back to Brian. "They're going to charge you, I think. You're going to be presented before a magistrate, then you're going to be spending time in the city jail. Don't talk to anyone—not the police, not a cell mate, not anyone. Can you do that?"

He gave me a lopsided smile.

"Good man," I said.

Chapter 9

The red and blue lights of the cruiser were still strobing the house and the small, boxy Honda that was in the driveway. James Jordan had paused in the doorway to say something to someone behind him, and I started up the sidewalk toward him.

"Hey," Hernandez said behind me.

Jordan came down the steps and stopped at the bottom to strip off a pair of latex gloves. The holly bushes along the front of the house, stretching out on either side of him, consisted of twisted branches with a few leaves sprouting from them.

"Where are you going?" Jordan asked me.

"Since we're working this case together, I thought maybe you'd let me have a look at the crime scene."

Behind me, Hernandez gave a snort. Jordan's upper lip rose, and there was something speculative about his gaze I didn't like.

"Have you ever been in this house before?" he asked me.

"I have not."

He nodded, almost to himself, as he pulled back on the latex gloves he had removed. "Okay, Starling. We'll go in."

I followed him up the two steps onto the porch, and Hernandez came behind me.

"Wait here," Jordan said. He went through the door and paused just inside to pull on a pair of baby blue booties over his shoes and tie them at his ankles, then he disappeared into the back of the house. Through the storm door and the picture window, I could see a threadbare Oriental carpet surrounded by a few pieces of worn furniture that might have been of the same vintage as the house. There was no carnage that I could see.

When Jordan came back carrying another set of booties and a box of latex gloves, Hernandez reached past me to hold open the door. I went through.

Jordan handed me the booties. "You know how it is, Starling. If any of your prints show up in this house, I want to be able to say they weren't put there tonight."

"These booties should help with that," I said as I bent to pull them over my shoes. I reached for the gloves, but he held onto them.

"You haven't been back there in the kitchen," he said.

"No. I told you I haven't."

"You haven't seen the body and haven't touched it."

I rolled me eyes and exhaled in audible exasperation.

"No?"

"No."

"Tara? We're ready for you," he called over his shoulder.

The woman who came out was wearing coveralls with a gold shield stenciled on the left breast. She had a utility belt around her waist and was carrying a plastic bottle with a spray trigger. A young man carrying a camera followed her.

"What is this?" I said.

"Just a little demonstration. I thought you'd like to witness a quick and dirty method for determining the presence of blood. Have you heard of luminol?"

I thought about the jeans I had handled, remembering the feel of the wet fabric. Had I touched the dark stain? "Yes," I said. "I've heard of it."

"Hold out your hands. See? They're perfectly clean. Nothing visible at all. Now turn them over. Still clean. Okay, Tara."

I could hear my heartbeat or maybe I was just feeling it in my neck as she sprayed the backs of my hands.

"Turn them over," Jordan said.

I followed instructions, and Tara sprayed my palms and the tips of my fingers. My hands looked wet, but still clean. I was drawing a deep, calming breath when the lights went out and I yelped.

"Keep your hands out," Jordan said. There was enough light coming from outside and from the back of the house for us to see each other, but only as shadows. "Turn them over."

"What are we looking for?" I asked.

Tara answered. "Luminol reacts with the iron in hemoglobin. If trace amounts of blood are present, it should give us a striking blue glow."

"A human glow stick," I said. "I don't see anything."

The lamp beside us came back on. Hernandez had a hand on the switch.

"Nope," Jordan said. "You're clean."

"I have to say it wasn't much of a demonstration."

"It was for me, and I have to tell you, I'm relieved, Robin, I really am." He handed me the latex gloves.

I put them on, taking a few more careful breaths as my heartbeat subsided to normal levels.

"Let's go back," he said.

We went through a dining room that contained a round table with a chipped mahogany veneer and four chairs. In the kitchen was a smear of blood on the black-and-white tile floor. Dr. Pavlicek, a doctor with the medical examiner's office, stood at the counter making notes on a clipboard. He wore a striped polo shirt under a bluish sports jacket that had a brown leather yoke and patch pockets. It looked about as stylish as it sounds. Bits of tape and powders of various colors were scattered here and there. Tara and her male assistant went back to their work, loading a measuring tape, plastic baggies of this and that, packets of gauze and wipes, and other oddments into a case that looked like a big tackle box.

"Where's the body?" I said.

"Taken to the city morgue."

"So this was all about testing my hands for the presence of blood."

"I wanted to reassure myself you hadn't been in here tampering with the crime scene."

"I wanted to see the crime scene."

"And here you are."

There was a small, rumpled rug in front of the sink, but the drawers were all pushed in, and no sharp object or weapon of any kind was in evidence. "I have to say it's a disappointment."

"Life is full of those," Jordan said.

"It was a blade of some sort, wasn't it? Not a gunshot."

"No, not a gunshot."

When we were back on the sidewalk, I stopped and said, "When are you going to take Brian before a magistrate?"

Jordan turned back toward me. "Could do it as soon as we finish questioning him."

"You're done. He's not going to be answering any questions."

"You realize this looks bad for him. He's got a lot to explain."

If Brian was telling the truth, there was blood in his apartment he couldn't explain. If it turned out to be Macy Buck's blood—and they'd be able to match the blood-type before the night was out—then the failure to explain that made all other explanations pointless. "Don't we all?" I said.

"We have to ask him to talk to us, make him go on record as taking the Fifth."

"What do you mean, go on record? His refusal to answer questions can't be introduced into evidence, and a jury isn't permitted to draw negative inferences from his failure to testify."

Jordan smiled. "I expressed myself badly. I mean, if we don't document ourselves asking him if he'll talk to us, our chief's not going to think we're doing our jobs. You're allowed to be there, of course. And a magistrate is available around the clock. We can get him presented, get bail set, get him transferred to the custody of the city jail—all tonight."

I sighed. "Okay, let's do it," I said.

By the time we were done, it was after two o'clock, and I was beat, but I'd left Deeks at Paul's apartment. I punched Paul's name on my phone as I crossed the James River.

"Hey, Robin. How'd it go?"

"Not good. You sound like you're still up."

"More or less. I walked Deacon. He's letting me lie on the bed with him."

I was too tired to laugh, but I felt myself smiling. "He'll push you around if you let him."

"No kidding."

"I'll be there in about five minutes so you can have your bed back."

"It's all right. I didn't mean to be in bed at all. I was going to nap on the couch while I waited for you, but it turned out there wasn't room on the couch for the two of us."

I did laugh, despite my fatigue. "I guess he thinks I left him in charge."

"Yes, and it makes him uneasy, being in charge. He keeps looking for you."

"Uneasy lies the head that wears a crown," I said.

"Is that Shakespeare?"

"Henry the Fourth, I think. One of the Henrys." I'd been an English major, but Shakespeare had written plays about four of the Henrys, and multiple plays about two of them. When he had a hit on his hands, even the great Bard himself hadn't been above putting out sequels. "I'm pulling in now," I said.

I parked, entered Paul's building, and took the half-flight of stairs down to his door. He opened it, looking almost skinny in gym shorts and a T-shirt, and Deeks ran past him and jammed his head between my knees, his tail going ninety to nothing. I leaned over to scratch the top of his head.

"Thanks for looking out for him."

"Glad to do it. You want to come in and tell me about it?"

"I'm beat, but the short of it is, Brian's in jail. They've charged him with first degree murder, and bail's been set at 750 thousand dollars."

"How did Brooke take it?"

"I haven't called her. I'm thinking she may be asleep, and it's not like anything I have to say will make her feel better."

He nodded. "You too tired to drive home? You can crash here, if you want."

"Better to wake up in my own place."

Deeks spun away from me and shot between Paul's legs back into the apartment.

"Deeks! Where's he going?" I went to the door and stood next to Paul as Deeks circled the weight bench in the middle of the living room, then darted back toward the bedroom. He reappeared holding something white with colored stripes at one end. It crackled as his jaws moved.

"What is it, buddy?"

He came and dropped it at my feet, and I bent to pick it up.

"Is this a tube sock?"

"I don't wear it anymore," Paul said.

"I don't blame you."

"I put a water bottle in it and tied a knot in the end. Kind of a homemade chew-toy."

It crinkled when I squeezed it. Deeks went up on his hind legs reaching for it, and I gave it back to him. He trotted back around the corner.

"Hey," I called. "It's time to go." I looked at Paul. "It's late."

"There's an IHOP out on Midlothian. I'll take you to breakfast if you're still here when I wake up."

"I don't think it's a good idea."

"I can lend you a T-shirt and pair of gym shorts to sleep in. And I have an extra toothbrush, never been opened."

"You've bought your next toothbrush, and you don't need it yet? Tell me the truth. You're half female."

"I do have an X chromosome," he said modestly. "But actually, I went to the dentist last week. They gave me a toothbrush, a small toothpaste, and some dental floss. You're welcome to all of them. You and Deacon can take the bed, and I'll sleep on the couch." His eyebrows were raised, his eyes appealingly wide.

"All right," I said. "I'll be magnanimous and let you sleep on the couch in your own home."

Paul had a full-sized bed with two pillows, a quilted spread, and rumpled sheets that looked like they hadn't been washed in a week. I looked at it and sighed, while Paul got the promised shorts and T-shirt out of a bureau drawer. I took them from him and went into the bathroom, stepping over Deeks, who was still crunching on his improvised chew toy.

The T-shirt was an extra-large, somewhat shrunken from many washings. I put it on and slipped my bra out from underneath, an entirely unnecessary precaution behind the locked door of a bathroom, but I was in a strange place. The shorts were skin-tight and didn't cover much more than my panties. I opened the door and went out.

"How long have you had these shorts?" I demanded. "Don't tell me they fit you."

Paul's eyes traveled down my legs and back up again. He grinned. "I think they came with the tube socks," he said. "I might have been in middle school."

"I'm going to need something a little bigger."

"Are you sure? That's a good look for you."

"No, it's a good look for you. But you've had your look, and I need something to sleep in."

He went back to his bureau, still grinning, and pulled out another pair of shorts. "These may hang off you, but you're welcome to them." He tossed them to me, and I snatched them out of the air.

I came out of the bathroom again with the shorts covering me, but only because I was holding them up by one hand. "You're a man of extremes," I said. "I don't suppose you have something in between this pair of shorts and the last one."

He shook his head.

"How about the ones you're wearing?"

He looked down, then back up at me again. "You're asking me to take off my pants?"

"I'm asking you to trade with me."

"Okay." He stepped into the kitchen out of my line of sight, and a moment later the shorts he'd been wearing hit the wall beside me. I picked them up, then, with my eye on the corner he'd disappeared around, let the over-sized shorts drop to the floor and stepped into the new ones. When I let go of them, they slid down a few inches, but my hips caught them and they stayed. I let the shirt drop over them, then stepped back into the bathroom to look at myself in the mirror. I was decent now.

"Hey," Paul called. "It's getting a little drafty in here."

"Sorry." I retrieved the big shorts from the hall. "Deeks!" I said, squatting beside him.

Deeks didn't get up, but his tail thumped the floor.

"Take it," I said.

He extended his chin over the sock-covered bottle and took the shorts tentatively.

"Go to Paul," I said.

He looked at me quizzically.

"Go to Paul." I gave his bottom a push, and he scrambled to his feet, his eyes on me.

"What's going on over there?" Paul asked.

I tilted my head in the direction of his voice. "Go to Paul," I said again.

Deeks looked at me uncertainly, then walked around the corner, his toenails scraping on the polished wood floor. "Good boy," I called after him.

"Hey," Paul said. "Did I put dog slobber on your shorts?"

"Get over it. I've got man cooties to deal with."

Paul came around the corner, one hand hooked in the waist of his shorts to hold them up. "Men don't have cooties," he said. "That's a female thing."

"Didn't those shorts used to fit?"

"I've been losing a little weight."

"You've been losing a lot of weight."

"You can tell a difference? It's hard for me to see it. I still have the same shape, really, just on a smaller scale."

I nodded, eying him critically. "You look like a teddy bear that's lost half its stuffing."

"Well that hurts."

He stood in the doorway, his hand on the light switch, as I slipped under the covers on his bed and Deeks hopped up beside me.

"You don't mind Deeks sleeping on your bed?" I said.

"What's a little dog hair between friends?"

"Dog hair, dog slobber, man cooties…"

He was shaking his head as he turned out the light. "Good night, sleep tight."

"Don't let the bedbugs bite," I said.

He laughed. As he went down the short hall, he said something to himself that I couldn't make out.

"What was that?"

"I said, 'All great things start from small beginnings.' "

"What does that mean?"

"It's Cicero. You were an English major. I was poli-sci."

"I mean, what does it mean in this context?"

"You're a smart girl," he called from further away. "You'll get it." There was a creak that might have been his sofa.

I turned over in his bed, making a face in the darkness. I was a smart girl. And I got it.

Chapter 10

We didn't make it to the IHOP the next morning. We intended to. We got dressed, fed Deeks, and went to the door, where I turned and told Deeks, "You stay here. We'll be right back." Deeks understood the term "right back." It's what kept him in the car when I ran into the store for something.

The problem was that Paul's apartment was neither Deeks' home nor my car. Wherever Paul and I were going and however long we were going to be away, Deeks knew beyond the possibility of any doubt that he was supposed to go with us. When the door opened, he darted at the opening. Paul closed it quickly, but incompletely, and Deeks wedged his nose into the opening and tried to force the door open. I dragged him back.

"Deeks," I said, squatting to be at eye-level with him. He turned his head to look at the door. "Deeks," I said again, turning his head toward me, but he pushed against my hand and rolled his eyes toward the door. "Deeks, it's all right, buddy."

To Paul I said, "You go on out. I'm coming."

Paul opened the door, and Deeks lunged for it. I held on and maneuvered myself between Deeks and the door.

"Deeks, you stay here. I'll be right back. Okay?" I straightened my legs, but stayed bent over to keep my hands on his head.

"Maybe we could take him with us, and he could wait in the car," Paul said through the door.

If the day was cold and cloudy enough, that would be okay, but I thought we'd feel rushed. "Open the door," I told Paul.

He did, and I backed through, my hands on Deeks' head to keep him inside the apartment. Paul closed the door until it was touching my arm.

"I'll yank out my hands, and you close the door," I said.

"You don't think he'll tear up my apartment?"

"He's never been destructive before."

"He chews on stuff."

"Just because he's bored."

"Great."

"Here goes." I gave Deeks a push, sending him sliding back a pace, and jerked my hands out, falling back against Paul as he pulled the door shut. Deeks was too quick for him. Paul stopped the door against Deeks' nose, which was already in the opening, nostrils flaring. I had slid down Paul's leg onto my keister.

"He knows he's supposed to go with us," I said, still sitting on the floor. "He thinks we're making a terrible mistake."

"We could go to Sonic instead of IHOP and eat in my car."

I smiled over my shoulder at him and pushed the door open with my foot. Deeks was instantly in my lap, giving me great doggy kisses of reconciliation. Looking past him up at Paul, I thought Paul looked resigned.

"You brought this puppy into my life," I reminded him.

"And you wouldn't change that if you could."

I pushed Deeks away and stood up. Paul was right, I wouldn't.

Anyway, we ate at Sonic that Saturday morning. While we were there, I got a call from Brooke.

"You didn't call me last night."

"I thought with any luck you'd be asleep. And…" I took a breath.

"And the news isn't good."

"No, it isn't. I'm sorry. Brian's in jail on a three-quarter-million-dollar bond."

"They think he killed her?"

"They think he killed her, and they think they can prove it."

I could hear her breathing. Finally, she said, "Where is he? Can I see him?"

"Yes. He's in the Richmond City Jail, and there are Saturday visiting hours. He is limited to one visitor a week."

"How about you?"

"I can see him more often. Every day if I need to. It doesn't count against his one-visitor limit."

"Well, that's something."

"Not much."

"He didn't do it, you know."

"I know."

"Tell me the truth. Do you think you can beat this?"

"Sure."

"How?"

"It's early. I have no idea."

Her breathing was becoming audible again.

"If it makes you feel any better, I never have any idea. The cases I've won, I just muddled around until suddenly I saw my way through."

After a pause she said, "It does make me feel better. A little."

"I'm sorry, Brooke. I really am."

"I like it better when you're representing people I'm not related to."

"Me, too."

I disconnected and looked at Paul.

"She gonna be okay?" he said.

I shook my head. "I guess she'll have to be."

"How are you doing?"

"Okay," I said, but I didn't want the rest of my croisSONIC breakfast sandwich. I took another bite, chewed, swallowed, then held out the rest of it to Paul.

"I've had plenty," he said.

"You've had one junior breakfast burrito."

"It's enough. You know who does want it." He jerked his head, and we looked at Deeks, whose eyes were locked onto my sandwich like a missile guidance system, a line of drool running from one side of his mouth.

I felt a pang of guilt. "I'm sorry, Deeks. Would you like my sandwich?" I held it out, and his mouth closed on my sandwich and three of my fingers.

Fortunately, he seemed to know what was breakfast and what was Robin, and I kept all three digits.

Afterwards we went back to Paul's apartment, and I didn't get home until midafternoon. Deeks and I were out on our evening walk when Brooke called again.

"I got in to see him, but he wouldn't talk to me."

"What, not at all?"

"Well, hello and that sort of thing, but he wouldn't tell me anything about what happened yesterday."

"I told him not to talk to anyone."

"You didn't tell him not to talk to me."

"No. I didn't mention you specifically."

"I'm his sister. I love him."

"You're not his attorney. Anything he says to you, you can be made to repeat."

"Not with a hot poker and a cat-o-nine-tails."

"With what?" Try as I might, I couldn't get a handle on that image.

"You know what I mean."

"I guess. If they couldn't make you talk, though, they could put you in jail, which would at least be inconvenient. Anyway, the main thing is that he's keeping his mouth shut, and that's a good habit for a criminal defendant to develop."

"Don't call him a criminal defendant."

"Sorry. A man falsely accused?"

"Don't mind me, I'm just upset. Also, I think he's hiding something."

"Because he won't talk to you?"

"It's not just that. There's something in his manner. I don't like it."

"Huh." I wasn't going to discount Brooke's intuition. There was blood on Brian's jeans that was completely unaccounted for. And I had found a glasses case in his apartment, almost certainly Whitney's. It might be a spare case she had left there some time ago, but it had her sunglasses in it. Suppose it was the one she always carried. Suppose Brian found it at Macy's house and carried it away, then panicked when he found the bloody jeans and left it behind when he fled.

"Robin?"

"Sorry. I was thinking. Can I call you back?" My thoughts weren't proceeding linearly, which was okay at this stage when I wanted to keep stirring up facts and ideas to see if they fell into any interesting patterns. I felt, though, that for a while I needed to stop thinking consciously about Brian and Macy and Whitney and the whole Walsh clan, so I called Deeks to me.

"Deeks! Deeks, old buddy."

When he appeared out of the darkness, I told him to heel. He was walking beside me looking up at me when I said it, and he kept doing it for another fifteen or twenty seconds before he started to run ahead of me. I just managed to catch his tail.

He looked over his shoulder at me inquiringly.

"No," I said. "Heel." I tugged him back to the appropriate position. "Heel," I said again, walking slightly bent with a hand on his head.

This time when he took off he went to the side. I grabbed at him and missed. "Deeks!" I called in exasperation. When he didn't reappear immediately, I shoved my hands back into the pockets of my jacket and kept walking. If I was going to teach him to heel, I was going to have to use a leash.

That night I was back in my own bed, alone except for Deeks, who was curled up against me, back to back, him on the outside of my covers and me underneath. I thought about Paul. It wasn't hard to imagine him in bed beside me. It was a little harder to imagine *sleeping* with him in bed beside me, but with a little effort I could sense him beside me, could feel the rhythm of his breathing and hear the whisper of air moving through his nose and mouth. He took a big breath and exhaled noisily…No, that was Deeks.

Sleepily I reached out to give him a pat. "You're a good dog," I murmured, and he licked my arm.

The next morning was Sunday. Deeks and I walked and ate oatmeal—actually, he had kibble—and my doorbell rang just as we were finishing up. It was Brooke, there on my front doorstep at eight o'clock on a Sunday morning.

"Hi," I said.

"Did you figure it out yet? What Brian's covering up? Hello to you too." That last was to Deeks, who had run past her and was piddling on a bush next to the front porch. He kept an apologetic eye on her as he peed, then ran back to the house.

"Brian thinks Whitney killed her or at least thinks she'll be accused of it," I said as Brooke scratched Deeks's head. "Come inside."

"You sound really positive," she said. "Are you, or are you just talking?"

"Oh I'm just talking. Look at this though." I opened the door of the coat closet and patted the pockets of the coat I'd been wearing Friday night. When I found what I was looking, I pulled it out. "Here. Whitney's glasses case."

She took it, but her eyes were on me. "What are you doing with it?"

"It was in Brian's apartment. How do you think it got there?"

"Whitney left it?"

"Maybe. Maybe she left it, or maybe Brian found it somewhere."

"At Macy's house?"

"It would go a long way to explaining Brian's panicky behavior, don't you think? That, and finding blood on his clothes he hadn't even been wearing."

"You're saying Whitney killed Macy."

"She doesn't have to have killed her. It just has to look that way. You up for a cup of coffee?"

"At Carytown Joe?"

"It's really good."

"Let's go."

Probably I should have walked Deeks across the street to Dr. McDermott's, but it was cold enough to see your breath outside, so I didn't have to worry about him overheating in the car. I got a beef rib out of the cabinet as we headed through the kitchen to the garage. It was wrapped in plastic, but Deeks followed close at my heel with his nose in the air.

When we got to Carytown and I'd found a parking spot on the street, I unwrapped the rib for him. We left him on the back seat with it clamped between his paws as he started gnawing at it.

"Getting that dog has changed your life," Brooke said as we headed down the sidewalk in the direction of Whitney's coffee shop.

"Reorganized it anyway, maybe as much as a husband would."

"A husband?"

"Okay, probably not as much as a husband would. I'm overstating."

"Are you and Paul…?"

"No, no. I don't think either of us has even thought about it. We certainly haven't talked about it."

"The lady doth protest too much."

"Hamlet," I said, and there must have been surprise in my voice.

"You English majors think you're the only people in the world who are halfway literate," Brooke said.

Whitney and another girl were behind the counter in Carytown Joe. I ordered a vanilla latte and, after a brief inner struggle, a pumpkin-cinnamon scone. Brooke got the latte and skipped the scone, which made me feel bad about giving into temptation so easily. I had, after all, already had my oatmeal that morning.

"We'd like to visit with you a bit when you get the chance," I said to Whitney as I paid for my second breakfast and got change for my ten.

She gave a nod. "If I get the chance." But it was only twenty minutes later that she joined us at our table, scooting in beside Brooke on the bench that ran along the wall.

"I've only got a minute," she said, tucking a loose strand of hair behind one ear.

I took out the glasses case embossed with the cat-eye frames, and I set it on the table next to the paper plate that contained the crumbs of my scone. Whitney looked from it to me, then picked it up.

"It is yours, isn't it?" I asked.

"Where did you find it?"

Her answer was nonresponsive, but I let it go. "At Brian's apartment. Friday night."

"Oh." She turned the glasses case over in her hands. She snapped it open, glanced at the sunglasses inside.

"Do you know where he picked it up?" I asked.

Her gaze flicked to mine. "I can guess."

I waited.

"You can guess, too, I imagine," she said.

"Tell me."

She took a deep breath and let it out. "I was at Macy's house Friday afternoon," she said.

"You didn't say."

"Brian said not to. He wants to protect me—and I didn't see what good it would do to tell."

"Why were you there?"

"She left a note at my apartment, tucked between the door and jamb. She said she needed to see me right away, that if she didn't hear from me she'd be back."

"Where do you live?"

"In half of a duplex on Grove, just about three blocks from here. The address isn't in the phonebook, but somehow she found it."

"It's strange she didn't look for you here."

She gave a brief, humorless smile. "She was looking to have a private conversation."

"Did you try calling her?"

"Yes. She said she'd be right over."

"And you forestalled that by going to her house?"

"I sure didn't want her coming to mine. Macy's not a big girl, probably no bigger than I am, but she's way scary. Was way scary."

"She strikes me that way, too," I said, nodding. "And I am a big girl."

"You're not big. You're just supermodel tall."

"That was the phrase I was looking for."

After a pause, Whitney said, "Anyway, I met her at her house. I tried to stay on the porch, but she didn't like that. She got me inside, offered me a beer, tried to make out like it was some kind of social occasion."

"Did you take the beer?"

"I don't really like beer. I asked for some water, and she got me a glass."

"What did she want to talk about?"

"What happened to the money that was in Uncle Robert's accounts."

"Do you know what happened to it?"

She shook her head. "I've told you that."

"Did Macy believe you?"

"No. She got loud. She stood over me. When I tried to leave, she grabbed me and twisted my arm."

"But you kept insisting you didn't know anything?"

"Uncle Robert and I were real close, but he stopped talking to me five or six weeks ago. I don't know why."

"So you didn't tell her anything at all?"

"I didn't have anything to tell her. I did say that if Uncle Robert had taken anyone into his confidence, it would have been his friend Jack Packard. But he may not have trusted even him at that point, you know?"

"Whitney?" called a voice from the counter.

She looked around, noticed the line nearly to the door. "I'm sorry. I've been longer than I meant to. I've got to go." Her hand closed over the glasses case, which she'd put back on the table between us, and she stood.

"I guess Macy was alive when you left the house?"

She leaned toward me. "You don't think I killed her, do you?" she whispered fiercely. "Killed her and left Brian to take the blame for it?"

"When did you leave her?"

"About three, I think. I found her note when I got home after we closed up here, and she doesn't live more than ten minutes away. I don't think I was in her house twenty minutes. I got out as soon as I could. Look, I've got to get back behind the counter."

When she'd gone, I looked at Brooke. "So, did she kill Macy?"

"I can't see it."

"She never actually denied it."

"Well, no. Did you notice her skin?"

I smiled. "She does have incredible skin."

"No pores at all that you can see, just that light dusting of pinpoint freckles on her cheekbones."

"No girl with such incredible skin could be a killer," I said.

"I just don't think she did it."

"I get the idea you approve of Brian's girlfriend."

"I did before this happened anyway."

Nodding, I took a sip of my coffee, but it had gone cold.

Deeks was glad to see us. Only about half of his beef rib was left. After he'd greeted us, he spun around for it, turned again, and presented it to me. I didn't know whether he was offering to share or whether he thought I might renew it somehow and make it whole. I took it from him, but he took it away from me again and jumped into the back seat with it.

"So what did we learn?" Brooke asked when we were on the Downtown Expressway.

I shrugged. "I don't know. If we believe her, then Macy was alive at three o'clock. There'll be a medical examiner's report that will tell us if that much is true."

"You haven't talked to Nathan, have you?"

"Not yet."

"If he and Macy were engaged, he's somebody you need to talk to."

"I know," I said. "Maybe tomorrow."

"I'll set it up." She got out her phone to search for his number. Just as we reached my exit, she said, "Here it is." She tapped the screen and held the phone to her ear. After a moment, she said, "This is Carly Price, calling from the law offices of Robin Starling. She needs to meet with you to talk about the death of Macy Buck." She gave him her mobile number. "Please call at your earliest convenience to schedule an appointment."

She punched off. "Do you think we'll hear from him?"

"Might," I said. "You never know."

We didn't hear back. We got to my house, talked a bit more, looked at each other, then turned on the TV. A church service was on, a local one we'd watched together from time to time back when we'd been roommates. Actually, we rarely watched more than the first half. We liked the music—the church choir was about sixty strong and accompanied by a small orchestra—the sermon, not so much. The pastor had one of those deep and resonating Baptist-preacher voices, which made it easier to mock than to listen to. When he started to preach, I clicked off the TV.

Brooke said, "So do you think Jesus was giving the okay to adultery?"

"What?"

"Didn't you hear the Bible reading? It was about the woman caught in adultery."

"I'm sure Jesus wasn't saying adultery was okay," I said, trying to recall the Bible reading. "He just didn't want the crowd to stone her for it."

"Because the punishment was too much, or because adultery shouldn't be punished at all?"

"Maybe he was just granting mercy in that particular situation."

"He didn't say anything about that particular situation. He said, 'Let the one without sin cast the first stone.'"

"He can't have meant it that way. It would go way beyond the issue of adultery."

"What do you mean?"

"It would be like saying, 'Everyone has sinned, so no one has the right to judge or punish.' It would undercut the whole system of criminal justice. It's all about judging and punishing."

"I think he was just talking about adultery."

"Let's see." I clicked back on the TV, and we listened to the sermon, but it was about forgiveness and mercy in general and addressed neither adultery nor the legitimacy or illegitimacy of sinful judges. When it was over, I turned off the TV again and said, "So who is he?"

"Who is who?"

"This married man you're thinking about having an affair with."

"I'm not thinking about having an affair with a married man."

I looked at her.

"I'm not." After a moment she added, "I'm just tired of being alone."

"You want to move back in with me?"

"It's not that. I want a man."

Deeks seemed to have worked his rib down as far as it would go. He left it and put his chin on the sofa next to Brooke to get his head scratched.

"A dog is a pretty good substitute," I said as she scratched him.

"No. It's not."

"Well, maybe not," I conceded.

"You've got Paul, and I like him a lot, but a lot of times I feel like you two let me hang around out of charity. I mean, I've got to be in the way."

"In the way of what? Paul and I can't always be pumping and grinding."

Her eyes went wide. "You and Paul..."

"No, no." I looked at her sideways. "I did spend the night at his place Friday."

She smacked me with a sofa pillow. "And you didn't say anything about it? Spill."

"There's really not much to tell."

"Robin…" Her tone was threatening.

"Okay, okay." I spilled what there was to spill, though of course it really wasn't much.

"You've got a talent for keeping a man on the hook," she said when I was done. "Really, I mean it. You give him next to nothing, and he pants around after you just like a second dog."

"Well," I said defensively. "I did pat his cheek when we said good-bye."

Chapter 11

On Monday it was back to work, though I was late, a bad habit that had been growing on me since Deeks came into my life. Carly was waiting for me. Before the glass-paneled door swung shut behind me, she had begun to vibrate behind the reception desk. "Guess who has joined us," she said, her fists quivering by her face. "Guess who your new suitemate is."

I raised my eyebrows.

"It's Rodney Burns!" she said, squeaking out the last word. "He moved in his computer and a box of office supplies this morning!"

I smiled. "And I get a commission?"

Her smile faltered. "Uh, no. You don't." Revving back up to full flutter, she repeated, "But you have a new suitemate. And he's here...right... now!"

"That's great, Carly, that really is. I'll go welcome him."

I went through the archway in the exposed brick wall. The door of my office, the rightmost in the group of three, was closed. Brooke's, in the middle, was open, and now the door on the far left was open as well.

"Hey, Brooke," I said, but she was on the phone and merely lifted a hand to me. I went next door and saw Rodney Burns, his feet already on his desk next to his computer monitor, his Edgar Alan Poe coffee mug held in the fingers of both hands.

"Hello, wanderer," I said.

"I hope you don't mind that I've joined you."

"I think I suggested it."

"I've got some background information for you on the various members of the Walsh clan … when you've set down your briefcase and have your coffee and are ready to hear it."

"I'll be right back." I opened my office to set down my briefcase and hang my coat on the coat-tree in the corner. In the suite's kitchen, I filled my mug two-thirds full of coffee with equal parts decaf and coffee from the pot labeled "6 Scoops." It would be all the caffeine I'd have for the day and was probably more than I needed, but at thirty-one I'd finally joined the human race with my morning cuppa joe. To confirm me in my new habit, a recent news story reported a study that showed coffee drinkers had lower mortality rates than noncoffee drinkers. Who was I to abstain from coffee and shorten my lifespan in the name of good health?

Back in Rodney's office, I dropped into a client chair, one that had come from his old office. He had his feet back on the floor.

"I see you kept the desk that was in here. What did you do with your old one?"

"Left it. My gift to the new owner." His face spasmed in a pained smile.

"When did you move your stuff in? All this morning?"

"I started over the weekend. I'll do a little each day and be moved in completely by the end of the week. To business?"

I nodded.

"We can do more small talk, if you want. I'm getting good at it. Carly was in here this morning for nearly an hour."

"By the end of the month, you'll be the best small-talker in the commonwealth," I said.

"To business then." He opened a folder on his desk, the surface of which was still relatively clear of the papers, yellow pads, pens, and stacks of folders that had cluttered his desk out on Broad Street. "You know Robert Walsh had his career in banking. Was with First and Merchants when it merged with Virginia National to become Sovran Bank, stayed with it when it merged with NCNB to become NationsBank, retired when NationsBank bought out Bank of America and took the new name for itself."

"Okay."

"At his death, he had about a half-million in retirement accounts, about ten thousand or so in his checking account, a hundred thousand in life insurance. He owned his house free and clear and had a ten-year-old 4Runner."

It was from the inventory filed with the probate court. I hadn't thought to give it to him, which meant I'd be paying him for his own trip to the courthouse. "According to his surviving relatives and their attorney, the assets should have come to a lot more," I said.

"I guess they're not laughing as hard as they expected to be."

"Huh?"

"Laughing heirs."

"Ah." Laughing heirs are beneficiaries who weren't particularly close to the deceased during his lifetime: Their joy of inheritance outweighs their sorrow at his passing. It did seem an apt description of Robert's surviving relatives.

"They hadn't planned to wait for his death to celebrate." He dug in a briefcase and came up with a manila envelope, which he pushed across the desk to me. I flipped it open.

It was a petition Jared Walsh had filed in the circuit court of the city of Richmond, petitioning the court to declare one Robert Wilson Walsh to be incapacitated and to appoint Jared Walsh as his conservator to manage his estate and financial affairs. The petition had been filed January 3 and served on Robert January 5. With it was a court order appointing Rupert Propst as Robert's guardian ad litem to represent his interests during the competency proceedings. I looked up.

Rodney said, "The hearing was set for last Tuesday." The day of Robert's funeral.

"Shouldn't there be reports here from the guardian ad litem and maybe an examining physician?" I asked.

"They were both under seal. I couldn't get copies."

"Things are beginning to fall into place." I told him about the safe-opening ceremony the previous week. "Evidently, Robert had begun emptying his financial accounts before his death. His nephews thought he was buying gold, but they can't find any of it."

"And Rupert Propst has gone from representing Robert Walsh's interests to representing..."

"His estate's," I finished. "Technically anyway. In practice he's representing Jared, Nathan, and Whitney, or some subset of the three."

"You know what would be nice to know," Rodney said.

"What?"

"What happened first. Did Robert begin pulling money out of his accounts, and that's what motivated this petition for conservatorship? Or did Jared Walsh file this petition, and that motivated Robert to start liquidating his assets to put them out of reach of his grasping relatives?"

"In other words, was Robert losing his mind or not?" I said.

"Exactly."

I tapped a finger on the petition for conservatorship, wondering whether Whitney could give me access to Robert's house and any papers he might have kept there.

Someone coughed behind me. It was Carly, being discreet. "I'm sorry to interrupt," she said, "but you didn't answer your phone, and there are people here to see you." She seemed to be looking at me. "A Rupert..." She hesitated.

"Propst?"

"That sounds like it. There's a younger man with him. Nathan Walsh."

Well, well. "Bring them back," I said, getting to my feet.

Rupert was wearing a gray cashmere topcoat over a double-breasted suit, a bright blue tie knotted at his throat. Nathan wore jeans and a parka.

"Have a seat," I said, standing behind my desk when Carly brought them in.

They remained standing behind my client chairs. Rupert said, "I know you're representing Brian Marshall, who's been arrested for the murder of Macy Buck." He smiled his shark teeth at me.

"Yes," I said.

"So I also know that you'll be looking for a scapegoat, someone you can implicate in the crime or at least someone you can smear sufficiently to create reasonable doubt. I know how you criminal defense lawyers work."

I opened my mouth to respond to this calumny, but Rupert barreled on.

"I'm here to serve notice that my client will not be your scapegoat. You are not to talk to him unless I am present, and any attempt to contact him should be through me."

"Which client?"

"You can't pretend to be so dim as not to know that I am representing Nathan Walsh, the young man who is standing right here beside me."

"Until this moment I had assumed you were representing the estate of Robert Walsh," I said, "having previously represented Robert Walsh himself as guardian ad litem."

His head went back. I try not to get mad unless someone is paying me to do it, and there was nothing to be gained by letting Rupert know I wasn't a clueless blonde—but, on the other hand, Rupert

Propst was about the biggest prick who had ever walked into my office.

"I assume you're representing Jared Walsh, too, personally and as executor of the estate?"

He inclined his head. "You assume correctly."

"Lot of fees there," I noted. "I guess you're not worried about a conflict of interest."

"There is no conflict of interest."

I looked at Nathan. "You probably know that a person convicted of murder can't inherit from the person he's been convicted of killing. If Jared was convicted of killing his uncle, for instance, your inheritance would increase by fifty percent."

Rupert gaped for a moment like a fish out of water. "That's outrageous," he said. "That's defamation."

"I was just giving a hypothetical example to illustrate a legal principle," I said. "I'm not saying Jared killed his uncle. I have no reason to think he did. I have no reason to think he'd try to frame his brother Nathan to increase his own inheritance, for that matter."

"I said you were not to address my client…"

"…except in your presence. I understand, but you've got to admit it's just the kind of conflict that can come up in cases like these. I understand your position, too. Three clients mean three fees. As a solo practitioner I certainly understand. If I had any clients that weren't locked up, I'd be trotting them around to lawyers' offices to make pointless declarations, too. A billable hour is a billable hour, after all. Isn't it, Rupert?"

Rupert had his hand on Nathan's elbow, pulling him toward the door. "We don't have to stand here and listen to these groundless accusations. And you won't get away with this. You'll be hearing from me."

"Something else to bill your clients for," I said, but Rupert had his client out the door, using his own body to shield him from my pernicious influence.

"You got me out of bed for this?" Nathan said, speaking for the first time.

"Now don't let her manipulate you. She'd like nothing better than to set us against each other. Nothing would serve her better…" They passed out of earshot, Rupert still going on about my manipulative, scheming ways.

I took a breath, and Brooke appeared in my doorway.

"Bravo," she said. Rodney was at her elbow.

"Is it always so exciting around here?" he asked.

"Only when I lose my temper." I tried a quick smile, and it evidently reassured them enough that they filed in and plopped down in my client chairs. I sat down myself.

"Did Whitney Foster have anything to do with that petition you showed me?" I asked Rodney.

"Not as far as I can tell. She may not have known about it."

"That's something," I said.

"Wait a minute," Brooke said. "What petition? I'm missing something."

We filled her in. When she had it straight, she said, "There's a lot going on here, and Macy Buck's death is tied into it somehow. Brian did not walk into her house and stick a butcher knife in her."

"His connection is through his relationship with Whitney."

"I think we need to know more about Jared and Nathan."

"Rodney's been working on it."

She turned to him. "What have you found out?"

He cleared his throat, looked at me. I shrugged, then nodded.

"Let me get my notes," he said.

He came back with a manila folder, sat, and crossed his legs as he opened the folder. "Okay," he said. "Jared Walsh, age 39. Married twice, the first time to a Valerie Johnson for a couple of years in his early twenties, most recently to a Jennifer Pace. That ended six years ago, about the time she was starting a residency at MCV and both of them were declaring bankruptcy."

"Jennifer is a medical doctor?" Brooke asked.

I was thinking about Jared's bankruptcy. I couldn't recall any reference to it in the petition for conservatorship, but it would have posed an obstacle to Jared's getting himself appointed.

"Internal medicine," Rodney said. "During their marriage, Jared was investing in real estate, mostly rent houses and small apartment buildings in the block or two south of the Fan."

"Marginal neighborhood," I noted.

"Transitional neighborhood," Rodney said. "Or it was. A decade ago, prices were climbing pretty fast."

"And Jennifer was part of this real estate empire?"

"I don't think so. She was in med school. As his spouse she signed all the loan documents, though, so when the real estate crisis came, it took her down with him."

"How long were they married?" Brooke asked.

"Four years. They have a ten-year-old son named Mason who's in the fifth grade at Southampton Elementary."

"Does Jared pay child support?"

"Three-fifty a month."

I said, "That doesn't sound like much for a man who lives in Jared's neighborhood."

"An unemployed man who lives in Jared's neighborhood. Actually, that figure was part of the divorce decree. It could have changed since."

"Is Jared unemployed or self-employed?"

Rodney inclined his head. "Depends on how you define it. He still buys and sells real estate, but it's all in the name of an LLC owned by two brothers named Strumpf. They made their fortune with a chain of pawn shops that was bought out by Cash America a decade or so ago. I've got copies of the articles of organization, and as near as I can tell, Jared has no equity stake in the LLC. He's working under some kind of commission arrangement."

He fell silent, evidently to allow for questions. "How about Nathan?" I said.

Rodney shuffled his papers, then leaned back. "Nathan Walsh, age 33," he said. "Started college at Virginia Tech, came home and took some courses at J. Sargent Reynolds, then enrolled at VCU and came within a course or two of finishing. Talked his dad into financing a business venture about five years ago…"

"Knockers?"

"You know about that. Yes. Kind of a Hooters knock-off, evidently. He was open less than a month. There was some kind of trademark infringement suit, some violations of city codes. The service was bad, the food was bad…Pretty clearly Nathan didn't know anything about running a restaurant."

"How do you know about the bad food and service?" I asked. "Internet reviews?"

His gaze stayed on his papers, but his ears turned pink.

"Rodney Burns," Brooke said. "You were a customer."

"Just the once." He flapped his hand as if to brush it away. "Food was bad, you know. The service."

"Does 'bad service' mean the girls were inefficient?" I asked. "Or that they weren't pretty?"

"They were okay, I guess, but, you know, slow."

I eyed him. "But you didn't go back."

"No. Like I said, it closed."

I shook my head. "Sometimes you think you know someone."

"How did they dress?" Brooke asked. "Did they wear undersized shorts, scoop necklines, cut-off T-shirts, that sort of thing?"

His ears had gone beyond pink almost to burgundy. My cell phone dinged, and I pulled it out of my jacket pocket. It was a text from Mike McMillan. "Paul at MCV, collapsed at work. Going now."

I stood up. "I've got to go."

Brooke said, "What is it? What's wrong?"

Rodney said, "I hope you don't…"

I sat down again and grabbed at my cross-trainers. "Not at all. You like pretty girls who smile at you. What man wouldn't? I'm sorry, I've got to go."

Chapter 12

The shortest way to MCV, the downtown hospital, went through the grounds of the state capitol. As I speed-walked up the hill, I fished out my cell phone and placed a call back to Rodney.

"What have you got on Jack Packard?" I asked.

"Nothing. Who's he?"

"Robert Walsh's best friend, from what they tell me. If Robert was fighting with his nephews for control of his estate, his best friend might know something about it."

"I'll look him up. Listen, Robin. I hope you don't think I'm one of those creepy, middle-aged men…"

"Time to let it go, Rodney. The damage is done." It was probably not the kindest way to end the call, and I regretted it immediately. I was crossing Broad Street at that point, though, and didn't have time to think about it.

Ten minutes after I'd left the Ironfronts, I was walking through the door of the emergency room. I couldn't have done much better if I'd gotten my car from the garage, and I couldn't have been certain of a place to park. At the desk was a woman in purple scrubs with red hearts all over the top, which reminded me it was Valentine's Day and I was going to have to do something for Paul.

"I'm here to see Paul Soldano," I said. "I understand he was brought in a short time ago."

Her eyes cut to her clipboard. "He's in room 82. Are you family?"

"Sister. Robin Starling. Do I need to sign something to go back? Which way is it?"

"Room 82," she said again. "Straight down this corridor, first left, third door on the left."

"Got it. Thanks." I sped down the hall, sidestepping an old woman in a wheelchair with an IV pole attached.

Paul was lying on a gurney and wearing a hospital gown. A tube from a bag of clear fluid ran to a needle in his left arm. Except for his disheveled hair and his sheepish expression, he looked pretty much like he had the last time I'd seen him.

"I hear you passed out," I said.

"Yeah. Stupid of me. I was feeling light-headed, and I should have sat down."

I looked at the IV bag and saw they had him on saline. "So you're dehydrated?"

"Evidently."

I took his hand. "How long has this been going on?"

"Has what been going on?"

"Your love affair with Scarlett Johansson. The dizzy spells, you dope."

He shrugged.

"Very communicative." I studied him. "How much weight have you lost exactly?"

"I don't know exactly."

"Give me an estimate."

"Twenty pounds. Twenty-five."

"In a month?"

"Or so. Five weeks, maybe."

"Are you counting calories? How many have you been getting a day?"

"Not many."

I thought back over the last several meals we'd eaten together: A burger without a bun, a salad without dressing—a junior breakfast burrito, for heaven's sake. "Fifteen hundred calories?" I guessed.

He looked uncomfortable.

"Twelve hundred?"

His expression didn't change.

"A thousand?" My voice had gone into its upper registers.

"About that. I have an app on my phone that helps me keep track, but there's some guesswork involved."

"A thousand calories a day for five weeks? Are you nuts?"

He smiled weakly. "That's what they tell me."

Mike McMillan came through the curtain. "I see reports of your death have been greatly exaggerated," he said to Paul.

"Hello, Mark Twain," I said.

"Robin Starling, English major."

"What's your excuse?" I said.

"Voracious reader." To Paul he said, "How was the ambulance ride?"

"Unnecessary. I was conscious before it got there, you know, but they wouldn't let me stand up."

"You hit your head?"

"I don't know. It is a little tender."

"So you left the Fed on a gurney."

"Pretty embarrassing."

"Did you know he was on a hunger strike?" I asked Mike. "A thousand-calorie-a-day diet?"

He moved his head. "I knew it was something like that."

"And you just let him do it? Why didn't you say something to me?"

"He was doing it for you."

"Doing it for me?" I looked back and forth between them. Paul was giving Mike a hard look.

"Oops," Mike said.

"I want to know in what way this is my fault," I said.

"Nobody said..."

Paul interrupted. "It isn't your fault, Robin. Of course it's not your fault."

"I'm going to step into the hall," Mike said. "You two can talk."

"About what?" I said. "What's this about?"

But Mike was gone. I looked at Paul. "So what have you told Mike that you haven't told me?"

Paul shifted his gaze. He took a breath and released it, like he was steeling himself for an ordeal. I waited. I had a question on the table, and I wasn't planning to speak again until I got an answer.

"You remember the end of your last big trial?" he said finally. "We had that big celebratory dinner at Enrique's, and afterwards you and I went to your house. We were on the couch and things were..."

"I remember," I said.

His gaze flicked to my face. "Things progressed right up to the point..."

"Yes, I remember," I said again, feeling a growing sense of foreboding.

"I know you do." He took a breath and looked at the wall again, then with an effort turned his gaze back on me. "I guess this is the part I need to say. Okay?"

My heart was pounding, and I didn't know why. I nodded.

"We progressed to the point that my shirt was open—I was wearing a T-shirt, like I always do, helps keep the flab from jiggling—and you were kissing me and…" He stopped and swallowed. "Your right hand was holding onto a big fistful of belly fat. And then it was over. You were getting up, straightening your clothes. I was buttoning my shirt. In fifteen minutes I was outside in my car trying to figure out what had just happened. Of course, I did figure it out. It didn't take any great leap to see you were disgusted by all that blubber, and I don't blame you. You thought you could overlook it, but when it came right down to it you just couldn't."

His bleak smile sent a stab of pain right through me. "Paul," I said. A tear broke from each of his eyes and ran down his cheeks, and my own eyes to start to leak in sympathy. I sat on the edge of his gurney. "I remember kissing you. I don't remember squeezing your belly fat. Do you remember what you were doing at the time?"

The hint of a smile quirked his mouth. "I guess I had my hands pretty much all over you."

"Pretty much, yeah. And you know where things were headed."

"I had my hopes."

"It wasn't time for that. I've been in a relationship before." I took a breath. "I've been in several relationships before. Once the sex starts—in itself, it's pretty wonderful, of course—it puts all kinds of pressures on the relationship. We have a good thing going, you and I. I wasn't ready to exchange it for something a lot less stable."

It's hard to maintain eye contact with someone when both your eyes and his are leaking tears, but I held on.

"Really?" Paul said in a squeaky voice. He cleared his throat.

"Really," I said.

"I'm not too fat?"

My mouth twitched. I leaned toward him until our noses touched. "Of course, you're too fat. You're too fat, and you leave the toilet seat up when you use the bathroom at my house. When you eat, I can hear you breathing through your nose. I've got problems, too, and I even know what some of them are. I'll bet if I gave you a pen and paper, you could fill a page."

"Actually, you're pretty perfect. I do wish you could be nicer to me sometimes."

"Paul." I took his head in both hands, leaned in and kissed him on the mouth. I took my time about it. When I pulled back, I raised my eyebrows.

"That was pretty nice," he said.

"For me, too. And I'll try to make more of an effort, if I can do it without getting your libido stirred up."

He looked at me, and I looked at him. The eye contact was excruciating.

At last Paul said, "Robin? Do women not have libido?"

Well, that stung. It did kick me loose of all the naked-soul sincerity. "Someday, if we get to that point in our relationship, I'll strip you naked and chase you through the house with a flyswatter. You'll see."

His breathing kicked up a notch. "Is that a, uh, particular fantasy of yours?"

"No," I said. "It's not. I'm a little disconcerted to realize it's one of yours."

"I'm in the E.R. and out of nowhere you start talking about stripping me naked and chasing me around the house. You went from zero to sixty in a hospital zone."

"Sorry. I didn't mean to go stirring up your libido." I patted his cheek and stood. "Where's your phone?"

"In my pants pocket. Folded up there on the chair."

I fished it out and punched it on. "What's your passcode?"

"Ah. Well, that's something else that's embarrassing."

"Why embarrassing?"

"Oh-nine-oh-eight."

My birthday. "What a coincidence," I said, punching it in. "And you've got your fitness app open." I tapped the little wheel for settings, tapped fitness goals… "You're trying to lose five pounds a week. You are insane." I changed it to one pound per week, tapped the screen again. "There, you can eat 2,000 calories a day. When I check this a week from now, I don't want to see that you've been under eighteen hundred calories, ever. Do you understand me? If you don't think you're losing weight fast enough, you can kick up the exercise."

"Yes, ma'am."

There was a tap on the door, and I opened it. It was Mike.

"Have you two got things sorted out yet? I'm getting strange looks out here."

"They're sorted. Paul needs to eat, so he and I are going to be having a big dinner at Enrique's tonight. Probably Brooke Marshall will be joining us. Are you in?"

"Sure. I don't usually get included in your little soirees."

My phone rang and I slid my finger across the screen, saying, "Maybe you don't try hard enough." Into the phone I said, "Robin Starling."

"Robin, it's Whitney. The police are here with a warrant."

"Where, the coffee shop?"

"Yes, Carytown Joe. They got here about ten minutes ago."

I looked at my watch. My car was across downtown. I was probably thirty minutes away. "Watch them. Pay attention to what they look at. If they take anything, they're supposed to give you a receipt."

"What about pictures? They're taking pictures."

"What are they taking pictures of?"

"Bills. Bank statements. Some printouts from QuickBooks."

"Keep paying attention. If they walk off with the computer, get a receipt. Find out when you'll get it back—tell 'em you need it to run the business. I'll get there as soon as I can."

I punched off.

"Trouble?" Mike asked.

"The police are searching Carytown Joe. Where's your car?"

"Parked on the street about half-a-block down."

"Can you give me a ride to my car?"

"What about him?" He jerked his head in Paul's direction.

Paul's eyebrows had gone up inquisitively. "Yes. What about me?"

"You can be back in twenty minutes, tops," I said to Mike.

He smiled crookedly. "Maybe twenty-five. I'll never find that parking space again."

"Paul will still be here. If they finish with him before you get back, they can leave him propped in a wheelchair by the door."

"Hey!" Paul said.

I smiled at him. "It wouldn't be for long."

Chapter 13

Even with the lift from Mike it took twenty-five minutes to get to Carytown Joe. Only two of the tables were occupied, one by an old man reading a Wall Street Journal and having a pastry with his coffee, the other by a couple of middle-aged women with lattes. No one was behind the counter, but when I walked around it, I found Whitney in a small office. There were no police.

"Did they run off your customers?" I asked.

Whitney was sitting in a padded swivel chair, white faced and looking as if she were about to throw up. She shook her head. "Business will start picking up again about eleven-thirty." She handed me a set of papers stapled at the top corners. It was the search warrant. I flapped back the top page to read the affidavit it was based on.

"The police have talked to you before," I said, looking up.

"They've been in here, just making conversation it seemed like."

"But you told them Brian had a key to the shop."

"He does. It's not like it's a secret or anything."

I took a breath. "You need to tell me when the police come by." The last page wasn't stapled to the others. It was a receipt for a woman's jacket, a dish cloth, and three assorted kitchen utensils. "Actually, from now on, you should not talk to the police except in my presence. Any question they ask, say you want your lawyer."

"My lawyer?"

"Me, until you find somebody else." I turned the receipt to face her and laid it on the small table she was using as a desk. "Tell me about the jacket they took."

"It's an old jacket that hangs on that hook by the back door. It's not one I wear very often. Sometimes I throw it on when I take out the trash."

"Why did the police take it?"

"I don't know. They seemed interested in something on the sleeve. A stain of some sort."

"And the utensils?"

She wet her lips. "A corkscrew, a food thermometer, and…a rusty looking ice pick they found on the floor between the counter and the wall."

"Which counter?"

"The one out there."

"Where any patron could have dropped it. When you say rusty looking…"

"The blade had dark splotches on it." Her expression was earnest. "Robin, I'm scared for Brian."

"Me, too," I acknowledged.

"I'm going to go down to the jail this afternoon. I need to see him."

I sighed. "You can't. He gets one visitor every seven days. His sister saw him Saturday."

"I don't know what I'm going to do."

"He seems to think he's covering for you."

"Covering for me how? Why would he think that?" Her eyes were on the desk, apparently focused on the arrest warrant and affidavit.

"He found your glasses case with a dead woman, and he took it," I said. "He tried to leave town, and now he's doing a good job of remaining silent."

"I thought he was running because things looked so bad for him."

"Taking off had the effect of directing suspicion to him—and, possibly, away from you. That may be why he left the glasses case in his apartment. He knew the police would catch up to him, and he didn't want it found on him."

Whitney got her glasses case from under the table, opened it, and extracted her sunglasses. She handed it to me. "Here. Do what you need to to save Brian."

I shook my head. "There's nothing I can do with it now. Once I took it out of Brian's apartment, it was too late for that. I could have gotten that case anywhere."

"You should have left it then."

Changing tack, I said, "You knew your cousin was trying to have your uncle declared incompetent, didn't you?"

"I do now. Mr. Propst said something about it in one of his phone calls."

"When we opened the safe? You didn't have anything to do with the petition?"

"No."

"Did your uncle seem in need of a guardian or someone to take charge of his property?"

"I wouldn't have said so." She hesitated. "Actually, there was one time I went by and he seemed a little loopy. I made it a point to go back the very next day, but he seemed fine then."

"Did you ever mention his being loopy to either of your cousins?"

She shook her head solemnly. "Brian and I talked about it."

"You talk to Jack Packard since the funeral?"

"I haven't seen him."

"I'm going to try to this afternoon."

"Why? What could he have to do with anything?"

"Nothing that I know of. I'm trying to get some insight as to what was going on in Robert's life before he died. Just in case there's any sort of connection."

"Between Uncle Robert's death and Macy Buck?"

There was a knocking from the counter out in the restaurant. "Hey, is anybody back there who would like to take my money?" Whitney had a customer. The lunch rush had begun.

She stood, and I stood with her. "You gonna be all right?" I asked her.

"I guess I'd better be, hadn't I?"

A half-block up from Carytown Joe I found a sandwich shop where I got a couple of vegetarian clubs—avocado slices, alfalfa sprouts, and so forth—on millet bread, which, the menu assured me, was gluten-free. I took them to my car. The sun felt good in the crisp, cold air, and I swung my arms as I walked. On a back-swing, a jogger appeared suddenly on the sidewalk behind me and got smacked in the groin with my sack of sandwiches before I realized he was there.

"Sorry," I called after him, but he was by me, hunched a bit but maintaining his pace. "I applaud your dedication," I called out to his departing back. He waved a hand, but didn't turn his head.

By the time I got back to my office, it was after twelve. I was afraid I'd missed Brooke, but she was still in her office.

"You haven't gone to lunch," I said as I came through the archway.

She swiveled her chair to face the door. "I was waiting for you. How's Paul?"

"It may have just been dehydration. He's been on some crazy kind of diet."

"I know."

"How do you know? I just found out about it."

"You hadn't noticed he's been losing weight?"

"Well, sure, I could see he was looking better."

"He's convinced he's going to lose you if he doesn't lose fifty pounds."

"Did he tell you that?"

"He didn't have to tell me."

"Somebody could have told me." I dropped the sack of sandwiches on her computer desk. "I brought lunch. If you knew so much, why is this the first I've heard about it?"

"I didn't want to interfere."

"Well next time, interfere. I can't have people pining away over me."

"What would you have done?" She opened the sack and took out the sandwiches. "They look good."

"Told him to stop."

"Oh, yes. That would have worked. 'Stop pining, Paul.' 'Oh, okay.' What are they?"

"The sandwiches? Veggie clubs on gluten-free bread."

"Sounds healthy."

"It's low-cal, except for the avocado. We're having a big meal at Enrique's tonight—you, me, Paul, and Mike."

"Mike McMillan? Paul's friend?"

"Yes. We're going to have a victory meal to celebrate however much weight Paul's lost, and we're going to rehydrate him in the process."

"Does that mean margaritas?"

"Well, not for Paul. Alcohol is dehydrating. The rest of us could have margaritas."

"Paul's not going to like that." She took a bite of her sandwich. "It's good," she said around the mouthful.

"Good." I took a bite of my own sandwich. "I think the avocado is the stand-in for meat."

"It works."

Rodney wasn't in his office, but he'd left a legal pad with Jack Packard's address and two phone numbers on my desk. I sat and called the one that looked like a landline, but it was no longer a working number. I could have gotten an address and a nonworking number from the phone book, I thought as I dialed the other number. No reason to hire a detective.

There was no answer at the second number either, but an old man's voice invited me to leave a message. I did, giving him my name and number and asking him to call me.

Packard lived on Arrowhead Road, not a street I knew. According to Google Maps, though, it was on the Southside. I tapped the desk with a finger. What else did I have to do, I thought.

Jack Packard's neighborhood looked like it had been established around 1960: Big brick homes with lots of trees, and winding streets with no curbs or sidewalks. Jack's house was a one-story affair with a patchy lawn that sloped down from the street. A ten-year-old Toyota SUV was parked at the bottom of his cracked and pitted asphalt driveway. He was home.

About halfway down the driveway, I parked, set my parking brake, and got out. There was a fence at the end of the driveway, just beyond Packard's car, but because of the slope I could see over it into a wooded backyard.

The sidewalk that curved from the driveway to the front door was flanked with the overgrown skeletons of some kind of bush. After one of the leafless arms snagged at my dress, I stayed strictly to the center of the walk, turning sideways at one point where they grew almost together.

The front door was a step above the level of the sidewalk, and the doorbell chimed like a grandfather clock. There was no answer. I opened the storm door and knocked, with the same results.

"Well, crap." I fished out my phone, found the working number I had for Jack Packard, and tried it again. Voice mail. It was a nice day for February, maybe sixty degrees and sunshine, but Jack's front stoop was in the shade, and I found myself shivering. I pulled open the storm door again and tried the knob, but it was locked, and the door itself was as solid and unmoving as if it were part of the wall it was set in.

I stepped back, letting the storm door fall shut with a bang. As I was winding my way back down the sidewalk, it occurred to me that Jack must not use his front door much. The thorns of the leafless bushes would tear at his clothes every time he went in or out. I bypassed my car and walked down the driveway to try a door that went into the house a level below the main floor: Jack had at least a partial basement. It was locked. There was a small, screened window next to the door, but I couldn't see anything through it.

The privacy fence at the end of the driveway had a gate—padlocked, natch—and I gave it a shake. The fence did have a little wiggle to it, but not enough to encourage me. I plodded back to my car.

As I was backing out of the driveway, I noticed a newspaper protruding from a paper box set on the post below the mailbox. Leaving my car running, I got out and walked around to pull out the paper. There were two other newspapers in there with it, Saturday's and Sunday's. Jack hadn't gotten his paper since Friday, which made it look like he had left home and had not come back—except that his SUV was right there at the bottom of his driveway.

Macy Buck had died on Friday.

I pushed the newspapers back into the box and stood looking down at Jack's house, the cool breeze catching at my skirt and hair. A shiver lifted the hairs at the nape of my neck.

I shook it off. After a quick glance up and down the street, I pulled open Jack's mailbox. He had mail, quite a bit of it. I stood there sorting through it. There was a bill from Dominion Resources, a statement from Bank of America, something from Gold's Gym that looked like a bill. The earliest postmarks were "10 Feb"—Thursday. The most recent were dated 12 Feb. Jack might or might not have picked up his mail on Friday, but he surely hadn't gotten it since.

A cloud passed over the sun, and I looked up as the day darkened perceptibly. I shoved Jack's mail back into the box, got into my car and sat with the car idling, the heater warming my bare legs. Jack might have two vehicles, I told myself, or he might have gotten a ride to the airport or someplace. He might have called a taxi.

Or he could be lying incapacitated inside his home, unable to reach the door or even his cell phone. He could be dead.

I put my car in drive and drifted back down the driveway, braking at the sidewalk. This time I skirted the sidewalk with its grasping rose bushes and walked around the front of the house, my heels, low as they were, sinking into the lawn enough to make walking difficult. There was a six-foot privacy fence on this side of the house, too, but no gate. There might be a gate at the back of the property, but trees and brambles and waist-high weeds grew all along the outside of the fence. In these clothes and these shoes, I wasn't going to make it back there.

Discouraged, I slogged back over the front yard to the driveway. Not only was the damn house impregnable, but I couldn't even get into the backyard.

I stepped up onto the rear bumper of my VW Beetle, bracing myself with one hand, trying to see something other than trees beyond the privacy fence at the end of the driveway. I won't tell you the possible courses of action that I considered and discarded, almost all of them highly inappropriate for a member of the bar. What I should do, I knew, was call the police and tell them Jack Packard had gone missing, then return to my office to await developments. Whether and how the police chose to pursue the matter was not my business. This was one occasion when I needed to behave prudently, and that's just what I was going to do, right after I tried one more thing.

I got the screwdriver out of my glove box and went to the little window by the side door, pushed the end of the screwdriver between the screen and the window frame, and levered out the screen. This was as far as I was prepared to go, I told myself as I propped the screen against the brick wall of the house. If the window was locked, I wasn't going to break the glass. I was going to return to my office and call the police.

Tucking the screwdriver into the waist of my skirt, I pushed up on the window sash—much harder than necessary, as it turned out. The bottom sash slammed upward in the frame.

I stepped back and looked up the driveway. It looked like I was going in after all, and suddenly I didn't want to. I got my cell phone out of my pocket and called Paul.

"Hey, Paul," I said when he answered. "Did you ever get out of the hospital?"

"Yes, Mike brought me home. Where are you? You never came back."

"Do you remember me mentioning Jack Packard?"

He didn't.

"Everyone says he was Robert Walsh's best friend, and I actually saw him at the funeral. He's a sturdy-looking guy with white hair he wears in a flattop. He read some scripture."

"And why are you telling me this?"

"I'm at his house. No one answers the door, and it doesn't look like he's been here for several days."

"Don't tell me you're thinking about breaking in."

"Well. I did just manage to get a window open."

He didn't say anything.

"Paul?"

"I don't guess it would do any good to tell you to leave it alone."

"You could try it and see."

"Robin. You need to leave this alone. Leave the window how it is. Just get back in your car and drive away."

I thought about it. "Not good enough," I concluded.

"Robin…"

"I'll just take a quick peek, then I'm out of here."

He exhaled audibly.

"You might call me back in five or ten minutes, just to check on me."

"If you don't answer, I'm calling the police."

"Don't be too quick to do that. I may still be trespassing."

It's not as easy as you might think for a woman who's five-foot eleven and wearing a dress to wedge herself through a tiny window with a sill about four or four-

and-a-half feet off the ground. Let's just say I managed it and that I'm glad no one was watching.

The first thing I did was grope for a light switch. An overhead light came on to reveal an old couch, an easy chair, and a flat-panel television. There was a burgundy area rug over a linoleum floor, and, incongruously, rich wood paneling that consisted of individual boards rather than the usual sheets of paneling.

I moved quietly across the room to a door and a straight staircase, going up. The door opened on darkness. When I found the light switch, I found myself looking at an unfinished basement with a wall of tools hanging on a pegboard, a row of shelves, and a several stacks of boxes. "Jack?" I called softly.

The furnace cycled off and plunged the house into sudden silence.

I closed the door as quietly as I could and remained standing at the bottom of the steps for several seconds, my eyes tracking a series of dark splotches that trailed up to a closed door. I leaned forward and touched one of the splotches. It was dry. I sniffed my finger, but it just smelled like a finger.

I climbed the steps into the silent house.

The hinges of the door at the top creaked alarmingly, and I stopped on the top step to listen. "Jack Packard," I called through the partially open door. "Are you home?"

If he was home, he wasn't saying. I stepped up into a recessed corner of the kitchen, feeling suddenly foolish. The man was out of town for a long weekend, and here I was prowling around his empty house to no purpose except to add wear and tear to my adrenal gland.

There were a few more splotches on the kitchen floor, more clearly visible in the sunlight streaming through the windows. The splotches here were black and uneven, perhaps with a reddish tint near the edges. I walked around the counter that separated the table and chairs of the breakfast nook from the kitchen proper and found a smeared splotch several inches across. When I crouched over it, trying to detect a pattern in the smear, I caught a whiff of a sharp odor and gagged. I put a hand on the countertop to pull myself up. I had no doubt that what I'd been looking at were dried drops of blood.

A siren whooped once from the front of the house and then was silent. Through the dining room windows I could see the flashing lights of a police car parked in the driveway behind my car. I turned and looked wildly around the kitchen. There was a phone on the wall by the refrigerator. I snatched it up, but there was no dial tone, and I remembered that it was no longer a working number. I fumbled for my own phone, dialing 9-1-1 as I ran for the front door and unlocked it.

"What is the nature of your emergency?"

"My name is Robin Starling. I'm at the house of Jack Packard at 4121 Arrowhead Road." The ring of the doorbell and the screech of the storm door sounded almost simultaneously. "He hasn't answered his phone or his door for several days." There was a pounding on the door. "Today I tried the door, and it was unlocked. The house is empty, but there's something that looks like blood on the floor in the kitchen."

"Open up. Police."

"Are you in the house now?" the emergency dispatcher asked.

"Yes, and someone's pounding at the door. I'm scared."

"Don't answer the door. Lock yourself in a bathroom and stay on the line. We'll get a patrol car there as quick as we can."

The knob turned and the door started to open as I hotfooted it down a hall that ran parallel to the front of the house. When I came to a bathroom, I went inside and closed the door and locked it. Already there were footsteps in the hall.

"I'm here," I breathed into the phone. "In the bathroom."

"Good. There's a patrol car in the neighborhood now. Someone's already called about a prowler. We'll just talk a few moments, and everything will be all right."

I remembered the screwdriver tucked into my skirt. I pulled it out, wiped it quickly on my blouse, then tossed it into the cabinet under the sink. I crouched to wipe the handle of the cabinet door with my untucked blouse.

The bathroom door rattled. "It's locked," a voice said, then continued more loudly: "Police. Is someone in there?"

They shouldered it open. Still crouched on the floor, I cried out and wrapped my arms around my head as two uniformed officers entered the bathroom, first one and then the other.

"It's all right, miss," one of them said. "We're the police. You'll be all right now."

I looked up. I still had my phone in one hand. "They're here," I told the dispatcher. "The police.

Thank God." I suppressed the twinge I felt at invoking the Lord Most High in my little deception, pressing End as I got to my feet.

There were not one, not two, but three police cruisers outside the house when we came out, two in the driveway and one in the street. Two cops were in the driveway along with a seventyish woman with short, henna-red hair. Another cop came out of the house just behind me and my two escorts.

"That's her," the woman said. "The woman I saw breaking into the house."

"I walked all around the house," I told the cops nearest me, trying hard to sound like a tremulous female. "I noticed the open window at the end of the driveway, but I went through the front door. It wasn't locked."

"She did spend some time casing out the house," the woman said, a bit dramatically in my opinion. "But she didn't go through the door. She went in through that window down there."

"I did lean in to try to get a look inside. The man who lives here, Jack Packard, hasn't been picking up his mail or answering his phone, but his car's here. I was worried about him."

"Something happened in the kitchen," said one of the officers who'd come out of the house. "There's something that looks like blood on the floor."

"Do you know what happened to Jack Packard?" I asked the woman, who was wearing a man's coat over her housedress and what looked like army boots on her feet. "Are you a friend of his? Is he all right?"

"I keep an eye on his house like any neighbor would," she said, more to the officer standing next to her than to me. "Same as I'd like to think he does for me."

"When did you see him last?" I asked her.

"Who is this woman?" she asked the cop. "And what is she doing here? That's what I'm wanting to know."

"My name is Robin Starling. I'm a lawyer here in town."

Evidently, none of them had heard of me, which I thought was a good thing. The cop I took to be the senior person present, the one who'd been standing with the old woman, came up the sidewalk and pushed past us into the house.

"I've been trying to get hold of Jack Packard for several days now," I announced to all and sundry. "He doesn't even answer his cell phone, and it looks like something may have happened to him in his kitchen."

"His car's right there," the old woman said, "and he only has the one. You keep looking, and I'm betting you find him."

I was getting tired of talking at cross-purposes with Jack Packard's intrusive neighbor. "You need to check the area hospitals," I said. "Maybe get your forensic unit out here to go over the house."

"What I think," the woman said, "is that you ought to take this young woman's fingerprints, see where she's been in that house and what she's been touching'."

The senior cop came out of the house. "I don't know what's happened here, but I think we'll need you both to come down to the station to make a statement," he said.

Great, I thought. There goes my afternoon.

I went home straight from the police station, but didn't make it any earlier than my usual time. It was too late to take Deeks on our usual two-mile run through the neighborhood. I fed him, wrestled with him, and then, having upset his little tum-tum too soon after eating, cleaned undigested kibble off the living room floor. Deeks helped with that, re-eating most of it despite my efforts to scoop it up. I mixed a solution for my Little Green Machine—very useful if you have pets—and spot-shampooed the carpet while Deeks circled me and barked at the noisy little vacuum.

"Okay," I said when I was done, eyeing the still damp carpet. I looked at Deeks. "Ready to go back to Dr. McD's?"

He wagged his tail, but a little uncertainly, I thought.

"I guess I could shower before I walk you over," I said.

Deeks barked, which I took as approval of the new plan, and dusk was falling as I walked Deeks back across the street.

When Dr. McDermott opened the door, Deeks trotted past him into the house like he owned it.

"Good evening, Deacon," Dr. McDermott called after him.

Deeks' tail wagged, but he didn't look back. He disappeared into the kitchen and began lapping from his water bowl.

"Probably thirsty after his gastro-intestinal upset." I told him about the messy aftermath of our wrestling match. "I can't seem to remember to give him time to let his food settle."

"If cleaning throw-up doesn't teach you, you're pretty hopeless."

"You sure you don't mind?"

"About an evening with Deacon? Not at all."

Deeks came back into the living room and lay down where he could look at us.

"You didn't have plans?" I asked.

"I'm a lonely old man. Why would I have plans?"

I must have looked stricken, because he smiled.

"I was going to read, but this is better. I hid some of Deacon's toys about the house. I thought I'd see if he could find them."

"What are you reading?"

"Arthur Conan Doyle."

"Sherlock Holmes?"

"No, I reread all those last year after I saw some episodes of the new series on PBS. Now I've started working through his other stories."

"Good?"

"I think so. Entertaining in a cerebral sort of way."

"I'll leave you to it."

Chapter 14

Brooke was already in the parking lot at Enrique's, her car running. I parked beside her. When I got out of my car, I could hear the bass notes of whatever song she was listening to. She opened the door as she killed the engine, and I recognized "Ace of Spades."

"Motorhead," I said. "The others here?"

"Not that I've seen. It's cold. Let's wait for them inside."

We got a table for four, and Paul and Mike came in just as the waitress was filling two ice-filled glasses from the pitcher of margaritas.

"You look good," Brooke said to Paul.

"Meaning I don't look as bad as you expected after hearing about my episode this morning?"

Mike smiled at the waitress, a pretty, twenty-something slip of a girl. "Could you bring us two more glasses?"

She smiled back, ducking her head and flushing, and went to get them. I noticed Brooke watching.

When the waitress got back, we ordered. Paul had an enchilada plate with potatoes instead of spanish rice. More concerned about maintaining my girlish figure than about passing out at work, I had a chili relleno a la carte, forgoing the beans and rice altogether.

"So how did your breaking-and-entering go this afternoon?" Paul asked.

They all looked at me as I sipped my margarita. "Not well," I said, wiping the salt from my mouth with the back of my wrist. "The police showed up. For a few minutes there I thought I'd be calling Mike about bailing me out."

"I don't really do that kind of work," Mike said.

"Sometimes you just have to get in there and figure it out." I told them the story.

"So what do you think happened to Jack Packard?" Brooke asked when I was done.

"I have no idea. Nothing good, I think."

Paul said to Mike, "Since you started practicing law, how many crime scenes have you stumbled on?"

"Zero."

"Robin doesn't practice law like other people. There's not another lawyer in Richmond who would go climbing in someone's window because she wanted to talk to him."

"You wouldn't expect there to be," I said. "There're not a million lawyers in Richmond."

"What?"

"With just three or four thousand lawyers in Richmond, the odds aren't in your favor."

Paul looked at Brooke and Mike.

"She's saying she's one in a million," Mike said.

Paul rolled his eyes and reached for his mug.

The pitcher of margaritas proved to be good for about five mugs. We each had one with the chips and salsa and were pouring out another quarter mug for each of us when the food arrived. The waitress served Mike first, and we ordered a second pitcher.

"Did you ever meet Rupert Propst?" I asked Mike as the waitress was clearing our plates.

"I've met him. I did some research, too, after you asked about him. Several of his clients have filed complaints with the state bar, and a couple of years ago he actually had his license suspended for six months."

"He came by my office today."

"Ooh," Brooke said. "I want to tell it." And she did, her face flushed and increasingly animated, Mike watching her with apparent appreciation.

"So he pretty much fled your office," Paul said to me when she was done.

"Brooke made me sound better than I was, but pretty much. I lost my temper."

When the waitress came back by to check on Mike and his needs, I ordered a platter of sopaipillas for our dessert. When we got them, I made sure Paul ate his share.

"I know we're fattening Paul up," Brooke said, "but what about the rest of us?"

"I skipped the rice and beans," I said. "I'm good."

"I guess I should say, What about me?"

"You're perfect," Mike said. He held up his mug, giving her the same sort of smile that had melted the waitress.

She opened her mouth and hesitated. "Thank you."

"Peaches and cream," he said, a hint of dreaminess in his voice. "And just a dash of spice."

Brooke turned pink and looked down at her plate.

"Tomorrow," I said to Paul, "you can go back to counting calories."

He held up his own mug. "Yippee."

"Just make sure you count high enough."

"Can do. One of the advantages of a good grammar school education."

I'd never had one of Enrique's sopaipillas, and probably I should have kept it that way. These were hot and flaky and crusted with sugar. With a drizzle of honey they made for a treat that would be hard to resist on my subsequent visits to the restaurant.

"I'll have to step up my running," I said.

"What?"

I looked around. Paul was licking his fingers like a starving man, but Brooke and Mike were looking at me. "Sorry. I was just thinking I was going to have to pay for these. I've noticed you don't talk much about your legal work," I said to Mike.

"Well, no. I figure part of what people pay me for is my discretion."

Paul elbowed him. "Oh, stop pretending you've got professional ethics. What he means to say is that nobody wants to listen to stories about some arthritic old coot who's applying for Social Security Disability."

"It gets a little more exciting than that," Mike protested. "Only last week, I represented a fifty-year-old woman who weighed in at a morbidly obese 450 pounds, and the week before that I had a 29-year-old client who was suffering from syphilitic anal warts."

He looked around at our startled faces. "Or maybe that's not such a great story for dinnertime conversation."

"Not a great one, no," Paul said.

"Probably the most exciting part of my job is cashing checks drawn on the U.S. Treasury," Mike said. "And on that note, I'll try to make amends for my conversational offense by picking up the check." He signaled the waitress.

His picking up the check actually did go a long way toward making amends.

It was nearly ten o'clock when I walked across the street to retrieve my pup. Dr. McDermott's lights were still on, and I felt bad about being so late. He was an old guy who was usually in bed by then.

He answered the door wearing pajamas and a bathrobe, and Deeks came out past him and jammed his nose between my knees.

"Sorry we kept you up," I said as I scratched Deeks's head.

"Not at all. I was just about to take him potty in the back yard."

"If I'm ever really late, you can go on to bed, and I'll come see Deeks in the morning."

"I know. I was going to give you until ten-thirty or so and then turn in."

"Glad I caught you."

He bent to put a hand on Deeks's head, and Deeks' wagging picked up speed. "See you tomorrow, buddy. We'll have us some fun."

"Got anything special planned?"

He straightened. "No, nothing special. Deacon always has fun."

"He does that," I agreed.

My cell phone woke me at 6:45 the next morning. It was Whitney Foster.

"Robin? Hi. It's Whitney." Deeks, on the bed beside me, stretched and yawned. "I'm afraid maybe I've done something I shouldn't have."

I pulled myself into sitting position, pushing a pillow into place between me and the headboard. "Tampered with evidence," I suggested.

"Not exactly."

Not the most confidence-inspiring disclaimer I'd ever heard. "What exactly?"

"I talked to the police last night. They dropped by my apartment, and…I thought maybe it was my last chance to help Brian."

I felt a creeping coldness, but it may have been just that my headboard buts up against the window. I pulled up the covers and tucked them under my arms. "What did you tell them?"

She took a breath. "That Brian and I spent the day together last Friday, the day Macy Buck was killed."

"What about you going to see Macy?"

"We went there together. I showed them the note she left me."

"What time did you tell them you went to see her?"

"I was kind of vague on the time."

"Don't say anything else," I said.

"The time was a bit of a problem, you know, because of course—"

"Shut up. Stop talking now."

178

"Oh." She sounded taken aback. "I thought you meant not to say anything else to the police."

"That, too, but they may be listening to this call. Of course I'm your lawyer, and everything you're telling me is for the purpose of obtaining legal advice." If they were listening, there was no harm in letting them know they were violating attorney-client privilege. "Where are you?"

She was at Carytown Joe, getting ready for the morning crowd. "I can leave, though, if I need to. Jennifer's here. She helps us out mostly on weekends, but she's here today, and she can handle a weekday crowd by herself if she has to."

"I'll swing by. We need to talk." I clicked off and threw back the covers, inadvertently burying Deeks, and the mound of blankets began to roil immediately. I flipped the covers off him.

"Sorry, buddy."

He looked at me reproachfully, but he couldn't hold the expression. His mouth opened, and his tongue came out, and he panted at me cheerfully.

"You're a great guy, you know that?"

His tail swished back and forth across the comforter. Evidently he did know that.

"I've got an early morning, I'm afraid." And God bless Dr. McDermott, I thought. Deeks would be miserable if he had to rely only on me for companionship.

I couldn't forgo my morning routine completely, though, not after the meal I'd eaten the night before. I lay on the floor by the bed, my hands extended over my head to grasp the footboard. My legs in the air, crossed at the ankles, I raised my hips off the ground, concentrating on shortening the distance between my hip bones and ribcage: lower, raise, lower, raise. The first ten were easy, the next ten were hard. I tried to squeeze out five more, but the last one proved impossible. I rolled onto my side to relieve the burning in my abdomen, and Deeks was there to bathe my face with his slobbery tongue. I pushed at him, spluttering. "You're a nuisance," I said, getting to my feet.

In response he gave me a happy bark. It's nearly impossible to insult a dog, I've found.

I dragged a Bosu ball out of my closet, set it flat side up, then stepped up onto it to see how many air squats I could do before I hit the shower.

It was eight-fifteen before I found a parking spot on Cary Street and got out of my Bug. I could see my breath on the air as I walked, but the clouds overhead were no more than ornamental, white bits of fluff in a china-blue sky, and the sun on my face was a kiss from heaven. I opened the door of Carytown Joe, and Whitney gave me a nod as she filled a coffee mug. She came around the counter with it.

"I see you're wearing sneakers," she said, handing me the mug. "Can we walk?"

"Sure."

I held the door for her, and we went out onto the sidewalk. "I blew it, didn't I?" she said after half-a-block.

I paused in my stride to take a sip of the coffee she'd given me. "Because you talked to the police?" I said.

She moved her head.

"Because you lied to the police," I said.

"I just can't stand the thought of Brian locked up in jail. We've got to get him out."

"I know. We will."

"When?"

"That's harder to say. What I'm afraid of right now is that the police might charge you with something." I kept my eyes on the shifting surface of my coffee as I walked, thinking that a to-go cup would have been more convenient than an open mug.

"Something like what?" Whitney asked.

"Obstruction of justice if they can prove you lied to them. Accessory after the fact, maybe murder one."

We walked for a time. I'd laid it on pretty thick, but thought she needed to hear it. "If they arrested me, would they let Brian go?" she asked finally.

"Not likely."

"There's no chance they're going to electrocute him or anything. Is there?"

"No. They haven't charged him with capital murder." Also, the default method of execution in Virginia was lethal injection. If you wanted the chair, you had to ask for it.

"That's something, at least," she said meekly.

"What police did you talk to last night? Did they come by your apartment?"

"Yes. A white man with a biker moustache…"

"…and a broad shouldered Hispanic man," I finished. "I know them."

"They seemed very nice. They'd found my fingerprints at Macy's house and wanted to give me an opportunity to explain."

"That wasn't nice, that was tricky. How did the police come to have your prints for comparison?"

"They took them yesterday when they were searching Carytown Joe. They had this big white card…"

I knew about the white card they rolled your fingerprints on. "You didn't mention them fingerprinting you when I saw you yesterday."

"They made it seem very routine. I didn't think it was important."

"When your boyfriend's locked up on a murder charge, everything's important." I managed another sip of my coffee, this time without breaking stride.

"What should I do now?"

"Nothing now. If you're charged with anything, you should get another lawyer."

"You won't represent me?"

"It's not that. Another lawyer might be able to get you off by throwing Brian under the bus. I couldn't do that. Conflict of interest."

"I wouldn't want to get off, if it meant Brian…"

"I know."

"And I don't think he…I'd like you to represent me if you're willing."

"We'll talk about it."

"I'm scared."

I stopped and turned to face her. "What's done is done, and there's no point in worrying about it."

She searched my face.

"We'll fight the good fight," I said. "It will turn out all right."

"How can you be so sure?"

I wasn't, but I said, "All things work together for good."

"Is that from the Bible?"

I didn't know. "It might be," I said.

"It might be," she repeated as we turned to retrace our steps to Carytown Joe. "I'll try to take comfort in an assurance that might or might not come from the Bible."

"I know you want to help Brian, but the best way to do that is not to talk about this case to anyone, not until all this is over. Can you do that?"

"Yes."

"Good. If the questioning is official, say you want your lawyer, that you're not going to say anything except in my presence."

"Then once you're there..."

"I can make sure you still don't say anything." My coffee had ceased to be hot. I bent to pour it on some weeds growing between the sidewalk and the curb. It occurred to me that Whitney might be offended at my pouring out her gourmet coffee. "It gets cold fast out here," I said by way of explanation.

She nodded.

As we approached the coffee shop, I slowed. The Ford Explorer parked against the curb looked chillingly familiar. The door opened, and James Jordan got out.

"Uh oh," I said.

"I'm afraid so," Jordan said. He reached into the car, and Ray Hernandez, sitting behind the wheel, handed him some papers. Jordan gave them to me.

I glanced at them. On top was an arrest warrant commanding any authorized law enforcement officer to bring Whitney Elizabeth Foster before a Virginia magistrate without delay. Like Brian Marshall, she'd been indicted for the murder of Macy Buck.

"What is it?" Whitney said.

183

"They're arresting you for murder." I handed the warrant to Whitney so she could read it. "Listen to me, Whitney. You're going to be tempted to explain things—explain away evidence against you, maybe try to straighten out apparent inconsistencies in your prior statements. Don't do it. You're charged with first-degree murder. There's going to be a trial, and nothing you say can make that trial go better. It can only make things worse. Do you understand?"

She nodded, dumbly. Jordan reached out and took the arrest warrant before it fluttered from her nerveless fingers.

"I'll go in the shop and tell Jennifer what's happened," I said. "See if she can't arrange for someone to come in to help her as needed."

Hernandez was out of the car now, flanking Whitney and me. He said, "We're willing to take her without handcuffs, because we're a couple of male chauvinist pigs who don't take women seriously. That okay with you?"

I nodded. "Thank you. Where are you taking her?"

"Courthouse. We'll get her processed, then take her before a magistrate."

Processing meant strip search, fingerprinting, mug shot, then waiting alone in a cell to be taken before a magistrate.

"I'll be fifteen minutes behind you," I told Whitney through Jordan's open door. "Try not to think. The mechanics of the arrest process aren't so bad if you don't think about them."

She didn't respond. I wasn't sure she'd heard me.

"Try not to think?" Jordan asked me.

"'There is nothing either good or bad, but thinking makes it so,' " I said.

"Is that some kind of new-age crap?"

"Hamlet."

"Ah. Old World crap," Jordan said.

"Hamlet's talking about how the world's a prison with many confines, wards, and dungeons. It seemed appropriate under the circumstances."

Jordan shook his head. "I don't know sometimes whether you're a genius or a nut job."

"I can't be both?"

"Maybe you can, Starling. Maybe you can." He got in the Explorer and pulled the door shut. I stood watching until it had crossed the Boulevard and disappeared in the direction of downtown.

I sighed and went into Carytown Joe to talk to Jennifer about what we needed to do to keep the business operating until such time as Whitney and Brian could return to it.

Chapter 15

Brooke Marshall's door was open. I went in and sat down. She typed another thirty seconds or so, finishing her thought, then swiveled her chair to face me. "What?" she said.

"Whitney's been arrested. She tried to give your brother an alibi, and it backfired. I was just at the courthouse for her presentation before a magistrate. Bail's been set at 750,000 dollars, same as Brian."

"Things aren't getting better, are they?"

"It's only been four days."

"It feels like it's been going on forever."

"How are your parents taking it?" Her parents lived in Virginia Beach, about ninety minutes away, but I hadn't seen them since Brian's arrest.

"They don't know about it. This would age them overnight."

I was silent.

"You think I'm doing wrong not to tell them?"

"Their son's future is at stake. Don't you think they have the right to know?"

"It would be better if they found out when all of it was over. You know, an amusing dinnertime story about what's been going on in our lives."

I didn't say anything to that either.

"You are going to win this," she said.

"We can't know that."

"You've never lost a murder case yet."

I rolled my eyes. I'd had three. "That's kind of like saying I haven't died yet, so I must be immortal."

"Well, maybe you are. The facts haven't proved you're not."

It seemed unproductive to argue the point. "I still think your parents ought to know."

After a moment's reflection, she said, "It means driving to Virginia Beach. I can't do it on the phone." She sighed. "Ah well. It's not like I have a friggin' life."

"You do, too. You have a very friggin' life."

"Easy for you to say. You've got the world's best dog and a boyfriend who worships you."

"You've got family."

"Brother in jail, parents who are going to collapse when they hear about it," she said.

"You've got your work."

"That's the best you can do? 'You've got your work'?"

"Friends," I said.

She put a hand on mine. "You are a good friend, you and Paul both, but I'm a third wheel, and we all know it."

"Third wheels are good," I said. "Where would a tricycle be without one? It would just fall over."

"It wouldn't either. It would be a bicycle."

"What would be a bicycle?" It was Paul, standing in the doorway.

"You and I would be, if Brooke weren't around to keep us company." I looked at my watch. "Isn't it early for lunch?"

"I'm at Xenith Bank this week, just a block down on Cary. The examiner-in-charge let us go early, and I don't have to be back until two."

"Who's the examiner-in-charge this week?"

"That would be me. So, where should we go to lunch?"

"You two go," Brooke said. "I'll get some work done."

"What gives?" Paul said. "You haven't been to lunch with us in a week."

"Brooke thinks she's a third wheel and she makes us a tricycle," I said.

"The third wheel on a tricycle is the lead wheel," Paul said. "It's important."

"You know what I mean," Brooke said.

"So get yourself a man, and we can be a four-wheeler."

"Easier said than done."

Paul tossed his jacket on the worktable. "You sell yourself short. Name a man you want, any man. How about Mike? You seemed to get along all right with him last night. I know he likes you. 'Peaches and cream, and just a hint of spice'? Just work a few of your feminine wiles on him, and he's yours."

"What feminine wiles?"

"Do I have to draw you a picture?"

"Maybe."

Paul stepped toward her and turned her chair toward her computer screen. "Okay. Lean forward slightly, looking at the screen. Tell me, 'Look at this.'"

"Look at this," Brooke said.

Paul leaned over her shoulder, his own eyes on the screen, his cheek almost touching hers. He cut his eyes toward her. "See?"

"You've got your man-boobs resting on my shoulder. Is that what you mean?"

He straightened. "No need to get ugly. I was just trying to help."

"I know. I'm sorry." She kissed his cheek as she stood. "Here, you sit. Let's see if I've got it."

"Okay." He took her chair, and she stood behind him.

"Give me my cue," she said.

"Look at this," Paul said, gesturing at the monitor and lowering a hand to the desk.

She leaned forward. "Wow," she said softly. Her breath seemed to touch him just behind his left ear. She leaned further forward to bring their cheeks together. "I think I see what you mean."

There were goose bumps on Paul's forearm.

"Would you take your woman-boobs off my boyfriend's shoulder?" I said irritably.

She turned her face toward Paul. "You're so wonderful," she breathed, her nose brushing his cheek.

"Cut that out," I said.

She straightened, trailing her hand along Paul's arm. His eyes rose to her face, and she gave him a smile.

He swallowed. "See?" he said hoarsely. He cleared his throat. "A casual touch here, a quick smile there. A flash of a little too much leg. You don't need me to teach you feminine wiles."

She fluttered her eyelashes at him, something I've never been able to come closer to than a rapid blink. It was a demure look that somehow gave the impression of her looking up at him, though he was sitting down and she was not. "I hit my knee on something last night, and I'm afraid it left a bruise. Do you see anything?" She put one foot forward and slid her skirt up her leg to mid-thigh as Paul's eyes widened.

When I saw his tongue appear between his lips, I stood. "Okay, that's enough. Reset."

I tugged at his chair, rolling it backwards. "Let's move you back from the desk about six inches." I went around him to sit on the desk directly in front of him. Paul's eyes cut to my legs before returning to my face, an automatic reaction that usually irritated me, but in this case was the reaction I had counted on.

I said, "Unconsciously you realize that by shifting your position just slightly you could look up my dress."

He smiled uncertainly and kept his eyes firmly on my face. "It's not that unconscious," he said, flushing.

"But of course I can't actually let you look up my dress. That would be low class and overtly sexual." As his eyes cut down again, I pushed off the desk and walked around his chair. "I have to be innocent and disingenuous. That's the way it works, isn't it?"

I leaned over his shoulder. "Wow," I murmured, almost in his ear. "Look at that." I put my cheek against his.

He cleared his throat again, and I glanced at his face. His eyes were closed.

"Maybe you're the one who should be more careful with her woman-boobs," Brooke said. "I think he's going into shock."

I nipped Paul's earlobe and straightened. Paul didn't move.

"I think we've been unkind," Brooke said. "He loves you, you know."

Looking down at Paul, I felt suddenly uncomfortable. "I know."

Still with his eyes closed, Paul said, "I'm still here, you know. I can hear you."

"We thought you'd gone into a coma," I said.

"I was just concentrating."

"Ah."

Brooke said, "So you think this kind of thing would work on Mike?"

"I can only envy him what's coming," Paul said, opening his eyes.

"I think I pity him," I said.

"There's a problem with your plan," Brooke said. "I hardly ever see Mike. It's not like he's ever asked me out."

"Easily resolved. Just one more exercise of feminine wiles. How come I'm the only one here who knows how to use them?"

"Think back to the first time we met," I said.

"But that was..." He stopped. "You are good."

"Still, I guess you're going to have to help us here. How does Brooke use her wiles on a man who isn't there to use them on?"

"I happen to know Mike's out of the office this afternoon." He looked at Brooke. "Call him at his office and leave a message. Just tell him it's Brooke Marshall and leave your number."

"And when he calls back?"

"When he calls back tell him you were going to see if he wanted to meet you for lunch tomorrow, but that something came up and you can't."

"And then what?"

"Then stop talking and wait."

"Wait for what?"

"Wait for him to say something."

"Suppose he doesn't?"

"A man can only be silent for so long. You wait. He'll talk."

"What will he say?" I asked.

"If I know him at all, he'll return the lunch invitation, and he might even make it dinner. Either way, he's putting himself in your hands."

After lunch, I worked in my office, which, I'm sorry to say, felt weird. It's a bad sign when disposing of blood-smeared jeans and climbing through windows seems like the normal part of the job. A little after two o'clock, a tap on my open door made me look up. It was Jordan.

"I'm almost surprised to find you here," he said, which as I've said was pretty much the way I felt about it myself. He came in and dropped into one of my client chairs, leaned back and crossed an ankle over one knee. "I just heard about your antics out at Jack Packard's place yesterday." He rocked back on the back two legs of the chair, evidently in no hurry to get to his point.

I settled back in my own chair, determined to wait him out.

"Nothing to say in your defense?" he said finally.

"I didn't know I needed a defense."

"That was blood on his kitchen floor and going down the steps to his basement."

"Human blood?"

"Now that's an interesting question."

I waited.

"Yes, it was human blood. Type O-positive. You don't know whose it was?

"Type O-positive belongs to about forty percent of the population. I think I need a little more to go on."

"We know you didn't go through the front door," Jordan said.

"I haven't been able to get hold of Mr. Packard. I'm worried about him."

"You know what my first thought was when I heard about all this? I thought, I wonder if it has any connection to the death of Macy Buck."

"I might fool you some time and work on more than one case at a time."

"Not this time. It turns out that Jack Packard was an acquaintance of Robert Walsh."

"He read scripture at the funeral," I admitted.

"And of course Macy Buck was Walsh's therapist. Walsh may or may not have been murdered; the pathology results are inconclusive. Jack Packard is missing, and he may or may not have been the victim of violence. He may be off somewhere for reasons of his own, completely oblivious to the comings and goings of lawyers and police officers at his home."

"Does Packard have O-positive blood?" I asked.

"Are you saying you don't know whose blood is in his house?" Jordan countered.

"That's what I'm saying. I'd like to know."

"Do you know where Jack Packard is?"

"No."

"What were you doing at his place on Friday?"

"You mean Monday. Yesterday."

"No, I mean Friday—the Friday Mr. Packard seems to have disappeared."

"I wasn't doing anything at his place."

He uncrossed his legs and leaned forward. "Come on, Robin. Let's be straight with each other. You know I'll cut you all the slack I can."

I knew he'd give me all the rope I needed to hang myself, but I said, "I am being straight. I wasn't there."

"A witness says you were."

"That old woman in the housedress and army boots?"

Jordan's mouth quirked despite himself. "Is that what she was wearing yesterday?"

"She had plenty to say, but she didn't say anything about having seen me there before yesterday."

"Her signed statement says she saw you."

"Well, she didn't."

Jordan was watching me closely. "I hope you're telling the truth."

I'd made my denials, and I didn't repeat them.

"The D.A.'s taking a look at it, trying to decide what kind of case he can make against you. I think he's decided to wait, at least for now, see if you get even more tangled up in things than you are already."

"Sometimes I don't think Aubrey likes me very much."

Jordan sat back with a bark of laughter. "No, it's safe to say Aubrey Biggs doesn't like you very much.

He's let it be known that every time your name comes up, he wants to hear about it."

I didn't like the sound of that. "I don't guess there's any way to make nice with him? He's not single, is he?"

"Far from it."

"What does that mean?"

"The woman he's married to is about twice his size and built like an NFL linebacker."

"Sounds like there's not much room to exercise my feminine wiles."

"Probably not," Jordan said. He slapped the desk as he got up, but in the doorway he turned back. "My impression of you is that you're fairly truthful…"

"Thank you."

"…but that I have to parse your words carefully. You said you don't know where Jack Packard is."

I nodded encouragingly.

"Do you know anywhere he's been in the last twenty-four hours?"

"No."

"Do you know whether he's alive or dead?"

"What kind of question is that?"

He waited.

"Sorry. Question avoidance is kind of automatic with me. No, I don't know if he's alive or dead."

"God help you if you're not being straight with me on this."

I held up my right hand, palm out. "So help me God," I said.

He studied me a moment longer, shook his head, went out.

When it seemed unlikely he was coming right back, I went over to Rodney's office.

"What are you working on?" I asked when he looked up from his computer.

"Nothing for you. Fortunately, I have a few other clients."

"I guess that is fortunate. Don't worry, though. With any luck, this will turn into a paying job for both of us."

"That is reassuring," he said with a completely straight face.

I took a seat in front of his desk. "Let me ask you a hypothetical question. If someone just walked away from his house…"

"Someone like Jack Packard?"

"How do you know about that?"

"It was in this morning's paper."

"Good grief." I was going to have to start subscribing to the Richmond Times-Dispatch. "Do you have a copy?"

He turned to one of the stacks on his credenza and extracted a folded newspaper from near the bottom. A picture of Jack Packard's house was on the front page of the local section. The headline of the accompanying article was "Local Man Missing"—innocuous enough.

> *Richmond man Jack Packard seems to have been missing from his home since at least some time Friday. Yesterday afternoon one of his neighbors called police after noticing suspicious activity at his residence. When the police arrived, they found Richmond attorney Robin Starling in the house and spatters of blood on the floor. Jack Packard's car was in the driveway, but he himself was nowhere in evidence. Starling, who told police she had*

found the door of the house unlocked, had dialed 9-1-1 only minutes before the police's arrival...

It went on for several paragraphs. Though it was a bit dramatic, the article was not as bad as it could have been. At least it didn't accuse me of breaking and entering.

"You were hypothesizing that Jack Packard walked away from his house," Rodney said.

I looked up. "Okay," I said. "Suppose Jack Packard walked away from his house, and he didn't want to be found. How long could he reasonably expect to stay in hiding?"

"Once the police started looking for him? Not long. As soon as he used a credit card or got money out of an ATM, they'd have a general idea of his location. If he rented a car he'd have to use a credit card, so the police would know what he was driving pretty quickly."

"Could you find him any faster than the police?"

He shook his head. "Not without some incredible piece of luck. I wouldn't count on it."

"Maybe he has more than one car. Could you find out?"

"That I can do," Rodney said.

I stopped in his doorway on my way out. "Jack Packard is old, but he's a big muscular guy."

"I'll be careful."

"No, that's not it. There was something from Gold's Gym in his mailbox. Could you find out if he's a member, and if he is whether he works out regularly?"

"Okay."

"And whether he's been in since Friday," I said. "If he's used to working out, he may not be able to give up his workouts for long."

"You should know."

I smiled. "Why thank you. I think."

I'd only been back in my office a few minutes when my cell phone rang. Dr. McDermott's name and face were on the screen, causing me instant alarm, because Dr. McDermott never called me at work.

"Is anything wrong?" I asked, raising the phone to my ear.

"I think we're all right. Deacon may have gotten bit by something he's allergic to, my guess is some kind of bug."

"A rattlesnake?" I felt a surge of guilt, having never gotten Deeks a shot the vaccine. My office phone buzzed, but I ignored it.

"I don't think so," Dr. McDermott said. "He's got bumps all over, and his fur is standing up in tufts, but it's not the localized kind of swelling you'd expect from a snakebite."

I was on my feet, slapping my laptop shut and stuffing it one-handed into its carrying case. "Are you on your way to the vet?"

"I've given him a couple of Benadryl wrapped in deli meat. If he's having an allergic reaction, the Benadryl may calm it. I'd like to give it an hour. If he doesn't improve, I can still get him to the vet before five."

Carly was at my door. "There're a couple of men," she whispered, rolling her eyes toward reception.

"I'm on my way," I told Dr. McDermott.

"If you'd like me to take him now, I will," he said. "They might be able to give him a shot that would act faster."

"Here to see you," Carly mouthed, almost silently.

I held up a hand to ward off further attempts at communication on her part. "Is he in pain?" I asked.

"He's restless, and he's rubbing up against things like he itches."

"I trust your judgment," I said, though I wondered whether dogs were allergic to Benadryl, and whether a retired people-doctor like Dr. McDermott would know it if they were.

"Well, I'm glad you're able to come. I'll feel better with you being part of the decision-making process."

I ended the call. "Who is it?" I asked Carly.

"Two men. I think they said Charles and Darrell?"

I shook my head. I didn't know a Charles and Darrell. "Can you make an appointment? My dog's having an allergic reaction to something, and I've got to get home."

"Little Deacon?"

I gave her a nod and a sick smile.

When I entered the reception area, two men who looked as if they were in their middle sixties stood, but I barely slowed. "I'm Robin Starling, but I can't talk now," I said. "My secretary can make you an appointment for tomorrow if you'd like." The outer door of The Executive Suites was swinging slowly shut behind me almost before I got the words out. I bypassed the elevator and pushed through the fire door into the stairwell.

I had seen those two old men before, but I didn't place them until I was at my car, swinging into the driver's seat. They were the two old men I'd seen with Jared Walsh at Robert's funeral.

Chapter 16

I parked on the street in front of Dr. McDermott's house and ran up the sidewalk to his front door. It opened as I reached it, and Dr. McDermott was there, Deeks beside him. Deeks's head was down, but his tail started wagging when he saw me.

I knelt and smoothed his fur as I looked him over. "It doesn't look as bad as I imagined," I said.

"It's better. I think the Benadryl is working."

"You don't think we ought to take him in?"

"I really think he'll be all right. You can give him another pill before you go to bed and another one in the morning."

"Benadryl's all right for dogs? You're sure?"

He nodded. "I'm sure. I looked it up."

"Okay. We'll go with it."

"I'm heating up a Costco lasagna, and I've got salad and of course kibble for the big guy, if you and Deacon would like to join me."

"We'd be happy to," I said.

Dinner would be ready at six, he said, so Deeks and I went to drive my car around to the garage.

Deeks walked slowly, though, and when we got to the car, he just stood at the open door and looked at me until I bent and scooped him up to set him inside. There's something about a woebegone dog that will just about break your heart. In the garage, I lifted him out of the car, and he followed me into the house.

He stayed on his feet as I changed into sweats and sneakers. It was already getting dark—and colder—when he and I walked back across the street and rang Dr. McDermott's doorbell.

"It's open," he called.

We found him in the kitchen. He offered me a glass of Chianti, which I accepted, and I sat at the kitchen table and sipped it as Dr. McDermott bustled about the kitchen, taking a sip from his own glass and setting it down to get a couple of plates, taking another sip before getting out the silverware. Deeks eased down on the floor by my chair, resting his head on one of my sneakered feet. I picked out what I thought was the most entertaining part of my day and told Dr. McDermott about Paul trying to teach feminine wiles to Brooke and me. He laughed out loud several times, throwing in a one-liner here and there that had me laughing, too. It was all very companionable, all very family.

By the time we finished our meal, Deeks was noticeably better. I got his kibble out of the pantry and put a cup of it in his bowl. Dr. McDermott started the decaf and got two more wineglasses out of the refrigerator that looked like they might be filled with banana pudding.

"What is it?" I asked.

"Banana pudding." He squirted whipped cream on his and held the can over mine, his eyebrows raised inquiringly.

"Please," I said. It proved to be pudding from a can, but it did have real bananas and real vanilla wafers added, and the presentation was nice. I ate the pudding to the bottom of the wineglass, resolving to start the next day with a three mile run. Then while Dr. McDermott sat and sipped his decaf, I cleaned up the kitchen.

"Thank you for dinner," I told him when everything was put away and it was time to go. "It's been a wonderful evening." I gave him a hug, then headed home with Deeks, Dr. McDermott standing in his doorway and hugging himself against the cold as we crossed the street.

When the doorbell rang, I was sitting on the couch with Deeks's head pillowed on my thigh where I could stroke his head and play with his ears. He wasn't completely himself, but this rare, lethargic interlude matched my own mood. How often do we take time to sit and simply be?

The doorbell rang again. "The world always intrudes," I murmured to Deeks, supporting his head as I eased it off my leg and lowered it to the couch. He followed me with his eyes as I went to the door.

Through the peephole I saw the two men who had been in my office and who had been giving Jared a hard time at the funeral. I stepped away from the door, glancing back at my dog. A Rottweiler he was not.

"Come see me in my office," I called through the door.

"We did. You seemed reluctant to talk to us."

"I had an emergency at home."

"Since we're all here now, why can't we visit a bit?"

"I'm not going to open this door," I said. I put a hand to the knob to make sure it was locked and turned the thumblatch to engage the deadbolt.

I went to a window and looked out at the street. A sedan was parked at the curb, maybe one of the big BMWs. Something that sounded like keys rattled at the front door. It was a scary sound, and it was followed by the sound of a key being inserted into the lock, which was even scarier. There was another jangle of keys, and my gaze ran over the room in search of a likely weapon. I had a softball bat in the front closet. I was heading toward it, but stopped when the doorknob turned. There was a tap, and the door opened to reveal the two white-haired men on my doorstep.

My phone was somewhere behind me on the couch or the coffee table, and I had an urge to turn and lunge for it. Instead, I said, "How did you do that?"

"We'll show you," the shorter of the two said. "My name, by the way, is Darrell Strumpf. This is my brother Charles." The door swung further open, and I saw that key rings hung from both the doorknob lock and the deadbolt.

I grimaced. "I would say that I'm pleased to meet you, but under the circumstances I'm really not. How did you get keys to my house?"

"They're not keys to your house," Darrell said, stepping to the inside of the door. "They're bump keys. Your doorknob lock is a Kwikset, and your deadbolt is Schlage. Schlage makes a bump-resistant lock, but this isn't one of them." He pulled the key out of the deadbolt. It looked like my key except that the stem was narrower.

His brother said, "You insert the key just one notch short of full insertion, then you give it a tap with a bump hammer." He pulled a flat tool with a rubber face from his pocket and held it up using only two fingers so as to better display it. "The driver pins bounce off the key pins for just an instant, and if you're applying a light rotational force to the key, the cylinder turns and, voila, you're inside."

"There's no damage to the lock," Darrell said. "No one can tell you've been inside."

I thought about Brian's apartment, where, if his story was true, someone had entered and left, leaving no trace other than a bloody pair of jeans on Brian's bed and a bloody T-shirt in his clothes hamper. Of course, Brian had had a spare key that seemed to have gone missing.

"Can you open any lock that way?" I asked.

"Pretty much any key-pin lock, as long as you have the bump key."

"Or a blank you can file down," Charles said. "We first heard about bump keys about ten years ago. Useful things for a landlord, let me tell you."

Deeks plodded past me, his tail wagging hopefully.

"Hey, you've got you a dog," Darrell said, squatting to rub his ears. "Labs are great dogs. I've had 'em off and on all my life. Don't have one now, though. How are you, little fellow? You're going to be a big thing, aren't you?" He straightened, saying, "I can tell by those big ol' paws of his."

"You might as well come in," I said, rather unnecessarily, since they were both already inside. When I had retreated as far as my couch, I saw my phone on the end table, and I snagged it. "What is it you want?"

"We don't want anything at this point. We just wanted to get a bit acquainted."

"You picked a heck of a way to do it." I'd thumbed my phone awake and was doing my best to tap in the passcode without being obvious about it. The phone vibrated in my hand, indicating I'd gotten it wrong.

"Never liked locked doors," Charles said. He took a seat in my club chair and crossed his legs. "Least not when we're on the wrong side of 'em."

"Now we find 'em more of a challenge than an obstacle, if you see what I mean," Darrell said. He leaned forward to rest his forearms on the back of the loveseat. I remained on my feet on the far side of the sofa opposite it, the back of the sofa just shielding my phone, I hoped. Deeks came and lay on the floor next to me.

"So now I know something about you. I still don't know what your interest in me is." My phone didn't vibrate, and I glanced down. I'd gotten the passcode right. I touched the phone icon.

"You're Whitney Foster's lawyer," Darrell said.

"Okay."

Charles waved a hand. "We know you're representing her on that murder charge, but we don't care about that. That doesn't affect us."

"It would if she were convicted of killing her uncle," Darrell said.

"She isn't charged with killing her uncle."

"She could be, depending on how this plays out. That would increase her cousins' inheritance by a good bit."

"Her cousin Jared?"

The Strumpf brothers glanced at each other. "It'd help both cousins equally, it seems to me," Charles said.

"Suppose Jared were convicted of killing his uncle," I said. "Then he wouldn't be able to inherit at all. You wouldn't like that."

"I told you she was smart," Darrell said.

Charles, enthroned in my club chair, nodded. I tapped 9-1-1 into my phone's keypad. I could tap *Call*, and I'd be connected, something that made me feel marginally better, though until I did I'd have to keep tapping my screen to keep it from going to sleep.

I said, "Did you know Macy Buck was telling a story about hearing Jared's voice in the backyard the afternoon of the day Robert Walsh was found floating in the hot tub?"

"Yeah, we heard something about that," Darrell said.

"Any idea whether it was true?"

"We figure it wasn't. What we figure is she was looking to get Jared charged with killing old Mr. Walsh, see if she couldn't increase the brother's inheritance. They were engaged to be married, you know."

"Be a good motive for her murderer. Shut her up," I said.

"How about you? You thinking to throw suspicion on Jared Walsh, too?"

"I was," I said, "until a couple of old codgers who have the same motive forced themselves on my attention. Jared does owe you a good deal of money, doesn't he?"

Darrell laughed, and Charles smiled faintly.

"You hear that, Charles? She's threatening us. She doesn't just have brains. This girl's got moxie."

I could feel sweat cold against my sides and prickling my brow. I glanced down at my phone, tapped the screen to keep it awake.

"You can't pin that one on us," Charles said genially.

"The two of you could have killed Macy Buck, then bump-keyed your way right into Brian Marshall's apartment to clean the blood off yourselves in his sink using a pair of his old jeans to do it with. One of you could have stripped off his bloody T-shirt and dropped it in his laundry basket. Brian lives just a few blocks away from Macy's house."

The two of them had stopped looking so damn smug. "We wouldn't like our names coming up in court," Charles said.

"Your names!" I said. "I was thinking I'd subpoena you, put you on the stand and see what I can do with you." I glanced down again, tapped *Call* on my phone. Maybe I was overreacting, but my heart was pounding, and I didn't like being afraid.

"She's threatening us, Charles," Darrell said. "Can you believe it? When was the last time someone threatened us?"

I raised my voice, hoping the phone I was holding against my leg would pick it up. "What do you expect? You break into my home at 1017

Beechnut. You won't leave. You won't tell me what you want."

Darrell straightened to peer over the couch. "What's that you've got against your leg? That's your dadgum phone, isn't it? Charles, she's gone and called the police on us."

Charles said, "I'd hoped we could come to an understanding."

"You should have made an appointment with my secretary," I said.

"What we want," Darrell said, "is to know whether Whitney was helping her uncle to empty all his bank and brokerage and retirement accounts. We know he wasn't as senile as Jared Walsh was making out…"

"We suspect he wasn't as senile," Charles corrected.

"…but he wasn't any hundred percent, either."

"Macy Buck may have had a hand in that, all the pills and powders she was getting him to take, but maybe he was already having his troubles," Charles said.

"He didn't just empty his accounts, he converted everything to cash and made it disappear," Darrell said. "Somebody helped him with that."

"We're thinking Whitney Foster. If she's convicted on this murder charge, she's gonna have trouble spending any of the old man's money she's squirreled away…"

"But if she helps us, maybe we can help you. She's only entitled to a third, you know. No point in trying to grab it all and getting herself locked up for the rest of her life."

"What do you know that might clear Whitney?" I asked, but already I could hear a siren in the distance, and the brothers Strumpf were moving toward the door.

"We gotta run. If you hadn't called the police on us, maybe we coulda come to an arrangement," Darrell said, holding the door for his brother. He went through it himself, and the door closed.

I put my hands on the back of the couch and sagged against it. Deeks was still lying at my feet, derelict in his self-appointed duty to see people to the door. When he saw me looking at him, though, his tail thumped the floor.

It was only a minute later that a knock sounded on the door. The cavalry had arrived.

I sat on the sofa, looking down at Deeks. The police had gone. Though I'd given them the names of Darrell and Charles Strumpf, I doubted anything would come of it. They might or might not have information about the case. If they did, I had the threat of a subpoena to use as a lever to pry it from them. Or I could forget about threats and just put them on the witness stand, though the Strumpfs were smart…at least collectively.

"On the witness stand, I could have a go at them one at a time," I told Deeks.

He rolled his eyes toward me, but otherwise didn't move.

"Want to go potty?" I said.

A single thump.

"Let's go potty," I said. I got up and went to the French doors to take him into the back for his nighttime wee.

On the postage stamp of a patio, I stood hugging myself as Deeks plodded past me to the dogwood in the center of the yard. He looked back at me.

"Go potty," I said encouragingly.

He lifted his leg against the tree, but when he was done just stood there as if gathering his strength.

"Come on," I called. "Time to go night-night."

He headed in my general direction, but veered off behind the rhododendron that grew against the house to one side of the patio.

"Deeks?" I followed him around the big bush and found him tugging at the edge of a tarp that covered a wheelbarrow.

I went closer, peering at it in the darkness. I had a wheelbarrow, but I was pretty sure it was in the garage. This one looked like it had a deeper bed than mine, and it had wooden handles. I didn't do a lot of yard work, but I thought mine had metal handles with plastic grips. At any rate, I hadn't left it out here with a tarp strapped over the bed with bungee cords.

Deeks gave up on the tarp and moved away a few paces to let me deal with the intruding lawn equipment. I went back to the house to turn on the floodlights, which revealed my breath on the cold night air, but left the wheelbarrow in the shadow of the rhododendron. I gripped the handles to move the wheelbarrow to the porch for easier inspection, but I couldn't move it.

"Holy moley," I said. I got a better grip and braced my feet. I got the legs supports off the ground, but only barely. If I tried to move it, I was going to turn it over.

"I'll be right back," I told Deeks, and I went inside for a flashlight.

The tarp was a small one, strapped over a pile of hard, lumpy stuff with crossing bungee cords that ran beneath the bed and hooked through the grommets at the corners of the tarp. Another much longer bungee cord that went all the way around the load. I unhooked that one, then lay down on the hard ground to unhook the other two. My shoulder caught the edge of the tarp as I rolled onto my hands and knees, and the tarp slid half off the wheelbarrow. I stood and shone the light into the bed.

The wheelbarrow was piled high with white cloth bags, tied off with cloth straps. I leaned closer with my flashlight. "Provident Metals" was printed on at least some of the bags, a compass in place of the "O" in Provident. I picked up one of the smaller bags. Even though I could almost close my hand around it, it weighed several pounds. The hairs prickled at the nape of my neck as I opened the bag under the patio floodlights.

All that is gold does not glitter, the rhyme goes, but this gold did. Holding the bag against my body, I reached in for a few of the coins. Eagles were engraved on one side, and on the other a woman with long flowing hair, a torch in one hand and an olive branch in the other. Liberty. I dropped all but one of the coins back in the sack and turned the remaining coin over in my hand: United States of America, 1 oz. fine gold ~ 50 dollars. But one ounce of gold wasn't worth fifty dollars; it was worth maybe twelve hundred dollars. If I was holding a five-pound bag, this one little sack was worth…I did the math in my head…one hundred thousand dollars? I tried again: Five times 16 gave me 80 ounces. Eighty times 1200, to make it easy say 100 times 1000…It was true. I was standing there with a hundred thousand dollars in my hand, give or take.

I looked back at the rhododendron, toward the wheelbarrow on the other side of it. There were bigger sacks over there than the one I was holding. How many five or ten pound sacks?

I went back and counted, laying them on the grass in piles, one pile for the smaller sacks, one for the larger ones. There were forty-five of the little sacks, twenty-five of the larger ones, all of them heavy. If the little sacks each had five pounds of gold and the big ones each had ten…that was roughly ten million dollars' worth of the stuff.

"This is crazy," I said to Deeks, speaking softly. "No wonder I couldn't move it." The question now was whether to move the wheelbarrow now that I had it empty. Did I want the gold on the patio? In my garage, my house? I didn't have a safe. If this came from Robert Walsh's estate, then Jared should be the one responsible for it, but I didn't trust him. Ditto for his shark-toothed lawyer, and the Strumpf brothers were out of the question.

What I needed to do, I decided, was decline all responsibility for the gold, at least until I could think what to do with it. I picked up two of the bigger sacks and put them back in the wheelbarrow, then I picked up two more. It took nearly fifteen minutes to get them all arranged as compactly as possible. I laid the tarp across the load and lay down on my back to secure the tarp with the bungee cords.

When I was done, I got up and looked down at Deeks, who was lying in the grass. "If you're not yourself in the morning, you're going to the vet," I said, and he got to his feet. I led him back inside, pausing with my hand on the switch that would kill the floodlights. Deeks stopped and looked back at me.

"We must never speak of this to anyone," I told him.

He wagged his tail in agreement.

Chapter 17

I was serious when I told Deeks we must speak to no one about the wheelbarrow filled with gold. I didn't tell Paul. I didn't tell Brooke. I didn't tell Brian or Whitney. As far as I knew, the only people in the world who knew it was there were me and whoever put it there—and, as far as I was concerned, I had never seen it.

But it's not as easy to forget about 450 pounds of gold sitting unprotected in your backyard as you might think. There was Deeks to worry about, too. He'd seemed better that morning, almost back to normal, and of course he had a retired physician watching over him. Still, between Deeks and the ten million in gold, I was distracted and jumpy at work, so much so that Brooke asked me what was wrong.

"Your brother's arraignment's tomorrow," I said, though that didn't weigh on me especially. Nothing much happens at an arraignment. The judge reads the charges and asks whether the defendant is represented by counsel; the defendant pleads guilty or not guilty; the question of bail is revisited; the date of the preliminary hearing is set. Momentous events to be sure, but I thought I could handle my part adequately even under heavy sedation.

"You'll do fine," Brooke said, touching my arm. "Try not to worry." After a few moments, she added, "Thanks for worrying."

I smiled at her. "Part of the job. Keeps me sharp."

Brooke went with Paul and me to lunch, but my mind kept drifting. "I'm starting to worry about our relationship," Paul told Brooke at one point. "You thought that was funny, right? Robin's stopped laughing at my jokes."

"No, that was a good one," I said. I tried a chuckle, but knew it was unconvincing.

"She's worried about the arraignment tomorrow," Brooke said.

I wanted to tell them about my golden wheelbarrow, but I remained firm in my resolution.

At the arraignment the next day, Judge Cochran read the criminal complaint against Brian Marshall, informing him that he was charged with murder in the first degree for which the penalty was not less than twenty years in the state penitentiary and with a maximum sentence of life imprisonment. Brian pleaded not guilty, confirmed that he was represented by one Robin Starling—that would be me—and the judge asked me and the attorney from the district attorney's office to address the issue of bail. I argued that bail should be reduced from 750,000 dollars to 75,000. The prosecutor, a thirty-something lawyer named David Miller, argued that bail should be denied altogether. The judge left the bail where it was.

We went through the same rigamarole with Whitney Foster. When it was done, Judge Cochran asked David Miller if he had any documents for me, and Miller presented me with a folder purported to contain Macy Buck's autopsy report, James Jordan's police report, and the transcript of a 9-1-1 call.

"No other statements from witnesses?" I asked.

"A few, I think. We're still pulling things together."

"Do you think you could have those for counsel by Monday?" the judge asked.

"I think so, your honor."

"In that case, suppose we schedule the preliminary hearing for Tuesday."

"Of next week?" I said.

"You can't be ready?"

"No, I can be ready."

"Good."

When the judge had left, I asked the sheriff's deputy if I could have a few moments with my clients.

"Sure. There's a conference room in the clerk's office."

"Thanks. If you could escort my clients, I'll meet you there."

I went across the aisle to introduce myself to the assistant district attorney. "Robin Starling," I said, holding out my hand.

He took it, smiling. "David Miller. I don't guess you remember me. Five or six years ago I bought you a glass of Perrier in the bar at the Tobacco Company. I remember you especially because you were in a bar and you didn't drink alcohol." He had a model's good looks, with dark, curly hair and dusky skin that made him look like he had a suntan even in the middle of

February. I didn't remember him from the Tobacco Company, though I couldn't imagine why not.

"I've relaxed a bit about the alcohol," I said. "I don't remember you, though. I'm afraid you wasted your money on the Perrier."

He laughed. "It's all right. I'm married now. Probably best for all concerned."

"I halfway expected to see Aubrey Biggs here."

"At an arraignment?" He glanced around. "He considered it, actually, then decided it would be beneath him. I'm sure you'll see him in the main trial, but you've got me for the preliminary."

The deputy sheriff was waiting with my clients in the clerk's conference room. "Let me know when you're ready," he said, and he stepped out and closed the door.

"Have a seat," I told Brian and Whitney, setting my briefcase on the table and dropping into a chair myself.

They looked at each other. Brian held a chair for Whitney, awkwardly in his handcuffs, then sat beside her. He rested his cuffed hands on the table. Whitney kept hers in her lap.

"How does it look?" Brian said. "Be brutally honest."

"I see some glimmers."

"What are they?"

I moved my head. "They're glimmers. Not much shape to them yet, but they're there."

"That doesn't sound like brutal honesty," Whitney said.

"Brooke always described you as a hopeless optimist."

"I hope she said 'hopeful optimist,' " I said. "Optimism is usually justified. Admit it: ninety-five percent of the bad possibilities you contemplate in life never materialize."

Brian's mouth curled. "I'm not usually on trial for murder-one. Surely you're not suggesting you have a 95 percent chance of getting us acquitted."

"Well," I said. "No."

"And the district attorney's office is filled with experienced lawyers, isn't it? Surely they think they have better than a five percent chance of a conviction."

"Most lawyers are not especially good at their jobs, just like most people." Though I thought David Miller probably was.

He let it go. "I know Whitney got into this mess trying to give me an alibi. I don't want her to suffer for it. Would it help her if you got us separate trials?"

"Maybe. They're trying you together on the theory that you conspired to do the murder together."

"I don't want a separate trial," Whitney said. She put her cuffed hands on the table so as to rest one of hers on one of Brian's. He looked at her, then back at me.

"Suppose I confessed and said I did the crime alone. Do you think you could plea bargain her out of it?"

"Maybe."

"Suppose I confessed?" Whitney said. "Same answer?" She looked at Brian, her chin slightly upraised.

He turned his palm up so he could close his hand on hers. The two of them looked at each other, and my eyes watered. They looked back at me.

"Ninety-five percent, huh?" Brian said.

I gave him a bleak smile.

In a preliminary hearing, the judge must determine whether there is probable cause to believe that a crime has been committed and that the defendant—in this case, defendants—committed it. If the judge finds probable cause, the defendant is bound over for trial.

From the defense standpoint, preliminary hearings provide a helpful look at the prosecution's case. I get to take a look at the prosecution's evidence and cross-examine its witnesses well in advance of having to try to knock holes in the prosecution's case before a jury. The witnesses testify under oath, locking in their testimony and making it very difficult for them to change it credibly at trial. Of course, the prosecution tries to limit the benefits to the defense by putting on only as much of its case as is necessary to ensure the trial will take place.

On the last Tuesday in February, the bailiff called the court to order, we all stood, and Judge Cochran swept in in his black robes. Before the bar, I seated myself at the table on the left with Whitney Foster and Brian Marshall. David Miller sat at the table on the right, alone. The spectators in the gallery—there were a dozen or so, even at this preliminary hearing—settled into their seats. Brooke Marshall was sitting in the row of seats directly behind us, alone because Paul was off examining a bank in Norfolk that week. Just a few rows behind Brooke sat the Strumpf brothers, Darrell wearing a plaid shirt and a jean jacket, and Charles wearing a plaid sport coat. Darrell waggled his fingers at me, but I ignored him.

"Mr. Miller," the judge said. "Do you have an opening statement?"

Miller stood. "No, your honor. I'm ready to call my first witness."

His first witness was a police officer named Wardle, who, in response to a call from the dispatcher, had gone to Macy Buck's house on Patterson Avenue. He found her body in the kitchen.

"Was the house locked or unlocked?"

"Unlocked. The door was closed, but not latched, and it came open when I knocked. When there was no answer to my knocking, I pushed the door open further, called 'Police' a few times, and went in."

"What did you find?"

"A young woman lying in the kitchen."

"Alive or dead?"

"She looked dead. Her shirt was soaked with blood, a big circle of it in the middle of her chest, some of it on the floor, her hands wet with it, some drops and smears of it on her forearms and her legs. I checked for a pulse in her neck and couldn't find one, then called the station for EMS and to report the apparent homicide." EMS would be the ambulance: Emergency Medical Services.

"Who was next on the scene?"

"EMS. The paramedics weren't able to find any signs of life either, so we waited for people to show up from the medical examiner's office and from homicide."

"Your witness," Miller told me.

I stood. "Did you step in any of the blood, Officer Wardle?"

"I don't think so. I tried hard not to."

"Did the paramedics?"

"I don't think so. I warned them about it."

"But either you or the paramedics might have left hair or fibers at the scene."

"I suppose so."

"You didn't mention a weapon. Was none in evidence?"

"Not that I saw."

"You said the dispatcher sent you to Patterson Avenue. What prompted that call, do you know?"

"I understood…"

Miller was on his feet, interrupting smoothly. "The answer to that question would be hearsay, your honor."

"Are you planning to call the dispatcher?" I asked him.

"Not at the preliminary hearing. I don't think she's necessary to prove what I have to prove to have the defendants bound over for trial."

"I've seen the transcript of the 9-1-1 call," I said. "The person who placed the call must have been in that house at some point, but he didn't give a name to the dispatcher, and he wasn't on the scene when police arrived. Do you know who he was?"

"I do not."

I turned to the judge. "No further questions of this witness, your honor."

The next witness was Victoria O'Neal, a woman in her mid-twenties who came to the stand wearing a navy skirt and a white blouse that were vaguely reminiscent of a grade-school uniform. After she had been sworn and had identified herself, Miller asked her if she remembered the date of Friday, February 11.

"Yes, I do. I'll never forget it."

"Why is that?"

"It's the day a woman who lived across the street from us was murdered."

"When did you find out about that?"

"Well, a police car came, and then an ambulance. And an SUV with two men wearing ties. They all kept going into the house, and no one was coming out."

"And that suggested murder to you?" I had to like Miller for that one, but the witness flared.

"It suggested something had happened," she said, her voice rising. "And since I'd seen a man running out of the house that evening, my husband and I went over to see what it was. One of the men wearing a tie told us it was murder."

"And you told him about the man you'd seen running out?" Miller asked.

"I did."

"Describe the man for us please."

"I don't need to describe him. It was that man sitting right over there at the table."

"The defendant Brian Marshall?" Miller asked, pointing.

"Yes. He ran out and flung himself into a low-slung sports car, a Corvette or maybe a Camaro or something, that was parked on the other side of the street. For a long time he just sat there. Then when he did go, he went pealing out of there."

I was thinking that a Corvette looked nothing like a Camaro, but Miller asked, "What time was this?"

"About six-fifteen. I was conscious of the time, because I was waiting for my husband Mark.

We've…" She paused, flushing. "We've only been married six weeks."

"This man you saw running, had you ever seen him before?"

"I had, about forty-five minutes earlier. I saw him walking up the sidewalk toward the house just before sunset."

"When you say just before sunset…"

"About five-thirty."

"Did you see the man go into the house, or did you just notice him on the sidewalk and pay no attention to him after that?"

"I just noticed him on the sidewalk."

"Where is your house in relation to Macy Buck's, Ms. O'Neal?"

"Right across the street. I can see her front door very clearly, but as I say I wasn't really watching when he went in."

"So you weren't watching the Buck house continuously?"

"I was reading by the window, glancing out from time to time, particularly when I heard anything that might be my husband coming home."

"So this man, the defendant, came running out of the house. What did you do at that point?"

"Well, as I said, he got into his car and just sat there, and it started making me nervous. I put down my book and stood at the window, watching the car. I couldn't see him."

"How long did he sit there?"

"Maybe as long as fifteen minutes."

"And you were standing and watching him the whole time?"

"Watching his car. Then my husband Mark pulled up to the curb on our side of the street."

"What did you do?"

"I hurried outside and down the sidewalk to meet him. That's when this man, the defendant, pulled out from the curb on the other side of the street and went racing away."

"Was that when you noticed the make of his car?" Miller was letting this build slowly as if he enjoyed teasing it out. So far she had identified a man walking away from her up a sidewalk on the other side of the street, then running in the darkness, but Miller's manner suggested more was coming.

"Yes. It was a dark car, black I think, some kind of sports car, but I was too busy getting the license plate to tell you any more about it for sure."

"And later that evening, when you crossed the street to talk to the police—"

"Right," she said. "I gave them the number."

Miller gave me a smile that might have been sympathetic. "Cross examine," he said.

I stood and went to the podium. My tentative plan was to play nice at the preliminary hearing and get from her what I could, then, if I needed to, break her down at trial. It doesn't make me sound like a very pleasant person, I know, but I was a trial lawyer—in the opinion of many, second cousin to a barracuda—and I had a job to do. "You say this was a Corvette or a Camaro. Could it have been another model of muscle car, a Dodge Challenger maybe?"

"Honestly, I thought Corvette, but I don't know cars."

"You said it was dark, and yet you identified Brian Marshall pretty definitively. Did he pause under a streetlight to give you a good look at him?"

"There was a streetlight, but he didn't pause. He was running."

"So he was moving fast, and for the most part his face was shadowed. Is that fair?"

"I suppose. Of course I'd seen him earlier, when it was light."

"That's right. You saw him walking up the sidewalk across the street. I guess from your angle you were looking at his back. Could you describe to us what he was wearing?"

She hesitated for the barest instant. "Jeans, I think. Jeans and some kind of jacket."

"What kind of jacket?"

"A bulky sort of jacket."

"Blue?"

"I don't know. A darkish color of some sort."

"A solid color or patterned?"

"Not a real obvious pattern."

I nodded. "Of course. You were across the street, looking out through a window pane. Was he wearing a hat when he went into the house? A cap of some kind?"

She hesitated. "No."

"What about when he came running out?"

"Definitely not when he came running out."

"So he might have been wearing something on his head when he went in. You can't say definitely."

"Well, no, but I don't think so."

"Baseball cap, hoodie…"

"You know, I almost think there was something on his head. I know it sounds ridiculous, but I want to say a coonskin cap."

"Like Davey Crocket wore?"

"I'm sure it was just the shadows. It was that time of evening, you know."

I nodded again, thinking her identification of Brian was shaky at best. On the other hand, if a coonskin cap turned up among Brian's possessions, he was screwed. "How about his hands? Was this man carrying anything as he walked up the sidewalk to the house?"

"Not that I remember."

"Or were his hands in his pockets?"

"They might have been. I didn't notice." She bit her lip. "I do think he had something in his hands coming out. In one hand, anyway."

I had a sick feeling, thinking she was about to name the murder weapon. "Really?" I said. "Could it have been a glasses case?"

"A what?"

"A case to carry eyeglasses in," I said, wanting to plant my own suggestion before she decided she'd seen Brian carrying a knife dripping blood.

"I suppose that could have been it."

Nodding, I picked up my yellow pad and started to leave the podium. I stopped. "Which identification are you most certain about, Ms. O'Neal—your identification of the car, the license plate number, or Brian Marshall himself?"

"The license plate," she said promptly.

"How certain are you about the license plate? One hundred percent, ninety-five—"

"One hundred percent," she said, interrupting.

"So you were somewhat less than one hundred percent certain about the make of the car."

"Oh, yes. As I told you, I really don't know cars."

"Are you as much as twenty-five percent certain it was a Corvette?"

"Maybe about twenty-five percent."

"And you're less than one hundred percent certain in your identification of the man you saw. It was someone about the same size and build as Brian Marshall, maybe the same hair color, but you're not as certain about him being Brian Marshall as you were about the license plate."

"I don't know that I'd say that."

"But you did say that. I asked you which identification you were most certain about, and you said the license plate." I gave her what I hoped was a friendly smile. "If you were more certain about the license plate, it follows that you were less certain about the identity of the man you saw. Isn't that right?" I tilted my head, gave my smile a lift at the corner.

"I suppose that's right. I'm still pretty certain though."

"Not a hundred percent certain," I said. "There were strange shadows. It was that time of day."

"Okay, not a hundred percent," she conceded. "More than fifty percent, though, for sure."

Fifty percent was a better number than I'd expected to get from her. "How can you be so certain about the license plate?"

"It was pretty distinctive."

"A vanity plate?"

"Not a vanity plate or anything, but the first three letters were KKX. At first I thought it said

KKK, you know, like the Ku Klux Klan, before I realized the third letter was an X. And the four numbers following were sixty-three hundred."

"Six-three-zero-zero?"

"That's right. The plate was KKX 6300."

"Thank you."

I sat down, glancing at Brian. By the luck of the draw, the Commonwealth of Virginia had issued him a distinctive, easy-to-remember license plate. Ordinarily, that would be a good thing.

Chapter 18

When the court recessed for lunch, Brian leaned toward me to murmur, "It was after dark when I got to the house. Whoever she saw going in, it wasn't me." He turned to Whitney and said something into her ear that earned him a glance and the flash of a smile. If I could keep them out of prison for the next twenty years, the two of them would be all right, I thought. There was something special between them.

Miller came to my table as the sheriff's deputies led Brian and Whitney off to their respective holding cells. "You didn't ask her whether your client was wearing glasses going in or coming out."

"No," I said, shaking my head.

"Does he even wear glasses?"

My smile was one that showed no teeth.

"What they say about you is true. You are a piece of work." He didn't sound upset about it.

"Based on what we've heard so far, I don't know why you've charged Whitney Foster," I said. "Your own witness tells us she wasn't there."

"She doesn't have to have been the one to do the stabbing." In a criminal conspiracy, each coconspirator is punishable in the same manner and to the same extent as for the crime itself. "Besides, she was there at some point. We've got her prints." He gave me his own smile and pushed through the bar.

Brooke was still in her seat just behind the rail, but the Strumpf brothers were gone.

"Lunch?" I said to Brooke.

She shook her head. "I couldn't eat."

"Keep me company. I need to take on fuel, something high in protein and fat to keep me going through the afternoon."

"So you want a hamburger?"

"Hamburgers are good."

She sighed and got to her feet. "Hamburgers it is," she said.

Brooke did bestir herself to eat some of my fries, but that was okay: I'd added them to my order primarily for her benefit. Mike McMillan came in when I was about halfway through my burger, spotted us, and hurried over. "Paul said you might be here. Neither of you answers your cell."

Brooke pulled her phone out and looked at it. "Sorry. I had the sound off."

"So how did it go?" He pulled out a chair and sat down.

"All right. We learned that another man was in and out of the murder house only minutes before Brian got there."

"Hey, that's great."

Brooke said, "We did?"

"Brian said it was after dark when he got to the house. Victoria O'Neal said she saw a man going in while it was daylight."

"Can we prove it was another man she saw?" Brooke asked.

"No. Not yet."

"So what good does it do us?"

"Gives us someone to look for."

When the elevator opened on the second floor of the courthouse, Charles and Darrell Strumpf were there.

"Well looky, looky," Darrell said, folding a stick of gum into his mouth. "If it isn't little miss hit-the-panic-button herself."

I stopped in front of them. "You can't blame a girl," I said. "It's a little unnerving to have a couple of tough old geezers walk through her locked front door."

Darrell cackled.

"It is a neat little trick, I'll admit," Charles said. "We're rather proud of it."

"Do many people know you can do it?" I asked. "Or is it a talent you try to keep under wraps?"

"We don't broadcast it. We may have shown a couple of people."

"Jared Walsh? Does he know about your bump keys?"

"Yeah, I think so. Him and Nathan."

"Did you ever give anyone a set of bump keys? Are they hard to come by?"

"We never did, but you can get 'em online, easy greasy."

"You two are amazing," I said. I left them there and went into the courtroom.

"Call Detective James Jordan." David Miller led Jordan through his academic credentials and his experience as a police officer, then through the preliminaries of arriving on the scene after the paramedics but ahead of the medical examiner. Jordan described the scene in Macy's kitchen pretty much the same way the patrolman had, though not so similarly to suggest they had coordinated their testimony. The gist of it was that there was a woman on the floor and that the front of her shirt was soaked with blood.

"Was she dead?"

"She appeared to be. My partner and I took the paramedics' word for it rather than check personally. The M.E. and the forensic unit hadn't gotten there, and we didn't want to contaminate the scene any more than it was already."

"So what did you do?"

"Talked to the paramedics. Looked around the house. After ten minutes or so, a Sean and Victoria O'Neal showed up talking about a man she'd seen running from the house. When she gave us a license number, I went out to my car to run it."

"What car did the license number belong to?"

"A black Corvette registered to the defendant Brian Marshall."

"What did you do with that information?"

What he did was use his iPad to tap out an application for a warrant to search Brian's apartment. "About fifteen minutes after I'd transmitted the application, Magistrate John Shields told me he'd signed the warrant. I called for a patrol car to meet me at the address on the defendant's car registration. It turned out to be an apartment in Malvern Manor."

"Was the defendant at home?"

"No. No one answered the door, so we used a pick gun to open it, and we went in and searched the apartment."

I was beginning to think that between pick guns and bump keys there wasn't much reason to bother with door locks.

"What did you find?" Miller asked.

"An orange T-shirt with blood on it down among the dirty clothes in a plastic laundry basket."

"Was this the T-shirt?" Miller went to his table to get a clear plastic bag, inside it a wadded up T-shirt that was a muted orange in color. He took it to the witness.

"This was the T-shirt."

"How can you tell?"

"The bag itself is tagged, showing the chain of custody. I also signed my initials with an indelible marker on the inside front collar of the shirt."

"Move for admission as State's Exhibit A."

"Any objection?" the judge asked me.

"May I see the exhibit?"

Miller brought me the T-shirt, still in its plastic bag. Inside the back collar were stenciled the words Dolce Vita, not a brand I had heard of. There was no indication of size. A metallic rectangle on the left breast also had the brand name etched on it. When I turned the bag over, I could see the dark stain along the bottom hem of the T-shirt and going up. "May I open the bag?" I asked the judge.

"Sure," Miller said.

I pulled open the zip lock, and put my hand in. It was a soft fabric, combed cotton or possibly something more exotic. I zipped the bag shut again, returned it to Miller. "No objection to admission," I said.

The bag was marked and the shirt admitted into evidence.

"Is this Brian Marshall's blood on the shirt?" Miller asked Jordan. "Or do you know?"

"It couldn't be Brian Marshall's. When we arrested him a few hours later, he didn't have any cuts or wounds on him serious enough to have produced that much blood—this blood had dried at the edges, but most of it was still wet. More significantly, the defendant's blood type is A-positive, and this blood is O-positive."

"What was the blood type of the decedent Macy Buck?"

"O-positive."

I stood. "Does Mr. Jordan have personal knowledge of these blood types, or are we relying on hearsay here?"

Jordan said, "The preliminary tests of both the defendant's and the decedent's blood were done with EldonCards, a dry-format card for blood grouping. I was present when it was done and observed the results."

I sat back down.

"Did you confirm the match with a DNA test?"

"We asked the medical examiner's office for such a test, yes."

"We will get those results from the deputy coroner. Thank you." Miller flapped over another page of his legal pad. "Back to the night of the murder, what did you do immediately after finding this bloody T-shirt?"

"Put out an APB on Brian Marshall's car and filed a complaint along with an application for an arrest warrant."

"The APB was for the defendant's Corvette, license number KKX 6300?"

"Yes. A Chevrolet Corvette, model year 2006, color black. It was the only car registered to Brian Marshall."

"Did the police find the car?"

"Yes, we did. It was parked in the lot behind St. Joseph's Catholic Church in Petersburg, Virginia. I got the call about ninety minutes after I put out the APB."

"How did the police come to look for the car at St. Joseph's?"

"It's a block or so away from the Greyhound Bus Station."

"I see."

"By the time the call came in, I had the arrest warrant, so my partner and I drove down to Petersburg. Brian Marshall had just boarded a bus to Raleigh."

"Did he make any statement when you arrested him?"

"No. He refused to answer questions and said he wanted to see his attorney, Robin Starling."

"He had already retained a defense lawyer?" Miller said, glancing over at me.

"I'm just telling you what he said."

Miller turned another page. "You subsequently arrested the defendant Whitney Foster, did you not?"

He got a confirmation and said, "What ties her to the crime?"

"Her fingerprints inside the victim's house, the murder weapon at her place of business, the false statements she made to police."

"Let's take those one at a time. You say the defendant Whitney Foster's fingerprints were found in the house of the murder victim. Can you tell us where?"

I stood. Jordan glanced at me as he started to speak, and I interrupted him.

"Officer Jordan has testified that he was in his car pursuing various leads that led him to Brian Marshall. Was he present when these fingerprints were found?"

"Officer?" Miller said.

"I was not."

"Objection, hearsay," I said. I wanted to cross-examine the witnesses who would be testifying at trial, not listen to Jordan summarize their testimony.

"Sustained."

Miller looked at his notes. "Officer Jordan, what can you tell us of your own knowledge about the murder weapon?"

"We found an ice pick under the counter at Carytown Joe, a coffee shop owned and run by Whitney Foster."

"How do you establish the ice pick as the murder weapon?"

"There was blood on the blade of the ice pick. We transferred the ice pick to the Office of the Chief Medical Examiner for DNA profiling of the blood, but an EldonCard test established that the blood was human blood, type O-positive."

"Remind us. The blood type of the victim in this case…"

"Was O-positive."

"And the blood types of the defendants?"

"Brian Marshall is A-positive. Whitney Foster is O-negative."

Miller was nodding. "You said Whitney Foster made false statements to the police. Can you tell us about those?" While Whitney's words were an out-of-court statement, because she was a defendant in the case they weren't excludable as hearsay.

"She said she'd gone with the defendant Brian Marshall to the house of Macy Buck early in the afternoon on Friday, that Macy Buck was still alive when they left together, and that they'd been together the rest of the day right up until Brian left to take a bus to Raleigh to visit friends."

"This is Raleigh, North Carolina?"

"That's right."

"Did he say why he was taking a bus from Petersburg rather than leaving from Richmond?"

"No. All he said was that he wanted his lawyer."

"So he was on a bus bound for Raleigh when you picked him up?"

"Yes, he was."

"So that much of Whitney Foster's statement was true."

"Maybe. Neither of them ever identified any particular friends in Raleigh he was going to visit. As for the rest of it, we have an eyewitness who puts Brian Marshall at the scene much later than early afternoon and who puts him there alone."

"Oh, yes. Ms. O'Neal." Miller picked up his pen and legal pad. "Your witness," he said, and left the podium.

I stood. "You said you found this orange T-shirt in Brian Marshall's laundry basket, is that correct?"

It was correct.

"Are you familiar with the brand name, Dolce Vita?"

"I am not."

"Were there any other T-shirts in Brian Marshall's apartment with the same brand name?"

"Not that I'm aware of."

"Any T-shirts of the same quality?"

"I wouldn't know. I don't have any expertise in fashion design." He held up the end of his tie. "This is a polyester clip-on." There was a titter of laughter from the gallery.

"Did you look at his other T-shirts?" I asked.

"I have a list."

We examined his inventory of items found in Brian's apartment. Among his items of clothing Brian had 34 T-shirts, 8 of them plain pocket T's, the rest unspecified. There were no brand names listed. "Were all the T-shirts in the apartment the same size as the one with the blood on it, or do you know?"

"They all seemed to be roughly the same size."

"Did you examine the orange T-shirt for traces of DNA other than blood? Flakes of skin, loose hairs?"

"The blood was all we found."

"O-positive blood, did you say?"

"Yes."

"There seems to be a lot of O-positive blood washing around this case—blood at the crime scene, blood on a T-shirt at Brian's apartment, blood on an ice pick at Whitney Foster's place of business. Were traces of blood found in the car of either defendant?"

"No. We checked them both very carefully."

"Was there O-positive blood anywhere else in Brian's apartment, or was it just on the T-shirt?"

"Just on the T-shirt."

"Was there O-positive blood anywhere else at Carytown Joe, or was it just on the ice pick?"

"Just on the ice pick."

"Both defendants work at Carytown Joe, don't they? Who else works there?"

He had to consult his notes. "A Jennifer Humphreys."

"Was her blood O-positive?"

"We didn't check. As I said, the ice pick went to the Medical Examiner for a DNA profile. That told us pretty definitely the source of the blood, but I understand someone from that office will be testifying about that."

"You were looking into the death of Whitney's uncle not long ago. Was his blood O-positive?" The blood type of Robert Walsh wasn't relevant to the current prosecution as far as I knew, and I expected an objection from Miller, but none came.

"There was an autopsy report," Jordan said, "but if it mentioned his blood type I don't recall."

"Then Jack Packard, a close friend of Robert's, disappeared under mysterious circumstances, and blood was found at his house."

Jordan's mouth twisted, and I thought he looked suddenly sad, but he said, "Yes, it was."

"Did you ever locate Jack Packard?"

"It's not my case, but I don't believe he's been found, no." It was a statement clearly based on out-of-court statements made by others, and again I expected an objection from Miller. Again, none came.

"Do you know what efforts have been made to find him?

Judge Cochran interrupted. "I don't see the relevance of this."

"Nor do I," Miller said.

"Is that an objection?"

"No, your honor. If Ms. Starling thinks it relevant, we're willing to give her the opportunity to establish that."

The judge's mouth tightened, but he didn't say anything.

"Detective?" I said.

"The question also seems to call for hearsay," the judge said.

Miller said, "If Ms. Starling wants to bring it out, this seems to be an efficient way to do it. The state has no objection."

The judge drew a long breath.

"Detective?" I said again.

"My understanding is that since February 11, the day of Macy Buck's death, Jack Packard has not used his cellphone, he has not made a withdrawal from his bank, and he has not used his credit card."

"He hasn't rented a car, at least in his own name?"

"No."

"Do you suspect foul play, or do you think he has resorted to flight for some reason?"

Judge Cochran said, "I think this has gone far enough."

I said, "Your honor, if Jack Packard resorted to flight immediately after the murder of Macy Buck, it could be evidence of a guilty conscience—and if he's guilty, my clients are not."

"Unless they conspired with Mr. Packard to commit the murder," Cochran said.

"Unless they conspired together," I acknowledged. "Though at the moment that seems inconsistent with the prosecution's theory of the case."

Cochran looked at Miller, then shook his head. "Proceed, counselor."

"Detective Jordan, where was blood found at Jack Packard's house?"

"There were spots of it on the kitchen floor and going down the steps to the basement."

"You sound like you're speaking from your own knowledge."

"I am. I went and looked at it."

"Do you know what blood type that blood was?"

"It was O-positive."

"So O-positive blood was found in Macy Buck's house, on a T-shirt in Brian Marshall's apartment, on an ice pick at Whitney Foster's coffee shop, and on the floor in Jack Packard's house?"

"Yes, it was."

"Were DNA tests performed on the blood found in all of those locations?"

"We turned samples over to the Office of Chief Medical Examiner for that purpose, yes."

Miller stood, "We intend to call Dr. Harold Pavlicek to testify about the results of the DNA tests.

What this witness has to say about the subject is based on hearsay."

"Is that an objection?" Cochran asked.

"Yes, your honor."

"Well it's about time. Sustained."

I said, "Let's turn for a moment to the statements Whitney Foster made to you. She said that she accompanied Brian Marshall to the victim's house early on Friday afternoon. You do believe she was in the house, do you not?"

Miller stood. "Ms. Starling herself has objected to using this witness to introduce evidence of the fingerprints found at the house."

"I'm not asking about fingerprint evidence," I said. "Officer Jordan could have multiple reasons for believing Whitney Foster was in the house at some point. If he does, we can then explore those reasons, some of which may be stronger than hearsay."

Judge Cochran rolled his eyes, which I didn't appreciate, but he said, "I'm going to allow the question."

"Yes," Jordan said. "We believe she was in the house."

"And based in part on the testimony of Victoria O'Neal, you believe Brian Marshall was in the house."

"We do."

"Did a witness come forward claiming to have seen Whitney Marshall going in or out?"

"No."

"So when she went to the house, she might well have been in the company of Brian Marshall. No one has said she went in alone."

"No."

"And you can't tell from a fingerprint when it was made, can you?" Conscious of Miller coming to his feet, I added, "I'm just speaking in general terms, not asking about what prints may or may not have been found in this particular house."

Miller didn't object, and Jordan said, "That's right."

"Any fingerprints found in the house could have been made early in the afternoon as easily as later in the day."

"Objection."

"Sustained."

There had been as yet no testimony as to whose fingerprints had been found in the house, so it was hard to argue that when they were made had any relevance to the case. I didn't pursue it. Instead I went on to make the point I'd been driving toward: "So Ms. Foster's statement that she and Brian Marshall went to the house together earlier in the afternoon might well have been true, as far as you know."

Jordan took a moment to think it over. "I suppose it might have been."

"Ms. O'Neal has testified that the defendant Brian Marshall ran down the sidewalk to his car shortly after dark, then he sat in his car for some minutes. Did she tell the police that the car was empty when he got in, that he was sitting in the car alone?"

Jordan shifted in his seat. "No, she didn't. As I understood her, given the light and the angle, she couldn't see into the car."

"So Whitney Foster could have ridden with Brian to Macy Buck's house and waited in the car for him when he went in. That wouldn't be inconsistent with her statement that she had spent the rest of the day with Brian, would it?"

"No. Not if that's what happened."

"So far then, we have no evidence that Ms. Foster made false statements to the police, do we? We know she made statements, but as far as you know, they may have been true. Isn't that right?"

He didn't answer, and I didn't wait for him.

"You also base your belief on her complicity in this crime on fingerprints found at the scene, but those could have been made earlier in the day, well before Macy Buck met her death. That leaves only the bloody ice pick to connect her to the crime."

Jordan said, "It's true that this piece of evidence or that piece of evidence might have an innocent explanation. It's when you look at all of it in combination…"

"As to her supposed false statements, you're relying only on supposition, and you've admitted as much. The fingerprints could have been made earlier in the day, or earlier in the week, or possibly as long as a month ago."

"Ms. Foster said the first time she'd been to the house was that day."

"I thought you were discounting her testimony."

Jordan was silent.

"So what we're left with is an ice pick with blood on it. Can you tell us exactly where in Ms. Foster's place of business that was found?"

"Between the counter and the wall."

"Is this the counter where various pastries are displayed for sale?"

"Yes."

"So the ice pick could have rolled off the top of the counter, or it could have been dropped to the floor and kicked into position from either side of the counter, couldn't it?"

"A customer might have difficulty doing either of those things unseen."

"But physically, a customer could have done it. He might just have had to wait for an opportunity."

Judge Cochran cleared his throat. "Ms. Starling," he said. "This line of questioning goes to the weight of the evidence, which is a matter for the jury. It's not anything I can consider in a preliminary hearing. If the decedent's blood was found in the defendant's place of business and the defendant's fingerprints were found at the decedent's house, then there's probable cause to find that a crime has been committed and that the defendant had some connection to that crime."

I inclined my head. "I'm sorry for wasting your time, your honor." I walked back to the defense table and sat down.

"No further questions of this witness?"

"I guess not, your honor."

"I don't mean to prevent you bringing out exculpatory evidence."

"I know you don't."

"Or probing the prosecution's evidence to test its validity."

I gave him a closed mouth smile, and Cochran sighed. He looked at the clock and sighed again. "Court is adjourned until tomorrow morning at nine a.m."

I had some work to do before I went home. The prosecution seemed likely to rest its case the next day, and as of yet I had no witnesses. Last week I'd gotten the court clerk to issue three subpoenas for me, signed but otherwise blank. All I had to do was fill them in.

Back in my office I did that and walked them over to Rodney. "You ever serve a subpoena?" I asked him.

He looked up, blinking. "Yes. It's been a while."

"There's another outfit I can use, if you don't want to do it. Maybe that would be better. I need help finding Jack Packard."

"You think he's alive then?"

"I don't know. But say he is alive and he's still in the Richmond area."

"He hasn't been back to Gold's Gym. I told you that, didn't I?"

"There are other Gold's Gyms in Richmond. Could he have been to one of those?"

"No. I checked them all."

"How do you check things like that?"

He shrugged.

"Doesn't anybody keep their customers' records confidential?"

"Sometimes you have to give something to get something." He smiled. "You have a date with one of the assistant managers this Saturday." He smiled again at my expression. "Just kidding. I was a son concerned about where his elderly father disappears to everyday. 'He used to go to the gym pretty regularly, but I've begun to suspect he isn't doing that anymore, that maybe he's meeting up with people who are looking to take advantage of him.' You know the sort of thing."

"Rodney Burns. You're a gifted liar. And you've got a sense of humor."

"It hurts to learn that's a revelation to you. If it helps, Jack Packard last worked out at Gold's on Friday, February 11."

"The day of the murder."

"Right. And before that day he was as regular as clockwork. He came in a little after six four days a week…"

"Six a.m.?"

"A.m., yes. Monday, Tuesday, Thursday, Friday. He's always gone by seven-thirty."

"Could he be going to another gym—Planet Fitness, World Gym, the YMCA?"

"Still working on your exercise-addict hypothesis?"

"It's what I've got. We're looking for a muscular old man in his late seventies with shoulders and a big, bull neck. He may or may not be using his real name. Works out in the mornings. Paid cash for his membership, or maybe pays by the workout. If he's hitting the same place every day, somebody has to have noticed him."

"Personally, I think he's dead or in California, but I'll do what I can."

Chapter 19

Aubrey Biggs, the district attorney, was sitting next to David Miller when I came into the courtroom the next morning. Nevertheless, it was David Miller who called the first witness of the day, Dr. Harold Pavlicek from the Office of Chief Medical Examiner. I had last seen him at the crime scene the night of Macy's murder. He came to the stand wearing a heavy sports jacket with elbow patches, a goatee, and glasses with round, owl-like lenses.

"Dr. Pavlicek. Could you give us your full name, please?" Miller asked him.

Dr. Pavlicek gave it and followed with his credentials, which included a residency in pathology and twenty-two years' experience with the Office of Chief Medical Examiner, Virginia Department of Health. He had arrived on the murder scene at 8:25 the evening of February 11 and found a dead Caucasian female lying on the floor of the kitchen. She had been dead between two and four hours, meaning she had died between four-thirty and six-thirty. Body temperature and the beginnings of livor mortis, or postmortem lividity, were used to establish the time window—which unfortunately included the time Victoria O'Neal had seen Brian Marshall running down the sidewalk away from the house. Pavlicek had also detected the beginnings of rigor mortis in the eyelids and jaw, which usually starts about two hours after death.

"The cause of death appeared to be exsanguination secondary to a penetrating wound to the upper right quadrant of the abdomen," Dr. Pavlicek said, an hour into his testimony.

Miller smiled. "Could we have that in English, doctor?"

"She died of blood loss secondary to a stab wound."

"Close enough. What can you tell us about the murder weapon?"

"It wasn't present, but it would have been a blade roughly four inches long with a point and no edge, possibly something like an old-fashioned ice pick. It made a straight puncture wound about four inches deep that penetrated the liver and caused extensive bleeding both internally and externally."

"How long after injury did death occur?"

"Probably thirty to forty-five minutes. She'd lost about half her blood. By the time the heart stopped pumping, the abdominal cavity had darkened considerably, making it look bruised, and as I said, there was a great deal of external bleeding, too."

"Did you take samples of her blood?"

"We did."

"And make a DNA profile from those samples?"

He'd done that, too.

"Did you also make DNA profiles from the blood on the T-shirt and the ice pick given you by Detective Jordan?"

"Yes. We were able to obtain enough blood from both sources to make adequate samples."

"The results?"

"Both samples matched the reference sample."

"And the reference sample was…"

"The blood taken from the body of the decedent."

That testimony alone might have been enough for the prosecution to make its case. There was probable cause to believe Macy Buck had been murdered, and probable cause to connect both Brian Marshall and Whitney Foster with the crime. "No further questions," Miller said.

I went to the podium. "I understand there was quite a bit of blood on the T-shirt, but was there really enough on the ice pick to make a DNA profile?"

"Oh, yes. We used to need about a nickel-sized spot of bodily fluid. That's when we first started making DNA profiles using restriction fragment length polymorphism…"

"Excuse me?" I said, waving a hand to stop him.

"It's a technique that usually goes by its initials, RFLP. It required a relatively large sample and often took as long as a month to complete. Now with PCR—polymerase chain reaction analysis—we can replicate a small amount of DNA to create a larger sample for analysis." He was just getting started. The first step in PCR was to add a special enzyme—the polymerase—to the DNA before heating and cooling it about thirty times. After the first step, it just got complicated.

When he came to a pause that might have indicated he was done, I said, "When you say there was a match between the various samples of DNA, what do you mean?"

He was still in lecture mode. "Each DNA profile consists of a combination of traits. When there's the same combination of traits in the reference sample and the evidence samples, we say there's a match."

"Were any of the traits in the samples especially rare?"

"No. Most of the traits occur in one-fourth to one-third of the population. It's the combination of traits that is rare. Take two traits and assume that each occur in one-fourth of the population. The chances that a given sample contains a single trait is one in four, but the chances that it also contains the other trait is also one in four—so the probability of a DNA sample containing both traits is one in 16. Do you follow? But of course, we were looking at many more than two traits here."

"Okay," I said. "What would the probability be of any two samples containing all of the traits you looked at?"

"About one in 7,000."

I frowned, having expected odds more on the order of one in a billion. "So if there are 1.2 million people living in the Richmond metropolitan area, that suggests there would be…a couple hundred people with this same DNA profile walking around town?"

Dr. Pavlicek's eyes cut to the ceiling. "About a hundred seventy," he said after a moment. "But before you get too excited, ask yourself how many of the hundred-and-seventy are likely to have bled onto a T-shirt of one of the defendants and an ice pick at the business of another. You can't consider the DNA evidence in isolation."

I thought for a moment, trying to decide if I could or I couldn't.

"The probability that a person is one in 7,000, left blood in both places, and left fingerprints in the decedent's house is vanishingly small," the doctor said.

Small enough to bind over the defendants in a preliminary hearing anyway. I let it go. "Did you compare any other evidence samples to the victim's blood?" I asked.

"Yes."

"Specifically, did you make a DNA profile of blood found at the home of Jack Packard and compare it to your reference sample?"

"Yes, we did. It was a match."

That was easier than I expected. "Thank you, Dr. Pavlicek. That is all."

At the prosecutor's table it was Aubrey Biggs who stood. "Call Wilma Henderson to the stand."

"Are you sure you don't want to rest your case?" Judge Cochran asked him. "I'm going to bind the defendants over." I stood, and he waved his hand at me. "Unless of course," he added, "the defense is able to produce video of someone else committing the murder and vacuuming up blood to squirt on various items belonging to the defendants." He gave me a tired grimace.

I sat down. I had no such video.

"Your honor," Biggs said. "The questions posed by counsel have suggested the possibility that a man named Jack Packard is implicated in this crime. We wish to rebut that suggestion."

"It isn't necessary for purposes of this hearing."

"We are not ready to rest our case," Biggs said.

Judge Cochran rolled his eyes, sighed. "Very well." He straightened, then, and his gaze focused. "I warn you, though, that we're going to stay on topic. Understood?"

"Understood."

I don't think Cochran believed him any more than I did.

The bailiff brought Wilma Henderson from the witness room. She was the old biddy who claimed to have seen me climbing in Jack Packard's basement window. Of course, I had been climbing in Jack Packard's window, so perhaps my resentment was misplaced, but that didn't keep me from feeling it all the same.

"Your name is Wilma Henderson?" Biggs asked her when she had been sworn in.

"It is. Wilma Alice Henderson."

"Where do you live, Ms. Henderson?"

She gave him the address, adding, "That's right across the street from Mr. Packard."

"Did you observe any activity at Jack Packard's house on Tuesday, February 15?"

"I did. I saw this young woman remove a screen from my neighbor's basement window and climb through it."

Having been an English major, I noticed the misplaced modifier. I had not in fact climbed through the screen, and if I were this woman's English teacher, I would let her have it.

"Which young woman?"

"That young lady sitting at the table there." She pointed at me, but of course Whitney Foster was also at the table.

"Which young lady?" Biggs repeated.

"The tall, skinny one."

My antipathy toward this woman was increasing exponentially.

"Could you see Mr. Packard's basement window from your house?" Biggs asked.

"No. His lawn slopes down, so I can only see the top part of his house. I had to come to the end of my sidewalk to see to the bottom of the driveway. The basement window I'm talking about faces the driveway."

"How did you come to move to the end of your sidewalk? Were you getting your mail, or was it something else?"

"I was not getting my mail. I had just seen this woman at Mr. Packard's mailbox going through his mail—adding some stuff to it, taking other stuff away."

"You saw Robin Starling, counsel for the defense, tampering with Mr. Packard's mail?" He was keeping a damper on the moral outrage, probably saving it for a full-fledged explosion. "That would be a crime unless Mr. Packard had authorized her to take care of his mail. Do you know if he had?"

"I know he could have. She had been at the house just a few days before, and he could have given her permission then."

I felt suddenly cold.

"When was Ms. Starling there, a few days before?" Biggs asked.

"She was there the previous Friday."

"Friday, February 11?"

"That would be the day."

Judge Cochran was beginning to look interested, which I took as a bad sign.

"What did she do at Mr. Packard's house on Friday the 11th?"

"I wouldn't know, would I? All I know is she drove down his driveway, and fifteen or twenty minutes later she drove out again."

"What time was this?"

"That I'm not sure of. Late afternoon, I think."

"No further questions."

The judge looked at me. "Counselor?"

"Could I have a fifteen-minute recess, your honor?"

He looked at the clock. It was 11:05. "Is there a problem, Counselor?"

Biggs said, "You see what this testimony means, your honor. Ms. Starling is most probably an accessory after the fact to the crime of murder. She had possession of the victim's blood on the very day of the murder, and she went to Jack Packard's house to sprinkle it around and talk him into leaving town on an extended vacation. A few days later, when no one had found the evidence she had planted, she was back at the house, where she dialed 9-1-1 to make sure the police did find it. I have the police report to prove it. Here at this preliminary hearing, yesterday and again today, she's done her best to bring out what was found in Jack Packard's house, injecting it into the case when she knows it has nothing at all to do with it."

"Do you intend to charge her as an accessory?"

"Possibly. At the very least, we'll be charging her with altering physical evidence, and we'll be filing a complaint with the disciplinary committee of the state bar."

The judge turned his gaze to me. "Ms. Starling?"

When at a loss, accuse the accuser. I took a breath. "Your honor, these personal attacks seem to have become a regular courtroom tactic of Mr. Biggs's."

"Just as playing fast and loose with the evidence has become of regular tactic of Ms. Starling's," Biggs said.

"Mr. Biggs is always going to make a complaint to the state bar, or he's going to charge me with some crime. He never has. His sole purpose is to intimidate me into providing a less-than-zealous representation for my clients—or maybe he's just throwing mud at me in an effort to smear my clients, I don't know. Either way, it's way outside the bounds of professional conduct. You should admonish him for it or even impose sanctions."

Biggs's his neck was puffed out like the body of a blowfish, and his face was reddening, but the judge held up a hand to forestall his outburst. "We're going to recess until after lunch. When we reconvene, we're going to proceed witness by witness and question by question, and we're not going to have any more of these personal exchanges. Is that understood?"

Biggs started to say something, then closed his mouth and nodded, tight lipped.

"Ms. Starling?"

"Yes, your honor."

"Mr. Biggs, I don't want another reference to any charges you're filing or planning to file against Ms. Starling. Is that understood?"

"Yes."

"Yes, your honor," the judge said. He tapped his gavel. "Court is recessed until one o'clock."

"You weren't at Jack Packard's house the day of the murder, were you?" Brooke asked me as we speed-walked toward our cars.

"No. I wasn't. I went home early to spend time with Deeks."

"So that awful woman is lying."

"Maybe."

"There's no maybe about it. She's just a twisted, miserable little creature, peering out of her windows all day like a big, bloated spider."

The description startled a laugh from me. "How about this?" I said. "Suppose she's involved in this whole sordid mess and is perjuring herself for reasons of her own."

"Involved how?"

"No idea." I fished out my phone and called Rodney Burns to ask him to look for possible connections between Wilma Henderson and Jack Packard, or Wilma Henderson and the Walsh clan, or Wilma Henderson and Macy Buck.

"That's a lot of possibilities," he said. "What kind of connection do you suspect?"

"None. I just need to rule out the possibility that there is one."

"It's your dime."

"Your rates have gone down," I said. "Thanks." I ended the call before he could clarify his fee structure.

"Where's Mike?" I asked Brooke as we got into my car. "He was there when we started up this morning."

"He slipped out an hour ago for a hearing at the federal building. He'll text me when he gets out." The federal building was just across the street from the courthouse. "So where are we going? Not to lunch, I assume."

I turned out of the parking lot. "Patterson Avenue. Macy's house."

"Not to Jack Packard's?"

"No. I can't think of anything to do there."

"What can you do at Macy Buck's?"

"Probably nothing. Her car was a boxy little SUV crossover of some sort. I've seen it twice, once when I met her for lunch the day she was killed and then again the night of the murder, but I really didn't paid any attention to it."

"You're thinking Wilma Henderson might have mistaken it for your Beetle?"

"I know. It seems far-fetched."

She didn't say anything.

The theory seemed more far-fetched when I pulled into Macy's driveway and stopped behind her car, which was a Honda Element, maybe five or six years old, burnt orange in color.

Brooke looked at me, and I gave her a shrug. We got out of the car and walked away from the driveway far enough to see both cars together. What we saw was a bubble-like Beetle, a dull red in color, sitting behind a boxy, orange car with dark gray cladding.

"What do you think?" Brooke asked neutrally.

"Suppose we look at them from the back?"

We moved toward the street to change our perspective. If I closed one eye to flatten the image into two dimensions, my car didn't look quite so bubble-like.

"Well?"

"It's a stretch," I admitted.

"Got any more ideas?"

I shook my head. "I'm going to have to do the best I can with this one." I continued to stand looking at the two cars until Brooke started getting restless. Finally, I got out my cell phone and took a picture of my car from directly behind it, being careful to keep Macy's car out of the frame. I took a few steps onto Macy's lawn for another picture, then handed my phone to Brooke. "Let me get my car out of the way."

I backed out of the driveway and parked on the street, then walked back and stood by Macy's car, my hand on the door handle. "Get some pictures of the car with me in the frame," I said. "Let's do several angles."

When she was done, I thumbed through the photographs, aware that Brooke was watching me with an expression of concern. I sent an email to Carly at the Executive Suites with several of the photographs attached.

"Print these on color printer," I tapped into my phone. "Three copies each. Will pick up on way to courthouse." To Brooke I said, "Let's hope Carly's not at lunch."

"Carly never goes to lunch."

"Let's hope she didn't start today."

Brooke drove. Main Street was parked up. Brooke stopped in the street in front of the Ironfronts, and I got out. "Drive around the block once, and I'll be back."

I took the stairs. Carly was at the reception counter.

"Did you get my email?" I said, a little breathlessly.

She gave me her simple-minded smile, then laid a manila envelope on the counter.

"Bless you, Carly," I said, and snatched the envelope.

When court reconvened, the Strumpf brothers were still in attendance, and Mike McMillan had rejoined Brooke. Wilma Henderson returned to the stand. "Hi, Wilma," I said.

She gave me a prune-faced nod.

"I remember seeing you with the police in Jack Packard's driveway. Did you call the police that day?"

"I did."

"I understand. You saw a stranger walking around the house, messing with the mailbox, and finally taking off a window screen."

She nodded severely. "And climbing through the window, don't forget."

I gave her a nod and a smile, not an admission the court reporter was going to get on his Stenotype. "Neighbors have to look out for each other," I said. "You recognize me, don't you, from that day in the driveway?"

"I certainly do."

"As I recall, you weren't wearing glasses that day."

"And I'm not wearing them now. Except for reading, I haven't needed glasses since my cataract surgery."

"That Friday, several days before we met in the driveway—do you remember seeing me then?"

"I got a glimpse of you."

"You told Mr. Biggs this was late afternoon. Had it started to get dark?"

"I could see well enough."

"Sunset's about five-thirty this time of year. I think the light starts to fade a bit maybe thirty minutes before that."

"Then this would have been before five."

"You got a pretty good look at my car?"

"I did. It drove into the driveway, and fifteen or twenty minutes later it drove out."

"So you got a pretty good look at my car." I took copies of one of my photographs to the prosecutor's table and another to the judge. "May I?"

Cochran nodded, and I took the third copy to Wilma. "This is the car you saw on Friday and again on the following Tuesday?" I asked.

She balanced the photograph on the rail in front of her as she got her glasses out of her purse. With them on, she studied the photograph. "Yes, it is," she said finally.

"When you got a glimpse of the young woman on Friday…"

"When I got a glimpse of you."

"Where was she? Getting into the car, getting out, going up the sidewalk?"

She hesitated. "You were getting out of the car," she said.

"I guess the car was in your field of vison more constantly than the woman."

"Than you, you mean."

"But the car was sitting in the driveway in plain sight the whole time, wasn't it?"

I heard whispers passing between Biggs and Miller at the prosecutor's table.

"I suppose it was," Wilma said.

"And you just got the one glimpse of me as I was getting out of the car."

"I saw you well enough."

I was suggesting that Wilma's identification was of a car rather than a person, and Biggs stood at his table, evidently seeing where this was going. "Your honor, I'd like Ms. Starling's assurance that this photograph she's presented to the witness is in fact a photograph of her car."

I smiled at him. "Your witness has identified it," I said. "I move that the photograph be marked and admitted into evidence."

"I object until we know more about this photograph and when and where it was taken."

"Your honor," I said. "I'm offering it merely as demonstrative evidence to illustrate the witness's testimony. She has testified that it fairly and accurately depicts the vehicle about which she is testifying."

"Is it your car?" Biggs asked.

"Your honor, I'm not under oath, and I can't authenticate the photograph. Only the witness can."

The judge looked down at Wilma Henderson. "Is this the car you saw?"

She now looked uncertain. "Yes, or one like it. Of course, it could have been a different car, but it was the same model."

"And the same color," I told her confidently.

Her nod was barely perceptible. "The same color," she echoed.

"Move for admission," I said.

The judge looked from me to Biggs. Everyone in the courtroom smelled a big, stinking rat, but finally he nodded. "Motion granted."

We waited while the photograph was marked.

I produced another photograph, this one without me in it, and handed copies around. Biggs smacked his hand hard on the table, as I asked Wilma, "Can you tell me if you've ever seen this vehicle before?"

"Your honor," Biggs exclaimed, jumping to his feet. "This is just the kind of evidence tampering I was warning you about. Ms. Starling knew good and well that the photograph she introduced into evidence was not a picture of her car."

"I didn't ask the witness if it was my car."

"You did."

"I asked her if it was the car she saw at Jack Packard's house."

"But it was your car at Jack Packard's house, and you know it. There were half-a-dozen police officers there in addition to Mrs. Henderson."

"That was on the Tuesday after the murder."

"But the witness also saw you on the Friday Macy Buck was murdered."

The judge cracked his gavel. "That's enough. Please address all comments to the court."

Wilma Henderson was bent over the photographs, peering at them side by side. "I think it may have been two different cars I saw," she said.

I smiled at Aubrey Biggs. "Thank you, Ms. Henderson. That will be all."

I went back to my table, and Biggs charged the podium. "Mrs. Henderson."

"Ms. Henderson," she said. "I'm not married, but I don't think it's really anybody's business whether I am or not."

"Ms. Henderson. Whether or not you are mistaken about the vehicle you saw…" Her nostrils flared. "…the fact remains that you saw Ms. Starling, the attorney for the defense, at the house of Jack Rupert on Friday, February 11."

She was glaring at him.

"Isn't that right? You saw Ms. Starling."

It was a leading question, but I held my objection.

"I don't know who I saw," she said.

"Oh, for the love of…" he threw up his hands and stormed back to his seat.

"My witness?" I asked the judge.

"Evidently. Yes, your witness."

I returned to the podium. "Both cars I showed you are important to the case," I told Wilma Henderson. "One of them is mine; the other belongs to Macy Buck, the woman who was killed. You can see why it matters which car you saw on that Friday."

She nodded.

"I'm five-eleven, pretty tall for a woman, and Macy Buck, the victim in this case, was probably six inches shorter. I know Mr. Packard's driveway slopes down from the road pretty sharply. From where you were watching, were you in a position to judge the height of the women you saw?"

Wilma chewed at her lip. "What color was this Macy Buck's hair?"

"It was blonde and straight, like mine."

"I reckon it could have been her then."

"Thank you, Ms. Henderson. We all appreciate your efforts to be scrupulously fair."

I returned to my seat. Aubrey Biggs was breathing heavily through his nose, and for nearly a minute we all sat and listened to him do it. Finally, the judge said, "Are you done with this witness?"

Biggs gave a nod.

"Ms. Henderson, you are excused. Mr. Biggs, are you now ready to rest your case?"

Biggs looked at Miller, who gave a slight, encouraging nod.

"The prosecution rests," he said.

"Very well." Judge Cochran picked up his gavel.

"Your honor?" I was on my feet.

"Ms. Starling," he said, rather ominously.

"I have served two subpoenas on witnesses who don't seem to be in court."

He put his gavel down. "Ms. Starling," he said again, "this is a preliminary hearing. Its purpose…You know its purpose. Let me tell you what its purpose is not. A preliminary hearing is not a discovery tool. You can't call witnesses just to hear what they have to say. The only evidence I'm going to let you put on is evidence that goes to the possible innocence of your clients—and given the evidence we've heard so far, I can tell you it isn't going to be enough. Your clients are going to be bound over for trial in circuit court, so we might as well get on with it."

"Does that mean you're keeping an open mind?" I said.

For about ten seconds or so, we got to listen to the judge breathing. "Who have you subpoenaed?" he said finally.

"Jared and Nathan Walsh."

"And who are Jared and Nathan Walsh?"

"Cousins of the defendant Whitney Foster. Since this is a preliminary hearing, the prosecution hasn't bothered to establish motive, but these two have the same motive they're going to try to show for Whitney—and, by extension, Brian Marshall."

"That goes to the weight of the evidence, which is a question for the jury," Cochran said. "You can't call witnesses here just because they'll be testifying at trial."

A voice from the gallery said, "I agree, your honor." We all turned to look. It was Rupert Propst, standing in the aisle by the back row.

"Who are you?" the judge asked.

"Rupert Propst, your honor, attorney for Jared and Nathan Walsh. As you've so clearly stated, there is no question Ms. Starling could ask them that would be relevant at this hearing."

"Mr. Propst, if they've been served with a subpoena, they don't get to make that determination. They have to appear."

"Both Jared and Nathan Walsh are busy men. To force them to come to court when there's no purpose to be served would be a waste of the court's time and theirs."

Cochran looked at me. "It's your call, Ms. Starling. Do you want them?"

"I do, your honor."

"I warn you, I'm not going to let you go on fishing expeditions. You're going to be limited to eliciting testimony of an exculpatory nature."

I was silent. Cochran sighed.

"Very well. Mr. Propst, produce your clients."

"They're not here."

"What time was specified on the subpoena, Ms. Starling?"

"One o'clock this afternoon."

"We'll take a short recess, while I issue the necessary bench warrants."

He stood, and Propst said, "I can have them here in an hour, your honor."

The judge looked at him for a long moment. "Come here, Mr. Propst." Judge Cochran remained standing while Rupert Propst came down the aisle and pushed through the bar. "Are you licensed to practice law in the state of Virginia?"

"Yes, your honor."

"Well, let me tell you, this isn't how it's practiced. I'll give you an hour, but if they're not here…" He looked at the clock. "If they're not here by three o'clock, you yourself are going to jail for contempt of court. Understood?"

Rupert's Adam's apple rose and fell beneath the waxy flesh of his neck. "Understood," he said.

Chapter 20

Rupert Propst brought Jared and Nathan into the courtroom with less than three minutes to spare. The judge hadn't come in yet, and after seating his clients in the front row, Rupert stalked over to me. "I know what you're up to, Robin Starling. You're out to smear my clients in an effort to exonerate your own."

I didn't stand up, didn't even look at him. "Go sit down, Rupert."

Instead he took a step sideways to move into my field of vision. "We've got to be careful with you, because you're tricky. I know. I've looked you up."

"The wicked flee where none pursue," I said, looking up.

"What are you saying? Is that slander? Are you accusing my clients of something?"

"It's a proverb, I think. Google it."

The bailiff called the court to order, and Judge Cochran came in. He sat, lacing his hands in front of him. "Are these your clients?" he asked Rupert.

They were.

"Ms. Starling, are you ready to proceed?"

I stood. "Call Jared Walsh," I said.

Jared came forward. He was wearing a pinstripe suit, a white shirt, a striped tie. In a bored voice he swore to tell the truth, and he took a seat in the witness box.

"Hi Jared," I said, giving him a smile he didn't return. "Could you tell us your full name for the record?"

"Jared Hunter Walsh."

"You were acquainted with the deceased, Macy Buck?"

"I object," Rupert said from the gallery, and Judge Cochran looked at him incredulously.

"On what grounds?" he said.

"On the grounds of relevancy. My client's relationship with Macy Buck has nothing to do with the charges against these defendants."

"He had a relationship with Macy Buck?" I asked.

"You see, your honor? See what she's trying to intimate?"

Cochran said, "She didn't have to intimate anything. You're the one who just told us Jared Walsh had a relationship with Macy Buck."

"I did not have a relationship with her," Jared said, speaking loudly.

"Mr. Propst seems to know a lot about this. I think I'd like to call him to the stand," I said. There were a few people in the gallery, and some of them laughed.

"She was my uncle's therapist," Jared said. "That's all."

"Did you know she'd been suggesting to people that you killed your uncle?"

"Don't answer," Rupert said, holding up both hands, and the judge banged his gavel.

"That's a lie," Jared said.

"Her suggestion that you killed your uncle was a lie?" I asked.

"Objection," Rupert said. "Don't answer."

"Your suggestion that she said any such thing," Jared said.

The judge said, "Mr. Propst, you have no standing in this proceeding. Another interruption from you, and I will have you removed from this courtroom."

"But you're honor, you can see what she's doing."

"Bailiff," the judge said.

"I'll be seated, I'll be quiet." Rupert moved to a seat beside Nathan in the front row and sat down.

The judge took a slow breath. "You've been warned, Mr. Propst. Counselor?"

"I'm not asking whether her comments had any basis in fact," I said, "merely whether you were aware of what she'd been saying."

"I deny that she'd been saying any such thing."

"You, at any rate, had never heard it."

"I had not."

"Your uncle lived right across the street from you, did he not? As his therapist, Macy Buck visited him almost daily."

"I saw her from time to time. I wouldn't know about the frequency of her visits."

"Did Macy and your uncle use your pool or your hot tub for water therapy or to soak tight joints or anything of that sort?"

"No."

"Not that you're aware of," I said.

"Not that I'm aware of."

"Your uncle was never in your hot tub before the day he was found floating in it. Is that what you're saying?"

"That's not what I'm saying. I don't remember seeing him in it, that's all. I don't watch either him or my hot tub every second."

"Did you know Macy Buck was engaged to your brother Nathan?"

He hesitated. "I did know it," he said.

"Your uncle was an old man who had several million dollars in assets. Her engagement to your brother might have given her certain expectations, mightn't it?"

"It might have. She was a conniving bitch."

I glanced at Nathan, but his gaze was fixed on the rail in front of him.

"And she might have known that if your uncle died and you were implicated in your uncle's murder, you would be barred from any inheritance yourself, which would have increased her own take."

In the gallery Rupert made a sound like he was in pain. His head was thrust forward, and his eyes were jerking as if to signal the witness.

Judge Cochran rolled his head on his shoulders as if loosening up for a fight. "Bailiff, please go stand right beside Mr. Propst. The next time he makes so much as a squeak, take him by the arm and remove him from the courtroom." He turned to me. "I warned you that I wasn't going to tolerate a fishing expedition," he said. "If you've got a point to make here, you need to make it."

"I wouldn't have put it past her to drown the old man and try to pin it on me," Jared said.

"But you don't have any reason to think she did."

"No. He could have passed out in his own bathtub, for all I know, entirely on his own. She found him floating there and carried him across the street to dump him in my hot tub. She wasn't a big woman, but she could have had help." He didn't even look at his brother Nathan, and Rupert flopped in his chair, banging the arm of his seat in an apparent effort to get his attention.

Judge Cochran nodded at the bailiff, who took Rupert's arm and pulled him to his feet. As they went up the aisle, Rupert twisted to call over his shoulder. "Remember, Nathan, what I told you. Answer no questions." The bailiff yanked at him. "No questions on the advice of counsel."

The bailiff pulled him through the double doors, and the doors swung shut behind them.

Cochran shook his head. "I've never put a lawyer in jail before," he said. "But that might have been a very good time to start." He sighed. "Ms. Starling, continue."

"I'm finished with this witness."

"Mr. Biggs?"

Biggs stood. "Ms. Starling has clearly abused the indulgence of this court," he said. "I for one will not add to the abuse by asking any questions of a witness so obviously peripheral to the issue before this court, which is whether probable..."

"Thank you for your restraint," the judge said, interrupting him. "Ms. Starling, it does seem that Mr. Biggs has a point. I won't say the testimony of this witness is irrelevant—it's clear you'll be calling him at trial—but it's not enough to change the disposition of the case in this courtroom. It's not in the ballpark of being enough. To succeed here, you've got to produce evidence that shows the defendants had no connection to the crime, and you can't do that. There's no evidence out there that can do that."

"I'm laying a foundation," I said.

The judge's head fell back against his head rest, his eyes closed. Without opening them, he said, "You may leave the stand, Mr. Walsh. Ms. Starling, call your next witness."

"Nathan Walsh."

Nathan was dressed more casually than his brother, wearing a blue suede jacket over a yellow T-shirt. The bailiff swore him in, and he took a seat in the witness box.

"What is your name, please?" I asked him.

He fished a business card from the front pocket of his jacket and held it up in front of him. "On the advice of counsel, I refuse to answer on the grounds that it might tend to incriminate me," he read.

"Telling us your name might incriminate you?" I said. "Is it not Nathan Walsh?"

"On the advice of counsel, I refuse to answer on the grounds that it might tend to incriminate me."

"Are you telling us you are implicated in the murder of Macy Buck, or is it some other crime?"

"On the advice of counsel…"

I looked at the judge, who pursed his lips. Following his gaze, I saw that the bailiff had returned and was standing just inside the double doors.

Nathan was still holding the card in front of him, and I stepped around the podium to get a closer look at it. "It looks like he's reading from the back of Rupert Propst's business card," I said.

Cochran nodded. "Much as I hate to say this—and I do hate to say it—bailiff, get Mr. Propst back in here."

The bailiff went out and came back a few minutes later behind Rupert Propst, who bustled down the aisle toward the front of the courtroom. "Thank you, your honor, thank you. I welcome this opportunity to represent my clients as this, this woman tries to sow discord between them and to smear their good names."

"This man on the witness stand is your client?"

"He is, your honor."

"And you have advised him not to tell us his name because the answer would incriminate him?"

"Well, now, your honor. I knew there was a chance I might be ejected from the courtroom as I attempted to offer my clients the best representation I was able. A lawyer can't make fine distinctions standing in the hall. I simply advised him not to answer any questions because I knew that this lawyer, this attorney for the defense, was going to do everything in her power to implicate him in matters he doesn't have anything to do with. In the courtroom she can say anything she wants to, she can make any assertion, cast any aspersion, ask any question no matter how unfair or how inflammatory, and the law protects her. She has an absolute privilege to say or imply anything she wants to, and we can't sue her for slander or defamation of any kind. The law protects her, and it doesn't protect my clients. I have to do that. I have to…"

The judge was holding up a hand. "Mr. Propst?"

"Yes, your honor?"

"Did you just tell me that this witness doesn't have anything to do with this case?"

Rupert's tongue appeared between his pale lips.

"If that's so, how can any testimony he gives possibly tend to incriminate him?"

"There are more crimes in the world than the murder of Macy Buck, your honor."

"And Nathan Walsh was committing one of them on the day she was killed?"

"I didn't say that, your honor. Please don't put words in my mouth."

The judge studied him. "Mr. Propst, unless your client is not Nathan Walsh and telling us who he is would implicate him in some crime, please instruct him to identify himself for the record."

Rupert hesitated. "Very well, your honor." To Nathan he said, "You may identify yourself."

I said to Nathan, "Who are you?"

"Nathan Walsh."

"Brother of Jared Walsh, nephew of Robert Walsh?"

He looked at Rupert, who nodded. "Yes," he said.

"Did you ever hear the decedent Macy Buck talk about hearing voices and splashing noises coming from your brother's backyard on the day your uncle, Robert Walsh, died?"

"Don't answer that," Rupert said. "You need to take the Fifth on that. Read the words on the card."

"On the advice of counsel…"

"Yeah, we've got it," I said, interrupting Nathan. I turned to Rupert. "It seems to me the answer is far more likely to incriminate Nathan's brother Jared

Walsh than Nathan himself. I know you're representing both of them, but that doesn't mean Nathan can plead the Fifth to protect his brother."

"You don't need to tell me the law, counselor. I know what I'm doing."

Judge Cochran said, "It's hard for me to see how an admission to having heard Macy Buck tell a story would implicate this witness in any crime."

"Once you see that, the damage is done, your honor. There's no putting the cat back in the bag once it's out."

"I don't like this," Cochran said. "I think you and your client are abusing the privilege against self-incrimination."

"Let me ask another question," I said. "Where were you the afternoon and evening of Friday, February 11, the day your fiancé was murdered?"

"Don't answer!" Rupert said. "You see what she's doing, your honor. This is just the kind of fishing expedition you told counsel you wouldn't tolerate."

"That's my concern, not yours," Cochran said. "The only acceptable grounds for this witness refusing to answer a question is that the answer would incriminate him."

"And that's what it would do. That's just what it would do."

"Because Nathan Walsh killed Macy Buck?" I asked. "Or was he engaged in shoplifting or assault or some other felony?"

Rupert's chin went up. "Your honor, this cannot go on. A person may reasonably fear prosecution and yet be innocent of any crime. The Constitution shields my client, the Constitution shields all

Americans, from having inferences such as these drawn from their failure to testify. This is America. My client is an American. God bless America!" To his credit as an actor, it did seem as if the fire of patriotism shone in his eyes.

Judge Cochran looked at me. I said, "Perhaps Mr. Biggs would offer Nathan Walsh immunity for any crime short of murder his testimony might point to."

Biggs half-stood behind his table. "Perhaps he wouldn't," he said, and dropped back into his seat.

"We seem to be at a standstill," Cochran said.

"Let me try one more time. Mr. Walsh, that's a nice T-shirt you're wearing under your blazer today."

Nathan looked at Rupert, then back at me. "Thanks."

"Is it a Dulce Vita?"

He held open his jacket to look at the left breast. "I don't think so."

"Let me ask you this, and you tell me if the answer would incriminate you."

"Your honor…"

"Mr. Rupert, the Constitution may allow your client to refuse to testify, but it does not give you the power to silence lawyers in my courtroom. I will hear the question."

I said, "On Friday the eleventh, did you Nathan Walsh go to the home of Macy Buck, find her dead on her kitchen floor in a pool of her own blood, and get blood on your Dulce Vita T-shirt. Did you subsequently return to your car and, before you could gather your composure enough to drive away, see the defendant Brian Marshall enter the house?"

One of Nathan's eyebrows had begun to twitch. "Your honor," Rupert began.

"I'm not finished," I said. To Nathan: "Did you then go to Brian Marshall's apartment and, using either the spare key you found there or a bump key your friends the Strumpfs had showed you how to use, let yourself into Brian's apartment and leave your blood-covered T-shirt in his laundry basket? Would the answer to that question incriminate you?"

For a moment there was silence, unbroken even by Rupert.

Nathan, both eyebrows going now, held up Rupert's business card in front of him. "I refuse to answer on the grounds that it might tend to incriminate me."

"Your honor," Rupert said in the softest voice he had used so far. "This is outrageous. This proceeding is making a mockery of the Fifth Amendment. To allow it to go on…"

"I'm not going to allow it to go on," Judge Cochran said.

Nathan was licking his lips like an old man with a neurological problem. Biggs, though, was on his feet. "As entertaining as all this has been," he said, "I must point out to the court that it constitutes misconduct on the part of counsel for the defense. She can have no basis for this wildly inventive fantasy that she's told. If it has a place at all, it's in closing argument at trial and not in a long, convoluted question propounded to a witness who has already invoked his Constitutional rights."

The judge gaze moved from Nathan on the witness stand, to Biggs, to Rupert Propst, standing like a sentinel at the rail. Finally he looked at me. "I think we're done here," he said.

"I have no further questions."

"You're excused," the judge said to Nathan.

Nathan got up, brushed past his lawyer as he pushed through the bar, and headed down the aisle.

"Nathan," I called.

He stopped, but didn't turn around.

"I know what you did."

As Nathan started forward again, both Biggs and Rupert started talking at once. The gist of their cacophony of argument was that I was guilty of misconduct and should face a variety of penalties that ranged from reprimand to being held in contempt to disbarment. Brooke Marshall got out of her seat and started down the aisle toward the door, followed moments later by Mike McMillan. For my part, I went to my table and sat down.

Chapter 21

I got reprimanded—scolded by the judge, essentially—but didn't get fined or jailed, and if I lost my license to practice law, it would be at a different time and before a different tribunal. From my clients' perspective, the important thing was that the judge recessed the hearing until the next morning rather than bind them over for trial. That might be coming—it almost certainly was coming—but we had lived to fight another day.

Since Mike and Brooke had left before me, I was able to think as I walked alone to my car, the cold wind cutting through my coat like it wasn't there. I had earned another day, but only one more day, and I needed to make the most of it. I pulled out my cell phone as I got into my car, using one hand to smooth my wind-blown hair as I pecked around for Detective Jordan's number with the thumb of my other.

He answered with "Robin Starling. What do you want?"

"Where are you? Are you at the station?"

"As it happens it's five o'clock and I'm on my way home."

"I was hoping you could meet me. Do you have any luminol with you?"

"Oh yes. I must have half-a-hundred chemical reagents lined up on my back seat."

"I'll take that as a no."

"What do you want, Starling?"

"Do you know where Macy Buck's car is?"

"Still in her driveway, I think."

"Was it searched thoroughly, do you know?"

"We looked through it. I don't think anyone combed it looking for loose fibers."

"Or blood stains? A witness today said she saw the car at Jack Packard's house the afternoon of the day Macy was murdered."

Jordan didn't answer.

"You see what I'm getting at, don't you? Macy's blood was found at Packard's house…"

"…and Brian Marshall's apartment, and Carytown Joe. Biggs thinks you're responsible for the blood at Packard's place, you know."

"He made that pretty clear. Let's assume for a moment though that I'm a reasonable person and not some nut-job who goes around dribbling the blood of murder victims onto every horizontal surface she comes across."

After a few seconds Jordan said, "I'm turning around. Let me call Ray. I think he's still at the station."

I got to Macy's house first and parked on the street in front of it. I stayed in my car. It was cold outside, and Victoria O'Neal was probably watching out her window for her new husband's imminent return. My phone began to play: Brooke was calling.

"Hey, Brooke. What's up?"

"Mike and I are on I-95 heading north. We just went through Fredericksburg."

"Are you eloping?"

"We're following Nathan Walsh."

"Where is he going?"

"Out of town. Do you think we should keep following him?"

"Do you want to keep following him?"

There was the briefest hesitation. "Okay, then. We'll stay on him," she said. "I'll let you know when he stops."

I punched off, smiling. Feminine wiles, I thought.

Jordan pulled in behind me and got out, pulling the zipper on his jacket all the way to his throat and stuffing his hands into his pockets. I lowered my window a couple of inches. "Thanks for meeting me," I said.

He nodded. "Oh, sure," he said. "I have no home life." It was getting dark, but the nearby streetlamp illuminated the white vapor of his breath.

A Ford Explorer cut across my headlights into Macy's driveway. I turned off my car and got out.

Ray Hernandez got out of the Explorer as we approached. "Which one of you brought the beer?"

"I really appreciate this, guys."

"Does that mean no beer?"

Jordan said, "Let's see if we can get this car open. Did you bring the keys?"

"Oh, yeah." He reached back inside the Explorer and came out with a plastic evidence bag. I saw a lipstick, a wallet, a small hairbrush, and a key ring with a fob in the shape of a four-leaf clover—evidently the contents of Macy's purse. As Hernandez got out the keys, Jordan opened the Explorer's passenger door and came out with a long flashlight. Hernandez pressed a button on the largest of the keys, and the Honda Element beeped.

He and Ray opened both doors of the Honda, then the rear-hinged back doors. The interior lights came on, and Jordan moved the beam of the flashlight around the car as we examined the various surfaces.

"Stain here on the passenger door," Hernandez said, and Jordan played the light on it.

"More of a smudge, really." Jordan moved the beam over the interior of the door then onto the seat and the seatback.

"Luminol?" I suggested.

"You watch too much CSI," Hernandez said, but he walked back to the Explorer.

"Actually, I don't think I've ever seen a complete episode. Are any of them still on?"

"Beats me. I watch SportsCenter," Jordan said.

Hernandez came back with a red spray bottle with a black top and a spray trigger. "Let's do this."

"Hang on. Let me get the camera." Jordan came back with a big black camera with an adjustable lens. "Okay."

Hernandez sprayed the smudge on the door, and the spot began to glow a faint blue. "Will you look at that?" he said.

Jordan's camera clicked.

"Try the seat," I suggested, and Hernandez gave it a few squirts, moving his arm to fan the spray.

Right where the seat joined the seatback, there was a spot that glowed blue.

"We need to get the forensic unit out here," Jordan said.

"And I need to get home to my dog," I said. "Can I count on you to be in court tomorrow, or do I need to serve you with subpoenas?"

"How come every time we try to help you out, it turns into a big old pain in the butt?" Hernandez asked.

"Thanks," I said. "I appreciate it."

The next morning at six a.m., I walked into the Shady Grove YMCA, the Y where I went for pick-up games of basketball and the occasional resistance workout. Rodney had called me on my way home the night before to tell me that of all the workout places in town, all the Gold's Gyms, World Gyms, Power Shacks, Fitness Planets, and YMCAs, only one had a muscular old guy who had started coming in the last month and was there almost every day.

"At least only one old guy who comes close to matching Packard's description," Rodney said. "He usually comes in sometime between six and seven in the morning and works out for an hour, hour and fifteen minutes."

"And it's the Shady Grove Y?"

"Yeah, the one on Nuckols Road."

"That's my Y."

"You haven't noticed this guy?"

"I don't go much now that I have a dog. I never did go much in the mornings."

This morning, though, I was there. I went to the free-weight room and started into a ten-exercise routine I used when I hadn't lifted in a while. It consisted of squats, Romanian deadlifts, bench press, and so on, one set each, and I could usually blow through it in about twenty minutes. Today I took my time and was doing upright rows when Jack Packard came in wearing sweatpants and a sleeveless T. I thought he started when he saw me, but he came in anyway, selected a forty-pound dumbbell from the rack in front of me, and sat on a nearby bench to do concentration curls. His biceps bulged like a cannonball each time he brought the weight up.

"That's an unusual exercise to start with," I said, watching him in the mirror. There were some people across the hall on the machines, but here in the free-weight room it was just the two of us.

"I'm thinking." There was a gravelly quality to his voice. He finished a set of ten or twelve with one arm and switched the dumbbell to his other hand. I put one of my dumbbells back on the rack.

"What about?" I braced myself on the bench nearest his and started doing kickbacks with my remaining dumbbell.

"You're Robin Starling, I'm Jack Packard. I guess you know that."

"I'd hoped."

He dropped the dumbbell on the padded floor, where it hit with a thump and didn't bounce. "How's the preliminary hearing going?"

"Not too well. Brian Marshall and Whitney Foster are going to be bound over this morning." I put the dumbbell on the bench, shifted my position, and picked up the dumbbell with my other hand. "The D.A. thinks I dumped blood on your kitchen floor…" I had to pause for breath. "…though at the moment he finds himself unable to prove it."

Packard nodded. "And what do you want from me?"

"Why'd you disappear?"

He shrugged. "I thought if everything went well, no one would even realize I was gone. If it didn't go well, better to be out of pocket for a while."

"There are some who think you're dead."

"Yes, after a certain attorney broke into my house and turned the whole thing into a circus. How'd you find me anyway? I haven't used my phone. I've paid cash for everything, selling a gold coin here and there when I had to."

"I saw you at the funeral," I said. "You looked like you worked out."

Brooke and Mike had tracked Nathan Walsh to a hotel in Georgetown. I considered making as much as I could of Nathan's flight to Washington, D.C.—call Rupert Propst to the stand, maybe force him to claim attorney-client privilege to keep from answering questions about Nathan's whereabouts. In the end, though, that would amount to no more than a sideshow. My plan to call Jordan to the stand as my own witness, use the evidence of blood in Macy's car to suggest she had been moved, was not much better. Biggs would claim I had planted the blood, and none of it was enough to defeat probable cause.

Now I had something. When the sheriff's deputy brought my clients in, I smiled and gave them a few vague words of encouragement. Aubrey Biggs sat looking at me until he couldn't stand it anymore, then he came over to tell me he wasn't done with me yet:

"You're an embarrassment to the profession. You know that, don't you?"

"I was about to say the same about you."

"I'm not finished with you, don't think I am." He turned and stalked back to his table. At last the bailiff called the court to order, and Judge Cochran came in.

I stood along with everyone else.

"Are you ready to proceed, Ms. Starling? Mr. Biggs?"

We said we were.

"Is there any chance we can get this wrapped up this morning, do you think?"

"I think there's every chance, your honor," I said.

"Then my prayers have been answered. Call your first witness."

"Jack Packard."

Biggs jerked around in his chair as Packard got out of his seat and came down the aisle. I swung the gate open for him. When he had been sworn and seated, I asked him his name.

"Jack Packard. No middle name."

"Kind of like Harry S. Truman," I said.

"No middle initial either."

So much for small talk. "Did you see Macy Buck on Friday, February 11th?"

"Yes. She came to my house."

"By arrangement? Did she call first?"

"No, she just showed up. She accused me of having secreted away the assets of Robert Walsh."

"Why would she be involved in recovering Robert Walsh's assets?"

"I don't know. She seemed to feel she had some kind of proprietary interest, having been his therapist or something. Now, I understand she's engaged to Nathan Walsh, but I didn't know that then."

"What's your connection to Robert Walsh?"

"We've been best friends since high school."

"Are you in possession of Mr. Walsh's assets?"

"I am not." It was true, I thought, at least technically. I was the one in possession of Mr. Walsh's assets, which had been converted to gold and left in a wheelbarrow in my backyard.

"Do you know why Jared Walsh, the executor of Mr. Walsh's estate, has had such a hard time locating those assets?"

"Because before his death, Robert went to a great deal of trouble to hide them. Jared Walsh isn't the executor, incidentally. I am. Robert wrote another will shortly before his death, disinheriting Jared and Nathan Walsh and leaving everything to his niece Whitney Foster."

"Why would Robert do all that?"

"Jared and Nathan were attempting to have him declared incompetent and have Jared appointed conservator of his property. When Robert got notice served on him, he immediately started emptying his accounts and putting his property where no one was going to be able to get hold of it."

"How was Macy involved in this, or was she?"

"Macy was giving Robert supplements that made him sleepy all the time and played hob with his memory. He was in a particularly bad state when a man came by who turned out to be a physician there to put together some kind of report."

"What kind of supplements did she give him? Pills of some sort?"

"Pills, powders, injections…I don't know how Robert let himself get talked into such nonsense, but she gave him all sorts of pamphlets about human growth hormone and so-called natural medicines that have names I can't even pronounce. I told him he was going to have to stop all that stuff cold turkey, or they'd have him in the looney bin."

"And did he stop?"

Packard took a breath and exhaled it noisily. "I think so. Stopped most of it anyway."

"Before he died, did he manage to empty his accounts?"

A smile passed over Packard's face. "Pretty much."

"And Macy Buck thought you had a hand in it."

"Yes, and that I had the assets, or at least knew where they were."

"Did she seem to expect that you'd turn the assets over to her?"

"Seemed to. The assets or information that would help her locate them."

"Why would you do that?"

He nodded. "She evidently thought she would drug me, inject me with something."

"Did she try to inject you with something?"

"She did. We were standing in my kitchen, doing a little verbal sparring, when she asked me for a drink of water. I turned away from her to get it, and quick as a flash she came at me with a big syringe with a needle the size of a sixteen-penny nail. Stuck me in the shoulder with it, might have driven it all the way to the bone if I hadn't jerked away from her and decked her."

"You decked her?"

He grimaced. "Caught her right on the cheekbone with a right cross, spun her around like a top."

"What happened then?"

"Well, she went down, and I stood over her waiting for her to move. I was planning to kick her all the way into next week if she came up with that steel spike in her hand." He sighed. "She didn't. I turned her over finally and saw it sticking out of the middle of her body. There was a little pool of blood on my tile floor."

"Was she dead?"

There was a tear running down one of the lines in his face. "No. Wasn't even unconscious. She just lay there staring up at me with blank eyes. I should have called the ambulance, but just as I picked up the phone to do it, she spoke to me. 'Help me to my car,' she said. 'I've got a friend who can help me.' "

"And did you? Help her to her car?"

"God help me, I did."

"What happened to the needle?"

"She pulled it out and handed it to me, meek as anything, and I tucked it in the side pocket of my jacket."

"Your jacket?"

"I don't keep my place too warm in the wintertime. I have an old windbreaker I usually wear around the house."

"Was Macy able to walk to her car?"

"With help. I carried her down the stairs to my basement, planning to put her down at the bottom, but ended up just carrying her on across the TV room I have there. I didn't set her on her feet until we got to the door. She made it from there to her car, but almost fell when we got there. I saw she wasn't in any shape to drive, so I laid back the passenger seat and put her in it, then I got behind the wheel myself. 'I'm not taking you to any friend's house,' I told her. 'I'm taking you to the ER.' I headed across the river toward St. Mary's, her lying back in her seat with her eyes closed, breathing steady—at least, she started off breathing steady. I didn't notice when she stopped." His gruff voice was getting hoarser and deeper.

"She died in the car?"

He nodded. "I pulled up to the E.R., jumped out and ran around to get her…but she was dead." I had to strain to hear him. "I thought maybe it would look better if she'd died in her own home, so I took her there. Put her on her kitchen floor, found an ice pick in one of her drawers, wiped a little blood on the blade and made sure her fingerprints were on the handle." He looked over at the table where Whitney Foster sat with Brian. "I didn't expect anyone else to get blamed for it. I thought everyone would assume she'd fallen."

"What did you do then?"

"Let myself out the back door, walked down the alley to the next street. When I was several miles away from there, I used my cell phone to call a cab."

Chapter 22

"Why did Nathan frame Brian and Whitney?" Brooke asked. It was late afternoon, and she, Brian, Whitney, and I were sitting around a table at Carytown Joe, ceramic mugs in our hands or in front of us. The coffee shop was closed, but all of us were having vanilla lattes.

"I don't know," I said. "My guess is he'd already been part of an effort to frame Jared for his uncle's death..."

"Do you think Nathan and Macy killed him then?" Whitney asked.

"No way of knowing. Maybe it was like Jared said. Macy found Robert drowned in his bathtub and thought Jared's hot tub would be a more profitable place for discovery of the body. That wasn't enough to get Jared arrested, so Macy started telling stories about hearing splashing and voices. If Jared were convicted of killing his uncle, he couldn't inherit. Nathan and she—and you—would inherit fifty percent more than you would otherwise."

"I got the sense there was no love lost between Nathan and Jared," Brooke said.

Whitney shivered. "In a way it's my fault she died. I think I told her that if anyone knew where Uncle Robert had hidden his money, it would be Jack Packard."

"But she was the one who went out to Packard's place with a horse syringe," I said. "You can't blame yourself."

There was a tap at the door of the café. It was Jack Packard, standing close to the door for shelter from the cold drizzle that had begun falling about midday. Whitney got up to let him in.

"They let you go," I said.

He unwound the scarf from around his neck and draped it on the back of a chair. "Is there one of those coffees for me?" he said as he unbuttoned his overcoat.

"I'll get it." Whitney went behind the counter.

"None of that sweet stuff in it," he said. "I will take the milk."

"They didn't charge you?" I asked.

"Oh, they charged me. For right now, it's obstruction of justice and involuntary manslaughter. I understand it might get worse, or better."

"So why aren't you locked up?"

"I called a bail bondsman and signed a bunch of papers."

"Did you get a lawyer?" I asked.

"Not yet. I'm planning to hire you, if you're willing."

"Sure." I felt a certain sympathy for Jack despite everything, and, of course, I needed the work.

"I'm going to pay for your work representing Whitney, too," he said. "You pad your bill as much as you think you can get away with, and whatever it comes to, I'll double it." He looked at Whitney. "I know I've behaved badly in all this, and I want to make amends. I wouldn't have let you go to prison. When they arrested you, I started to come forward, then I read up on your lawyer here, and I thought I'd wait out the preliminary hearing and see what she could do."

"Brian and Whitney waited it out in jail," Brooke said.

He made a face. "I am sorry about that. I know money can't make it up to them, but it's all I've got." He accepted a mug from Whitney and sat back, sipping it. "Of course, Whitney's going to be a rich woman."

"If Robert's will stands up," I said. "There's evidently a physician's report out there that says he's incompetent."

"We made a video recording of Robert talking to his lawyer about his will and signing it. I don't think anyone can watch him talking and joking with his lawyer and conclude he didn't know what he was doing. Plus, as his executor, I plan to hire top-notch legal talent." He gestured at me with his coffee mug.

I said, "The first thing I'd advise you to do is find a safer place for the ten million dollars' worth of gold you've got sitting in that wheelbarrow in my backyard." The comment called for the story about Deeks and me, and how we had found the gold-laden wheelbarrow one night after the Strumpf brothers walked into my living room through a locked door.

"It's been giving me the willies every time I think about it," I said.

"I can understand that," Brian said.

Jack nodded. "It's not ten million dollars, though. Just a little less than eight."

"Still," I said.

Brooke walked out with me to my car. We belted up and were still rubbing our legs to warm them when she said, "Mike asked me to marry him."

"Whoa."

"Yes. We spent last night at a hotel in Alexandria, and…"

"Double whoa."

"We'd followed Nathan to Georgetown and were coming back. It was late, and we were tired. You know."

"Did you, uh…"

She colored. "No, and Mike was very decent about it. After we kissed a little, he said he ought to sleep on the other bed, and I let him, though I don't know that either of us slept much. Getting showered and ready the next morning—of course, neither of us had a change of clothes—was very … I don't know, domestic." A certain dreaminess had come into her voice. "For a thirty-two-year-old lawyer, he looks pretty good with his shirt off."

"You saw him with his shirt off? Did he, uh, see you…"

"He did not. Well, not completely off."

"Brooke Marshall, you little vixen."

"On the way back, we got to talking, and he asked me if I'd marry him."

"Congratulations."

"I haven't told him yes."

"What have you told him?"

"I mean, we've only been dating two weeks."

"You've known him the better part of a year."

"I wanted a boyfriend! And here I may have a husband, and it's going to turn my whole life upside down, and who knows what it's going to do to my friendships and everything."

"Sounds like you shouldn't have used those feminine wiles at full strength." After a moment I added, "You can probably string him along a good while, you know, kind of like I do Paul."

"You treat Paul just awful."

"Ah. Well, you could string him along, but try to be nicer about it." After a pause, I added, "I could try to be nicer, too."

She looked at me sideways. "You could, you know. Paul's a great guy, and he loves you."

I sighed, nodded, then put the car in gear. "Let's go home. I've got a little guy there I've been neglecting, and Paul's supposed to be back in town. You want to come over?"

She shook her head. "Mike's coming to my place."

"Be careful," I said.

"How can you be careful when, when..."

"When you're in love?"

She nodded, but her smile was bleak.

"I know just how you feel," I said, nodding my head for emphasis. "Just...how...you...feel."

ABOUT THE AUTHOR

Michael Monhollon took out a semester in college to write science fiction stories and collect rejection slips. His first book sale, a legal thriller, came at the age of 31 at about the time *The Firm* was coming out in paperback. Its sales fell short of *The Firm*'s, though, and he continues to work for a living. For a dozen years he practiced law. Currently, he is the dean of the Kelley College of Business at Hardin-Simmons University in Abilene, Texas.